# MANMADE MONSTERS

# MAN MADE

# MONSTERS

### Andrea L. Rogers

illustrated by Jeff Edwards

## LQ

LEVINE QUERIDO

Montclair | Amsterdam | Hoboken

For Elena, Ana, and Angie.
My life is an honor song for you.
etsi

For Emilee, Lisa and my 12 dogs — All that I do
I do for you. Thank you for being in my life,
without you I would accomplish nothing. Love you guys.
Jeff Edwards

This is an Arthur A. Levine book
Published by Levine Querido

www.levinequerido.com • info@levinequerido.com
Levine Querido is distributed by Chronicle Books LLC
Text copyright © 2022 by Andrea L. Rogers
Illustrations © 2022 by Jeff Edwards

Library of Congress Control Number: 2022931796
ISBN 978-1-64614-179-1
Printed and bound in China

Published October 2022
First printing

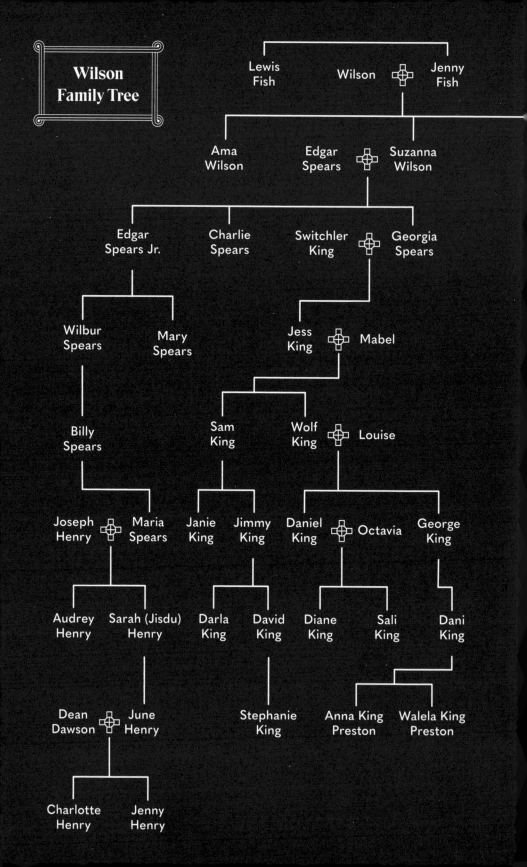

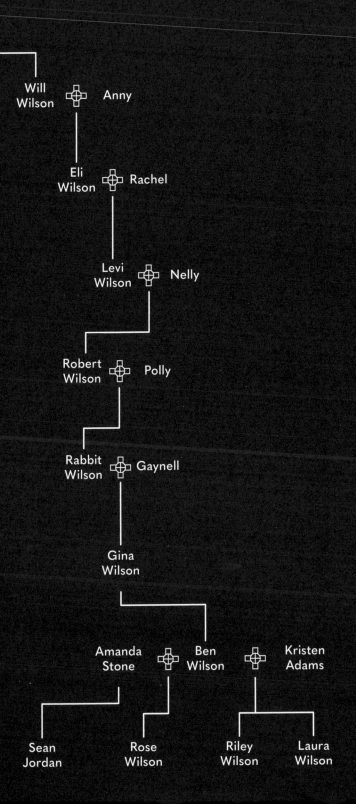

# Stone
# Family Tree

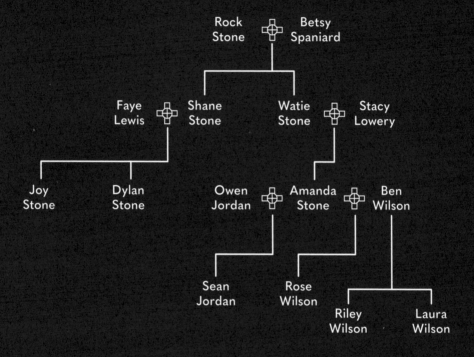

Rock Stone ✛ Betsy Spaniard

Faye Lewis ✛ Shane Stone

Watie Stone ✛ Stacy Lowery

Joy Stone

Dylan Stone

Owen Jordan ✛ Amanda Stone ✛ Ben Wilson

Sean Jordan

Rose Wilson

Riley Wilson

Laura Wilson

Cherokee speakers view the world as a large room that one enters by one door at birth and exits by another at death. Given the grammar of Cherokee, in this room there are all the things that have happened, will happen, or could ever happen . . . people move through the room over the course of their lives . . . behaviors that people engage in today are witnessed by their ancestors . . . the events that affected their ancestors are also visible here in the room. . . .

In the Cherokee view there must be consequences for violating the principles that hold everything together in balance.

Heidi M. Altman and Thomas N. Belt
"Reading History: Cherokee History
through a Cherokee Lens"
*Native South*, University of Nebraska Press

# An Old-Fashioned Girl

*1*

Ama Wilson
Kuyegwona 15, 1839
07/15/1839

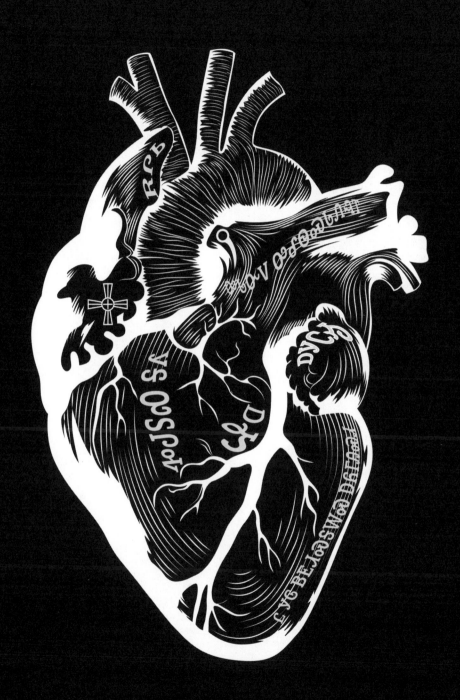

Tsalagi should never have to live on human blood, but some-
times things just happen to sixteen-year-old girls. My name,
Ama, means "water" if you say it right, and "salt" if you don't.
DᏉ. Etsi gave birth to me during the Hunting Moon.

One day after our band fled Texas for Indian Territory, my
little brother took sick. Knowing that the Texas Rangers were
at our heels and unable to delay, our band of Cherokees and
other Indians continued north without us. I held my baby sister,
Suzanna, and we watched our people disappear. When all was
silent, Etsi drove our wagon and two horses off the rutted Texas
road and hid us as best she could behind a thick stand of squat
mesquite. We hoped to set up our tent only long enough to gather
medicine and let my brother, Will, rest. That plan changed in the
middle of the night when we heard the Texas Army pass by, less
than a day's ride behind our tribe.

Edoda had been captured in Mexico a year earlier, but before
that, there had been a baby a year for Etsi. None but the three of us
children had lived long, and sometimes, it seemed Will wouldn't
make it either. Suzanna, born under this year's Bone Moon, was

a baby who thrived, though. Edoda was just called Wilson, but Etsi was Jenny Fish.

Etsi and I didn't talk much the next day; our hearts were split between our little family and the danger our people were in. Though he slept a lot, Will seemed to be feeling better. I went to dig roots and gather rabbitbrush to make a bath for Will's fever. Etsi watched over him while she nursed Suzanna. Etsi seemed to know what Suzanna needed before she cried with wanting. Some mothers are like that. It made for a quiet baby.

Toward dark, Suzanna fell asleep and Etsi handed me her rabbit-skin-lined basket. I placed it next to my pallet in the wagon and covered the whole thing with a lightweight cotton cloth we had woven. Our horses whinnied and their ears and bodies turned toward the road. My small pinto flicked her eyes from me to the road and back again, her feet stamping nervously. I turned in the direction they looked. Soon, we heard the clomp and rattle before we saw the small bone-white covered wagon turn off the road and clatter toward us.

A skinny, pale young man held the reins of the horses. He drove them to stop on the other side of our campfire. He didn't call out or wave, he just stared into the glowing coals. He was a silhouette with the sun flaming out behind the wagon.

I carried Suzanna's basket, quickly walking over to put it in the tent to hide her. The stealing and selling of women was common enough that it was my first fear. There was no shortage of the worst of the Texas Rangers and other bandits riding into villages, especially Indian and Spanish communities, stealing women, children, horses, and whatever else they could use or sell.

"Etsi, we should go," I whispered, leaning in between the flaps of the canvas tent.

Etsi frowned and Will's eyes twitched open. "Sleep, Chooch," she told my little brother.

Etsi patted Will as she stood up. She checked for the small knife she always kept tied to her waist and then followed me outside.

※

The sun had disappeared from the sky, leaving bands of orange and pink. A man in a dark suit climbed out of the back of the wagon. His sharply triangular beard and red-brown mustache seemed nearly attached to the stovepipe hat on his head. He was dressed like a dandy with ruffled collars and sleeves. He raised his hat to us. "Guten abend, Fräuleins."

In German, he ordered his boy to see to the horses.

The man approached Etsi, switching first to Comanche, then trying Apache. We understood a little, but when he switched to Spanish, Etsi bade me translate. She understood several languages, but only felt comfortable speaking Tsalagi. I had learned Spanish from some of the others in our tribe and understood a little German, but not enough to speak. I could certainly talk to him about food, water, and roads in Spanish. He said his name was Dr. May and he was headed for Indian Territory. He offered us dried beef in exchange for the use of our fire. The chance to add some meat to the corn soup my mother had been feeding my weak brother was attractive, so Etsi accepted. I was uneasy, but there was nothing to do about it.

The young man with the freckles and the nearly colorless eyes laid his blankets out on the ground next to the fire. I watched his dirty hands spread the blanket out and felt unease. He stretched out and stared into the flames, silent. He never spoke, just seemed to take orders. The man gestured toward him. "Está malo," he explained.

"¿Mudo?" I suggested, thinking he had chosen the wrong word.

Herr Doktor shrugged.

When the corn soup was ready, the stranger gave Etsi his bowl. She filled it for him. "Danke schön," he said, stirring the soup with a silver spoon.

"¿Tiene hambre?" I asked, gesturing toward the boy with a nod of my head.

A smile spread slowly on the man's face, bunching slight wrinkles near his eyes for a moment. "Immer," he muttered. Then, quickly, "Nein, nein, er kann keinen Mais essen," as he settled down near the fire.

"¿No puede comer maíz?" I repeated back, but in Spanish. For a moment he looked confused, then he realized I understood his German. He smiled and nodded. His smile was the opposite of comforting.

I explained to Etsi that the boy couldn't eat corn and she frowned. She filled tin cups with soup for herself and Will and disappeared into the tent. I took my tin cup to the wagon. I watched the man stir his bowl a bit longer. I never saw him taste it, but he stood up and stretched and disappeared around the back of his wagon. After rummaging a bit he returned carrying a long black greatcoat. He squatted near the fire. I wondered how he could stand the heat and keep the ruffles on his sleeves from burning.

"¿Tu nombre es Alma?"

I frowned. Even though he claimed he didn't speak Cherokee, he had paid enough attention to Etsi talking to me to figure out a version of my name.

"Ama," I said.

"Alma," he repeated, not hearing the difference.

The Doktor threw a stick into the fire and watched it burn. A smile played on his lips and he repeated my name again as he understood it in Spanish. "Alma, Alma, Alma."

I frowned. I didn't like his practicing my name.

"¿Y ustedes son indias?"

In the dark, I nodded.

He smiled. "Dile a tu mamá que la sopa estuvo buena," he said as he stood up.

He pulled out a small book from his pocket and a pencil. He told me he was also a travel writer and wondered if he could ask me some questions.

"Mañana," I said, intending to be gone before sunrise.

A frown flickered briefly across his face, then he nodded and smiled.

He pulled on the frock coat despite the heat, raised an unlit pipe to me from one of the pockets, said, "Por supuesto, mañana," and disappeared into the dark prairie. I turned and caught the boy watching me. It reminded me of the way a wolf will watch from the forest. Cold crept up my arms, forcing the hairs to stand on end. I decided to keep watch that night. I didn't want to worry Etsi more than I knew she was already worried. In the morning we could leave early, and I'd sleep while Etsi drove the wagon.

While eating, though, I began to feel tired. My mouth felt full of cotton. Involuntarily, my eyes blinked more and more. I got up and rinsed out my cup. I felt off balance as I dried it and returned to the wagon. It occurred to me that I had never been so tired. I climbed into the wagon and leaned against the headboard, keeping my eyes on the fire. Fighting sleep, I drifted in and out of dreams, my brain processing what had led to this moment, the violent pressure on our band to leave Texas. Sam Houston's efforts to secure us a deed to our land had failed. Our tribe was being driven out, toward Indian Territory.

In my nightmare, once more the Texas Army rode past us on the road, a parade of armed white men that never seemed to end. An endless parade of flags and cannons and guns and bayonets stretched down the path ahead and behind us.

Mother's brief scream jerked me awake. I sat up and looked around. The fire still burned strongly, but no one sat near it anymore. I struggled out of the wagon, nearly tumbling out, and staggered toward the tent. At the doorway, I collapsed. The tall man stood over Etsi. He had stabbed a needle into her throat. Beside him, the boy stood, carefully stabilizing a long glass jar attached to the end of a glass syringe filling with the blood of my etsi. I struggled to stand up and keep my eyes open.

My mother's moans weakened as the flow of blood into the jar slowed. The man extracted the needle from her neck and let her fall to the ground. His shirt was unbuttoned to his navel, his white ruffs splattered with blood. All the hair had been shaved from his chest. He plunged the needle deep, slowly emptying the jar into his heart. I forced myself up on to my elbows and crawled, trying to reach Etsi.

The man growled, an unholy sound that nearly weakened my resolve, but then I saw Will crying, lying beside Etsi. Tears seeped from beneath his long, beautiful lashes, and he shook with terror. The brute shouted something to his companion and the boy kicked me in the side. I lay there stunned. When I opened my eyes, the man was removing the needle from his chest. He pressed a handkerchief over the spot of blood and stared at me. Etsi was no longer making any noises or moving.

The pain in my ribs was worse than any pain I had ever felt, but I began to crawl toward my little brother.

The man spoke to the kid again, and he reached down and picked Will up. The boy clasped him to his shoulder with one arm and in the other he carried the jar with the large syringe.

"Willi!" I screamed.

The dandy reached down and forced me to sit up with his left hand, then slapped me hard with his right.

I placed my hands at my side and tried to back away from him, but he dropped down in front of me. He put his arms around my shoulders, pulling me to him. His dead breath was dry on my neck, cooler than breath should be.

"Silencio," he whispered, as he tilted my head back, and paused. "Esta es la manera tradicional." He sunk his teeth into my throat. I felt the skin and veins and muscles tear, his shaved face scraping my skin. The right side of my neck throbbed. I stared into the light of the lantern in the tent, and it seemed to flare, the pain making it burn like a bright sun. Then the light began to fade. I willed myself to join my family. Was my father dead, too? Surely Will was next. Suddenly, I heard Suzanna cry.

The evil doctor smiled.

A moment later the boy came to the tent carrying my wailing sister.

"¿Para beber?" he asked.

"Vender," the man answered.

There was no time for relief. This wasn't the kind of man you begged for mercy. "Ahora serás como yo," he whispered. I didn't want that, but I had no voice or strength. His sharp teeth tore at my throat a few minutes more before he dropped me. He pulled a shaving razor from his trouser pocket and cut a cross above the hole he'd previously made in his chest with the needle, just over his heart. He lay down next to me and softly stroked my long black hair away from my face. He pulled me to him and placed my mouth near his nipple. Rough stubble poked my cheek.

"Toma," he whispered.

I resisted as he pressed my lips over his nipple. But then the taste of salt and copper touched my tongue. The hands of the doctor pressed my head against his breast and only relaxed as I began to drink. I felt dizzy, thinking of Etsi feeding Suzanna. In my confusion, the blood tasted first of salty water, then milk. I found myself sucking in spite of my horror, and as I sucked, hunger gave me a strength rooted in satiating my thirst.

The monster ran his fingers over my braid, pulling its leather tie loose and spreading it over my shoulders. He whispered words in German I didn't understand. As I drank the blood, a tension spread over my skin that caused a tingling wherever he touched me. Only the thirst for his blood overrode the sensation. I slid my hands behind him and began to suck harder, my teeth itching to bite into his flesh.

His tender caresses stopped, and he grabbed my hair, pulling me away from his breast. I grabbed back at him, fighting to return to drink, and he countered with his unnatural strength, throwing me onto my back while tearing back the front of my shirt.

"Sigue siendo mi alma," he spoke softly, his razor suddenly at my ear. The tip pressed into the skin between my ear and hair, as if he might skin me.

I stilled.

Over my breast he cut two small lines. My heart pounded in my ears as he pressed to me and began to suck. Before feeding me, he had filled his heart with my mother's blood, and taken mine as well. Now it felt like he took much of it back. The tightening in my body relaxed and I felt as if I had fallen from a great height and landed in a pool of warm water. Ready to die I closed my eyes. The blissful feeling was unexpected, unknown, the heat of the sun in darkness. When he stopped, I noticed. His head rested on my chest.

I turned my head away and felt the renewed shock of my dead mother. The boy stood over her, brandishing a large knife. He knelt at her skirt and yanked it up. His back was to me, but I knew his work. I had heard of bodies skinned like this by Texas Rangers. Indian scalps were sometimes trophies, sometimes sold like animal skins. Sometimes it was shorthand for an Indian attack that had never happened. There was less blood than usual in the skinning and scalping of Etsi. I wondered if I would be dead or only dying when they skinned and scalped me.

My mind drifted in and out of the tent. Tears filled my eyes as I listened to Suzanna, her crying out in the doctor's wagon an angry wail. My mother's beautiful thick black hair hung from the boy's belt. He gestured toward me with the knife. I reached up and touched the spot above my ear where the monster had shaved a small strip of my hair. My hand came away lightly blooded.

The doctor sat up and shook his head at the boy. He covered my torn blouse with a soiled buffalo robe.

"Vámonos," he said, standing up. Then he switched to German and told the boy something I didn't understand. The boy frowned and reached for the knife in his belt.

Neither moved.

"Muevete," the monster hissed.

The boy turned and left the tent. The white man picked me up easily, still wrapped in the buffalo skin, and dropped me next to our campfire. While I slipped in and out of consciousness, I could hear him and the boy rifling through our belongings. The doctor carried Suzanna around in an effort to keep her from crying. When she stopped, I gave up and slipped into sleep.

I slept near the fire, fitfully. It began to feel as if I were covered in ants. They bit me and left me aflame. When I managed to open my eyes there was only my skin reflecting the firelight, no dosvdali. Eventually, I lost control of my bowels, soiling my dress and the blood-covered bison robe. I believed the doctor had infected me with the bloody flux. If so, with no one to care for me, I would surely be as dead as I wished I was, within hours. My jaw and lips hurt, and I shook with chill before losing consciousness for the rest of the night.

Toward dawn I awoke. In the fire, grease popped and smoke from burning flesh permeated my hair and clothing from the burning of my family. I shook. I had never felt so cold, and though it stank with my dying, the buffalo skin was my only comfort.

Later I woke again. On shaky legs, I stood. The smell of my family hurt my heart. We were supposed to be rejoining my mother's clan, her family, her brother, Lewis Fish, and his wife— not dying in Texas. It appeared that once the man and the boy had taken everything they could use or sell, they loaded the bodies of my family into our wagon and drove it over the campfire. Stabbed next to the fire was a Comanche lance.

I walked unsteadily to it and pulled it out of the ground. Using the lance to poke at the smoldering blanket, I tried to count the skulls in the dying fire. They lay together, lumps of burned flesh that looked to be the two small, burned pairs of feet of my brother and mother, barely recognizable as human in the ashes. There didn't seem to be a smaller body. In the ashes my mother's knifeblade was blackened and handleless. I fished it out. I cut a strip from the buffalo robe and wrapped it to give it a temporary handle.

Leaning against the lance, I stared into the last of the glowing coals. As the sun began to burn on the horizon in the direction from where we came, I squinted. The sunlight was like a fiery dust that burned my eyes. I pulled the buffalo skin up to protect my face.

As the sun rose, I had trouble seeing, almost as if it were night. Eventually, I would learn to protect myself in the daylight. Exposure to the sun causes us to need to feed more often. The tracks of the horses confused me. I was unsure if they had continued on our original route or pivoted toward Mexico.

In each direction I turned, breathing deep to taste the wind. From the southeast, I smelled nothing but death.

Death had taken our horses and left a Comanche lance to make it look like we died in a Comanche raid. Death followed the wagon ruts of the Texas Army. The Texas Army dogged our people who were fleeing toward Indian Territory on the other side of a country that had decided the only good Indian was a dead one.

I began to walk northeast toward those United States.

In the past my tribe burned the homes of the dead. I wondered if Herr Doktor had immolated my family because he knew that, or simply to destroy the evidence of his feeding. I thought of the pony he had taken, the pretty spotted pinto. I had ridden her since I was small. Exhausted, I imagined riding her now, laying my head down to weep into her neck. I did not think about how much blood pumped through a horse's body as she ran. Not yet, at least.

My people had been headed for the brush thicket around Caddo Lake. The darkness of the scrub called me as clearly as a song. I thought of our people and wondered about my father imprisoned in Mexico. I thought about the family of my mother that I might never see unless I kept moving.

Walking in the early daylight, I felt weak and cold. The sickness chilled me, leaving me burning up with fever. I felt as if it were the coldest of winter days. I had experienced a few blue northers, when streams turned to rushing ice and freezing winds killed livestock left unprotected, but none had frozen me to the bone like this. Shaking from the chills slowed me down even more. By evening I reached the wetlands and, exhausted, I began to stumble between the roots of the cypress. I thought of the water monster, Uktena. I wondered if that giant deer-horned serpent had ever made it this far inland. I have heard it said that if you see Uktena, it is a warning that the world is about to change. In my case, it would be a belated message.

In between the tree's long bony roots were various nests and burrows. I found a large, somewhat dry and empty rabbit den.

I crawled into its dark heart, an animal lair in which to wait for death.

But death never came.

I thought of the times I had been sick and how my mother had cared for me. Once I had been fevered and she had brought me tin cups of cool water, begging me to drink. "Hadita, Ama," she pleaded. I thought I was too dry to weep, though. Without water, tears cannot come, so I waited to die, to join my family, and as I slept, salty tears slipped down my cheeks unbidden. When I felt warm, wet air blow on my damp cheek, I awoke staring into the curious eyes of a doe. Her brown pupils were dark and her soft pink tongue darted tentatively to taste the salt on my cheek. The soft fur around her nose and muzzle touched my face like a light kiss. I stayed very still. I stopped breathing. Her tongue flicked out more quickly and drank the salt and blood on my cheek. She licked hungrily, but I didn't move.

Finally, she paused and turned her head away, and in that moment, I struck out. The scent of hot blood just beneath her skin gave me a will where I had lacked strength. I embraced her neck and heard my mother's voice say clearly, "Hadita, Ama."

As I had slept, the muscles of my jaw strengthened, and my teeth had grown sharp. I tore through the deer hide as easily as if it were boiled greens. Hot blood splashed onto my face, but I hung on to her neck while she trod backward, frantically trying to get away. She stumbled, her eyes now full of terror, and then she fell back onto her side. Her legs kicked fruitlessly in the air and I slipped in between them.

My feeding was inefficient. The "manner traditional" is no way to empty an animal, if you are really hungry. And I was. I lay on top of her still-warm body, sucking from the wounds in her neck. When no more could I drink, I sat up feeling hungry and disgusted. The deer would have fed several families for days. How many times had we needed meat, been grateful for a butchered deer brought to us when our kettle was empty? It made me sick to leave the venison to rot on the ground.

Instead, I used my sharp teeth to tear into her soft belly. Now that I had fed, my hands were stronger and able to rip easily through her hide. My teeth razored through the buckskin and then the heart and muscle with ease. I easily separated the bones of her rib cage and grabbed the lukewarm heart. I bit into the organ and sucked at the same time. Within moments I had pulverized and swallowed the whole heart. I sat back and viewed the work of my frenzy. A pack of wolves would have been cleaner and more efficient.

My physical regret followed closely. The heart came back up along with blood I could not spare. I vomited the scarlet tissue onto the forest floor. My body emptied violently and completely. I crawled away from the mess and waited. With more spirit, I might have wept. Even in daylight the forest was dark, but not as dark as it would be that night. I would wait to leave and find clothes and better food. I went to the water to wash. Seven times I dove into the water, praying for purification. Still hungry, I washed the blood-soaked buffalo robe and shook it out to dry.

As the sun dipped out of the sky, I began to follow what I hoped was the road to Herr Death. My people were out there, followed by a murderous army. My baby sister was out there, taken by a monster. Between the two of them they had tried to destroy me and stolen my heart to sell.

My Tsalagi family had tried to escape to Indian Territory in order to survive, in order to live with our people and be left alone. Still, treaties were broken, and we were chased by human monsters, monsters who lived on blood and sorrow.

Blood is thick salt water—the life-fluid of the earth.

Water, blood, power, life.

I was once unconscious of these things, but now they are everything. There are plenty of bad men to feed on and that is what I decided to do. Greed and avarice have no mercy.

I became merciless, too.

# Man Made Monsters

Suzanna Fish {born Wilson}
Anvhyi 3, 1856
3/3/1856

**Raven Hollow, Indian Territory**

Dear Georgia,

I was so happy to find your letters and the books waiting on me when I arrived home! Wado, oginalii. Aliheliga. I am grateful.

Obviously, I am back in Indian Territory. You may remember me telling you this, but the closest town is Tahlequah, the capital of the Cherokee Nation.

Father continues to spend time in Washington away from my stepmother, Lila, and their son, Charles. He has been working as a delegate for the Cherokee Nation and serving as the Assistant Principal Chief. John Ross and my father are meeting with as many Federal government officials and state representatives as they can, trying to get the government to pay what it owes our Nation. Still, Lila can't help but take Father's absence personally.

For many citizens, the sporadic payments for the seizure of our lands in the south creates a hardship citizens shouldn't encumber and can't afford. Our people were promised money for the soil and homes and livestock left behind (though not for the children and elders who died on the tortuous walk to Indian Territory). Money could never compensate for our dead. Father says the Cherokee Female Seminary will not be able to enroll students in the fall, as the Nation can't continue to pay teachers or cover the students' board. He said there was no point in sending me for only one term and that I am already more than qualified to either teach, marry, or work in the office of the *Cherokee Advocate* when that paper starts publishing again. Money woes caused our newspaper to stop printing two years ago! Can you imagine me as a teacher? I would soon be the mad woman in the attic Currer Bell wrote about in *Jane Eyre*.

Lila seemed to be under the impression that marrying a man who was a step away from the Nation's Chief would be akin to being the wife of a president, or at least a senator, in Washington. The balls, the dinners, teas in fancy drawing rooms. She misses being an heiress in Philadelphia. It was quite the scandal when she followed my father back to Indian Territory five years ago while my sickly mother still lived. Lila has settled in comfortably, though. Without consulting my father, she had a large house built close to my father's land. They had a bit of a row about it when it was finished, and my stepmother insisted that they move in as soon as she and my father could reasonably marry after my mother's death. I will live there, by God, she said, stomping her well-heeled foot until he relented. I can't be a bit upset about it, though, as within the year Charles was the result of their odd union. My father is less comfortable with the posh life. I think he sees a bit of sin in the lavishness of my stepmother. He is the son of a Cherokee Baptist pastor, after all. However, he has let both his wives run the household while he is busy with politics or preaching. He only insists that everyone attend church each Sunday.

The house is huge, much like the plantation homes my Eastern-born stepmother claims to abhor. There are rooms we never go in and yards and yards of velvet. Though she spoke derisively of the institution of slavery while she lived in Philadelphia, once here she had cabins built for the people my mother had owned. Before she died, Mama had promised to free Peter, Mary, and Dolly, but failed to do so. Dolly won't even speak when Lila's around since Lila threatened to sell her for speaking Cherokee with me. Dolly pretends she doesn't understand English, forcing Lila to fumble with Cherokee or call someone else to translate. Mary and Peter are the same age Mother would be if she lived still. Dolly, the cook, is their aunt, I believe. At least they call her Aunt Dolly. Mary accompanies us to church on Sundays, but Dolly goes off to work on other farms in order to earn her own money.

Until a few days ago, old Dr. Henry lived in the two-story carriage house. Previously, his main patient was my mother, but Father felt his medical knowledge was of value to the area even after her passing. Herr Doktor delivered Charles and many other babies. He was an odd fellow, obsessed with that book *Frankenstein* by Mary Shelley. He claimed it was based on a true story about a German alchemist named Johann Konrad Dippel. One could not speak with him regarding literature for more than a few minutes before he would turn the conversation to the *Modern Prometheus* and raising the dead through medical means. It quite disturbed Father. Were it not for Dr. Henry tutoring Charles and me in German, Father might have found another medical man to install in Raven Hollow. In truth, I found his ideas fascinating. He would talk of science and medical experiments and get a glazed, nearly rabid look in his eyes. Alas, he has retired from medicine and gone to the German colony in Bastrop, Texas, to help manage the family brewery. Before he left, he gifted Charles and me with an albino rabbit, a huge white bunny with red eyes (and a litter she would soon deliver). Rabbits are generally food in these parts, not pets. Lila suggested I move into the upper rooms of the carriage house to care for it only moments after Dr. Henry vacated. It's still cool this March but I like the privacy. I'd rather get up in the middle of the night and stoke my own fire than be in Lila's house.

As for me and little brother, Charles, all is well. My step-mother ignores us most of the day, as she sleeps late when Father is gone. By the time she gets up, we've had breakfast and packed a picnic lunch to go exploring. The redbuds are blossoming, their fuchsia buds brightening the otherwise bare limbs of the trees. Charles is so good about amusing himself while I lie in the sun-shine and read Ellis Bell's *Wuthering Heights*. How I love his novel. I have fond memories of the summer vacation with your family in Atlantic City. Raven Hollow is nothing like Atlantic City, but it is our home.

I am grateful I was able to meet you at Mount Holyoke before Father asked me to return to the nation to help with Charles. How I miss having you for a roommate.

I am enclosing a drawing Charles has done of a rabbit. Doesn't he have a skill beyond any five-year-old you know?
Until another day, oginalii,
Suzanna Fish

March 17, 1856
Raven Hollow, I.T.

Dear Georgia,
I have moved into the carriage house. The spring brought with it misery and I have spent a good deal of time inside these last few days. My nose runs and my eyes water. I'm miserable outside and in but have no fever. You have never seen a boy as kind as Charles. He attends to me daily until his mother notices his absence. I hesitate to tell you how pretty he is, as he is a

light-skinned boyish version of me, though I have always been more handsome than pretty, much like our father. I try to send him away after he follows Mary, when she brings me hot tea and toast with butter and honey. He curls up next to me as I drowse. I awake to find him brushing back my hair or kissing my cheek with his long eyelashes. This morning his mother swooped in and ordered him to stay away from me on threat of a beating. Mary told me Lila doses him with small drops of laudanum when his energy gets to be too much for her, or when she has one of her headaches.

Fortunately today, my father sent word he would be coming back early, and she forgot about Charles, and he was back to comfort me. He pretends to read me some of the books that Dr. Henry left. There are old German ghost stories among his many titles. If Charles could really read them, he might never sleep again. There is quite a treasure trove of scientific papers and books and unguents and equipment tucked away in a large wooden crate. Dr. Henry told me I could do as I wished with the boxes and crates. I hope to further my own studies in medicine. As you know, I am ever interested in science, though Father encourages me to write for a newspaper or teach. Cherokees do not, generally, have the low opinion of women's intellect I see so prevalent in American society. It is only that nation-building is so important. And words build nations.

Donadagohvi,

Suzanna

March 20, 1856

Lovely Georgia,

I am well within a few days of my last letter. It's a good thing, too, because the rabbit delivered her kits! There were four in all, but one died, and I had to hide it before Charley saw it. The mother had kicked it away. I was glad she hadn't started consuming it! It is a lot of work keeping Charley from pestering the mother bun.

While Charley naps, I sneak in and sort through Dr. Henry's boxes. There are some interesting scientific papers from the Royal College of Surgeons in London. There is a paper on "Observations on Apparent Death from Drowning, Hanging, Suffocation by Noxious Vapours, Fainting-Fits, Intoxication, Lightning, Exposure to Cold, etc., and an account of the Proper Means to be employed for recovery" published in 1815 by James Curry. Dr. Henry filled several margins of the articles with notes and drawings. There are also jars of strange liquid and a giant, well-preserved toad! It floats, a warty creature of green and silver. The outside of the jar is marked with the number 13 and other notes I cannot read in the lamplight. I placed the jar in the window of my room that faces the sunset. The other strange unguents I set next to the large iron tub in the room downstairs. In there is a small stove. It takes many trips to the well for Peter to fill the bath basin.

After what I have read about women having to undergo the knife in order to give birth, I believe Charley will be as close as I come to being a mother. The horrors that women go through only to give their husbands an heir! The pain and sadness that comes with bringing forth the generations. You would have wept to have seen my poor mother when she ailed after losing yet another baby boy in the year before she died. Her guilt over the deaths of my many siblings. She was but seventeen, only a few months older than I, when she lost her first child, a daughter, in the year after they came from Georgia. Mary helped Dr. Henry deliver the baby, then after Mama sat with the body a week, that baby was the first Fish to go into the cemetery on my mother's family's land across the road. Mary says Mother was never well after they left Georgia. How cruel to give life to a fragile child! How I used to worry over Charles when he was a baby, his thin thread of breath, his tiny beating heart. To have a child is to become twice as vulnerable to the world's vagaries. To relive the death of the beloved over and over . . . at times before they even pass. I don't know if I will ever have a child, but if I do have a daughter, I shall name her after you.

Please take care, my beloved friend,

I've no one to share my worry, but you.

Suzanna

March 25, 1856
Raven Hollow, I.T.

Dear Georgia,

I hardly know how to explain what I have seen. Yesterday, I surprised Charles with the preserved toad and then we put it back in the large windowsill facing the west. In the afternoon, he and I took a long walk to Spavinaw Creek. The chilly air was exhilarating. Toward suppertime it looked as if a storm was rolling in over the hills, so we hastened home. I had asked Mary to build a fire in my room when we departed, and my room was very warm. The sun was on its descent and light streamed through the toad's jar. Streaks of sunlight shot through the golden liquid.

As I reached for the jar, I could have sworn that the creature was turning slowly. I assumed it was caused by the jar's warming liquid and qualities of pressure, the property of which I know not, but as I held it out for Charles to observe, the toad's eyes blinked in tandem. Open, then closed, then open once more, wide and rolling. The creature stared into my eyes and then kicked as if to swim away.

I dropped the jar and it smashed onto the floor. The toad was not paralyzed for an instant, though I cannot say the same for Charley and me. He glistened with the slimy fluid. On green-silver legs, he hopped with abnormal speed toward Charley. Charley stood gaping but unmoving and upon reaching him, the toad reversed direction, giving me enough time to yank off my wrap and toss it atop the bolting amphibian.

Charley recovered and laughed, running to scoop up the shawl with the toad beneath it. I told him no. I am rarely sharp with him, but I was terrified for him to touch it, I know not why. When he asked me to explain, I lied and shared a fear of warts.

I grabbed the shawl and ran to get an empty jar from Dr. Henry's crates. I reached in blindly for something to cover it, wrestling out a thin leather-bound book by the German alchemist Dippel. I dropped the toad into the jar and topped it with the tattered journal. In hindsight, I realize how foolish and illogical it was to want the toad out of the house, out of the yard, far from Charley and me.

Charley followed me as I carried it down the stairs. The toad settled down and looked around. I tried to explain his existence to myself. If this was a trick by Dr. Henry, it was terribly cruel. How could he know I would find the toad while it lived? And how had it lived nearly two weeks in the strange fluid, within a seemingly airless jar? I am no expert on amphibians, but it seemed unnatural. And yet, here he stared at me, his color poor, his eyes looking as if a veil of gauze covered them. Then the toad jumped, hitting the book covering the jar, causing it to tilt precariously off the jar's top. I spread my fingers around the top of the jar, straining to hold the book down and support the glass's edge as I carried it to the creek. The toad kept hitting the top of the jar. My heartbeat quickened, filling my ears with a sound like crashing waves.

Suddenly, the book dislodged violently and I dropped the jar.

The toad disappeared into the grass in one long leap. It crashed through the brush. We stared after it until we heard it no longer. I knelt to pick up the glass, and Charley picked up the book and began to flip through it.

Poor Charley, he didn't recognize the lovely script was German. I told him who the journal had belonged to and made a poor attempt to explain alchemy. I think I told him alchemy aimed to perfect the imperfect. Perhaps I am really not called to be a teacher.

I flipped through the journal. A lovely, familiar hand and complicated equations filled the first third of the book. Progressively, the writing became nearly indecipherable, blurred in places, and scratched and inked out. I found the last page in a distinctly different hand. Written in much neater script and in English, the journal's final words read: *Johann Konrad Dippel passed from this world while aboard my ship on April 25, 1734. Captain Robert Walton.*

At the time I froze, processing this information slowly. As I write you, I understand my terror at the evidence. Seemingly, the writing on the toad's original label and the diary were the work of one man. Was it possible that the supernatural toad had been captured more than a hundred and twenty years earlier?

We hastened back to the house and I carefully gathered up the glass still covered in the oil, using a piece of vellum, then some crockery to hold it. The toad's label, indeed, was in Dippel's own hand and the date confirmed my fears. The year of collection was listed as 1732. Georgia, I will write more when my thoughts have calmed. Please, speak of this to no one, or they shall think me mad.

Yours ever,

Suzanna

March 28, 1856
Raven Hollow

Dear Georgia,

If only you were here to comb through these notes and reports and books with me. There is so much here. All of Dippel's notes he made in self-study and later at the University of Giessen. Dr. Henry's later copies of the Royal Society reports, especially articles on the resuscitation of the drowned. Lists of minerals and herbs. Jars of decayed plant matter and mineral samples. My own learning is a mere by-product of my father's benign neglect. I have gone without the benefit of true tutoring for the last several months, and now I feel its lack greatly. I am stumbling blindly, reading everything, without knowing if it is at all worthwhile.

I find myself becoming annoyed with Charley as he wants me to play, while I hunger for an end to my ignorance. Finally, I gather several papers and we go out to explore the streams that lead to the lake. I bribe him to search for crawdads and the strange toad, regretting its release. But it is difficult to read deeply and keep a watchful eye on Charley.

Today, I feigned a headache so we might return home. Charley tried to comfort me, taking my basket so that I might not have to carry it while in pain. It was much too big for him, but he could not be dissuaded, the sweet little gentle man. I felt terribly guilty.

We found the house in a flurry of activity. Word had come that my father has broken an ankle in a fall. Lila is preparing to make the long trip to be at his side. She bribed Charley into her lap and talked to him about how much his father loved him. She stroked his curls she wouldn't allow anyone to cut. She asked if he wanted to go with her, but he shook his head, looking at me. When she thought I wasn't looking she slipped him candies from her pocket as if it were a secret, but Charley offered me one immediately, anyway.

It occurred to me that I would have opportunity for quiet study time now that Charley's mother desired his companionship, so I politely refused the candy and slipped away. I shall miss Charley and I hope my father is well soon, but I look forward to a little bit of solitude.

I hastened to my room. Georgia, Dippel sought an end to death! What a benefit to mankind he might have been. According to his notes, some of the golden oil is the very oil of the wise men: myrrh. He wrote of drowning the toad in a bath of salt and blood and ground bone. The liquid would allow the toad to rest in a state of suspended animation, he claimed. Once warmed to body temperature, the amphibian awoke from a very long sleep. No older or worse for wear, if Dippel's postulations are correct.

He wrote, *"I gave the frog enough Laudanum to cause death. But before it breathed its last breath, I held it down in the liquid in the jar. How horrible to feel it writhe in agony, as all creatures fear death, even in its sedated state. Finally, I simply placed the stopper in the jar and put it in the cool saline bath in the dark, for I could no longer stand to watch it die. An hour later I checked on it and it was cool and still, writhing no more. I waited a week to be sure and then brought it slowly to room temperature. I had to be careful not to boil the poor creature. Eventually, I placed the jar in the window as the sun rose. It seemed the toad began to move about languidly. I took the poor creature out and warmed it more aggressively, wrapping it in warm cloths before the fire. Within the hour, it had begun to hop about and seemed well recovered from its week of death."*

Georgia, can you imagine? It is not as if resurrection is without precedent. Why would he write such a thing if it were not true? Think him mad? I would, had I not seen the toad leap away myself.

I close here Georgia.

I have much to learn and think about.

Love,

Suzanna

April 1856
Raven Hollow, I.T.

Dear Georgia,

My letter and your package seemed to have passed each other in the post. First, I must thank you for the Hawthorne book. Lila's home does not quite have seven gables, but I'm enjoying the read when I steal a few moments for leisure reading.

In the time since I last wrote, I am closer to understanding the experiments of Dippel. I have mapped out their patterns and successes and failures. He did a terrible thing following the incident with the toad. He began to make a man from parts of other men. How envious is man of woman's ability to create life! His energies could have been focused in the medical field, in preserving the lives of those unfortunates who meet with accident or illness. I have attempted to create more of the oil by separating out the solution I salvaged from the toad's jar. It is a difficult recipe. I have several jars of possible solutions and no way to test them. I've used so much salt from the storehouse and myrrh from the kitchen, I fear Dolly has noticed.

Lila and Charley have returned. Charley was thrilled with the tiny rabbits which are almost ready to be weaned. Lila pays attention to Charley one day, treating him with presents. The next day she comes to the carriage house with lunch and quickly leaves him behind, so that she might enjoy her supper alone. While they were away, she bought him a little pedigreed dog to play with, and I hate the beast. It charges at the chickens in the yard and bites at Peter and Mary. It steers clear of Dolly, though. I wish I knew her secret. I must keep the door latched when I leave, or I find the dog wreaking havoc in the carriage house upon my return. Charley has no control over the creature and can merely chase it and shriek. However, he loves the terrible thing.

A letter from Father tells us he is well and has decided he wants us all to go with him next school year. I will get to rejoin you in Massachusetts. I hope that I am not too far behind. Please advise me and continue sending me books to read, oginalii. I'm making a special trip to town to mail this to you.

Suzanna

May 1856
I.T.

Georgia,

I doubt that I shall ever see you again. It is possible this is my last letter to you, and I hardly know if I am brave or mad enough to send it. My hand shakes to confide in you, even, weeks after the events have passed.

I returned to my room one morning to find Charley sprawled out on my bed, drawing over Dippel's journal. His little beast was nowhere to be found, but I heard a screaming and snarling in the stairwell. There I found the dog shaking the last baby bunny dead. I kicked him across the room, and he struck the wall with a yelp. Charley came running in and grabbed his pup, yelling at me not to hurt him. I had picked up all the dead rabbits by then, warm and not so bloody, but quite dead. I scolded Charley. He ran out of the room and down the stairs, and, beast that I am, I let him go. I cried over the bodies of the rabbits for several minutes. But then, God forgive me, I thought of the experiment.

I took the kits to the room with the bath and I began to heat up the water. I placed each jar into the bath so that they would all warm up slowly, the scent of myrrh filling the room. I rubbed some of the oil into the rabbits' mouths. There were three bunnies, so I was only able to test the three most likely solutions. I placed each rabbit upside down into the separate cylinders. I was very careful not to lose track of which solution was which. Within the hour, one rabbit's eyes seemed to twitch. I focused all my energy on this rabbit. I placed my hands into the cylinder and rubbed the ointment and heat into its head and ears and belly. In my vigor I splashed it into my eyes. I squinted as they burned. Salted tears touched my lips, and I tasted the ocean.

Finally I removed the rabbit from the jar and placed it on a quilt over the cast-iron wood stove, warming it more quickly. It opened its eyes. Soon, Mama rabbit was nursing the formerly dead rabbit and cleaning it furiously. My joy did not remain such, for long. The poor rabbit's broken neck remained so and I am no surgeon. Repairing an injury such as that is beyond my ken. Yet, the poor kit lived. She lives still, for in the month since this happened, I haven't had the heart to dispatch her. Mama rabbit abandoned her shortly after that night. I keep them separate in fear the mother will eat the small helpless creature. I feed her milk by hand and hope that her bones will repair themselves.

I am sure my behavior shocks you.

I wish this were the worst I had to tell you.


I went into the kitchen in the house later that night to eat. It was almost morning, and Dolly was busying about starting the fire and breakfast. She frowned to see me. I asked her where

Charley was sleeping, and Dolly said he was alone in his room. This surprised me for we have spoiled him so, and he always sleeps with either me or his mother. She then told me that earlier he had come back into the house crying and inconsolable, so his mother gave him a big dose of laudanum and sent him to bed.

Angrily, I dashed upstairs to get him. He was snoring heavily. I tried to wake him, but he would not wake. I shook him repeatedly and the snoring stopped. I carried him downstairs and called for Mary and his mother. His mother would not come down until she was dressed. She told Mary I was being hysterical. We laid Charley on a blanket in front of the fireplace and his breathing was slow. His heart seemed to not be beating as quickly as it should have been, either. Peter was sent to fetch the nearest physician. Mary began to search the house for ammonia or smelling salts. I was sure there was ammonia in the bath of the carriage house, but I ran to get it myself as the experiment had yet to be cleaned up.

As I passed the small broken bunny, wrapped alone in its blankets, I thought I heard it cry piteously and that cry filled me with terror. When I got back in the house, I found my stepmother weeping over Charley. Her light-colored eyes were streaked with red. Their hair blended together, so I could not tell where one ended and the other began.

I hissed at her and made a comment about her selfishness. I handed her the ammonia and told her to remove his shirt and rub some on his chest. I held a cloth with it under his nose, but he did not respond. Mary stoked the fire and we wrapped him in warm blankets, talking to him constantly. At length, the physician arrived. I retreated to my room to clean up the failed bits of the experiment. I had one good cask of oil and a barrel of salt, and Charley was small. I didn't yet know what I might do.

When I entered the kitchen, I saw the look on the doctor's

face. He told us that if Charley made it through the night, there might be hope. His face seemed doubtful. We took turns sitting with him through the day. I was loath to leave him with his own mother. Still, I wanted to make sure I had everything I needed should the worst happen. I set the cask of the successful solution on my wood stove to warm. It would be enough to fill the bottom of the bathtub.

I returned to the kitchen and found my stepmother sleeping.

Charley was no longer breathing. His eyes had flicked open, and he stared, unseeing, with terror at the ceiling. I grabbed Charley's tiny body and wept silently. I would save my brother. I would not let this innocent child die, if I could help it. I carried him to my little house, undressed him, and then wrapped him in wool blankets. I had to move Dippel's journal, and I saw that Charley had written on a blank page in the back, "Suzanna=EℲGT." My tears came loudly then. My heart hurt and I wept and prayed for God to let Charley live. I was willing to trade my life for his. How would I live if the last thing I said to him was in a rare moment of anger?

I returned to the tub and filled it with water and salt. I stirred in the heated oil. I carried Charley in, unwrapped him, and placed the blankets next to the stove. I placed Charley facedown in the tub and began to rub the warm oil onto his body. I pressed on his back, causing his lungs to empty and inhale. I flipped him over and continued to rub the oil onto him, trying to warm him, forcing some oil into his mouth and nose, letting it run into his eyes. I saw a movement behind his eyelids first, then heard a choking sound. I yanked him from the tub and took him to the fire, where I wrapped him in a buffalo robe and blankets. I sat with him in my lap, rubbing him and talking to him in our father's language, praying to Creator, whispering and humming softly against his skin.

Finally, he seemed to stir. Alas, his look was one of confusion and madness. I spoke to him, but he said nothing back to me. Tears ran down his cheeks, and he shrank from my touch. I dressed him and told myself this was temporary. That he had suffered death and that he was bound to eventually recover. He was languid, his eyes tracking poorly. I told him how much I loved him and how glad I was that he lived.

I picked him up and he was unresisting. Back in the kitchen, I laid him down on the blanket and kissed him.

The doctor came back the next morning and looked him over. He congratulated us on our care of Charley. He came back every day for a month. Charley seemed to grow stronger, but he didn't speak. I tried reteaching him our syllabary. However, when he became upset, he only wailed. It could be as simple as not getting a sweet or getting a bite from his dog. Either way, his response was loud and increasingly violent. At the end of the month, the doctor pulled my stepmother aside and suggested Charley's fit had damaged his brain. He suggested that a nurse or an asylum might eventually be needed if Charley didn't show improvement soon. I had watched Charley's mother grow increasingly irritated with him. After the doctor left, I cornered her alone in her room, and told her this was her fault and that she would be a mother to him, or I would tell everyone what she'd done. My stepmother's face grew red, and she ordered me out.

I found Charley downstairs staring into the fire. I patted his head and he looked up at me. Charley and I went to the kitchen, and I proceeded to make an apple pie and a great mess to entertain him. I poured flour on the table and showed him how to write his name, but he just made crazed marks and pounded on the table, making clouds of flour. He had grown stronger—physically stronger than any five-year-old should be—and I had to distract him with spoons of sugar to get him to stop banging on the table. I put the apple pie into the oven. I let him play with the extra dough, showing him how to make little creatures. Finally, I left the room for a moment to retrieve a broom to start to clean up our mess. While I was gone, Charley ran over to the oven to pull the pie out with his bare hands. From the hallway I heard his shriek of pain, but his mother reached the kitchen before me. He ran to her, wailing, salty tears streaming down his wan cheeks, his flour- and dough-covered hands reaching for her. She slapped him. Charles shoved her impossibly hard, and she fell back on the stone floor, her head hitting with such force that it made the most awful sound, and then bounced again with a sickening, wet finality. Charles immediately ran out of the room as Dolly and Mary ran in. I lied and told them that Lila had slipped. I leaned over her and held her eyelids open, looking for movement. I felt blood oozing between my fingers as I cradled her broken head. My explanation was simple. Charley ran to hug her, and she slipped in the flour and hit her head. By then Peter had come into the house and I asked him to summon the doctor. I did not go find Charley until after the doctor arrived and declared her dead. He was hiding in the bath in the carriage house. He was holding the still-living broken rabbit. I do not think either of them will ever get any better. At a loss, Suzanna

~~July 1856, Indian Territory~~
~~Dear . . .~~
~~August 1856~~
~~September 1856~~

February 1857
Raven Hollow, I.T.

Dear Georgia,

Finally, there is some good news. The bunny's tail twitched in response to being petted the other day. I watched to see if it was a mere reflex, and if it was, she does it when she is pleased, as a fresh strawberry elicited the same reaction. Progress for the kit and Charley may ever be slow. All I can offer my brother is my love and protection.

My father came home in June to fetch Lila's body and take her back to be buried with her people in the East. He has not returned since then. We rarely write each other for there is little happy news. Occasionally, I send him messages from Peter about the farm. None of us go to church on Sundays. There is no question of us going to be with Father at this time. I do not know if Charley will ever be older than he was when I put him in the bath. In the months since then, he is nearly unchanged, as far as I can tell.

Every day I instruct him in our syllabary and try to teach him the names of things around him. I am never far from him, as I can't trust him to not lose his temper. Also, I fear for how he will be treated by others. I have moved into the house and we sleep in a large bed, with the moon lighting our room. A few minutes ago, I awoke and heard his first words. He was whispering in the dark to the tiny rabbit, "Jisdu gvgeyui Suzanna gvgeyui Jisdu gvgeyui Suzanna gvgyui . . ."

Yours,

Suzanna

# An Un-Fairy Story

Edgar Spears, Jr.
Kawohni 1, 1866
04/01/1866

My etsi died ten years ago of tuberculosis when I was five years old.

This is the story of what happened shortly before she died, while my grandmother was caring for me and my little brother. My eduda, Preacher Spears, had asked his wife to come from back East to care for me and my brother and sister in those last months of my mother's life. Grandmother is a white woman from up North. She and my grandfather met at a religious seminary in Connecticut. When they married it was a scandal.

They came to live in Indian Territory when we were removed from our homelands. Eventually, though, she took my father up North to raise him with her people, to put him in white schools. Shortly after grandmother came back to Cherokee Nation all those years later, my Etlogi Ama, who I had never met before, showed up to take my mother to Hot Springs. There were rumors the mineral waters could cure the consumption that was killing Etsi. My baby sister, Georgia, was too young to leave my mother, so they took her with them.

Charles, who is named after my mother's brother, was about

three at the time and my grandmother adored him. He is lighter-skinned than me, and I have been told, the spitting image of my father who was killed in the War between the States. Grandmother recently put him in a boarding school up North and I don't know when I'll get to see him again. We exchange the occasional letter. Maybe one day I will tell him this story.

It was a bright and sunny morning when the four of us returned home from church and found an owl on our front porch. It gave me and Eduda pause, but my grandmother just shooed it away. I felt sure it meant my mother's death was at hand. My grandmother does not put stock in Indian beliefs, but she did tell my grandfather that she was going to write my mother and aunt at Hot Springs and let them know she thought it best to take me and Charles back East for what she called a "proper" education.

Her son, Edoda, had a proper Northern education and he did not care for it at all. He came back to Indian Territory as soon as he could get. Hearing her talk this way put me in a mood and before long I had irritated her enough that she ran me out of the house. Carrying my blowgun, I ran off into the woods between our land and the church. I shot at squirrels and birds and anything that moved until every creature in the woods seemed to know I was there and they all got hid.

That made me even angrier, and I'm ashamed to say it, but I started to cry. I missed my mother and I didn't want to leave my home or my grandfather. I didn't want to go to some boarding school to learn a trade, where the only family I might ever get to see was my grandmother. I cried something awful. I was a small child, and small children are apt to cry when they have feelings too big to hold inside.

When I finally quit crying, I looked up and there was a white rabbit sitting in front of me. I slowly loaded my blowgun, but before it was even to my lips, the rabbit was gone, hightailing it into the darker parts of the woods. I jumped up and chased him, but he was fast. I ran and ran, not even knowing why I was following him. That rabbit was so fast that sometimes I lost sight of him. Sometimes when I blinked I thought he was a two-foot-tall person with long black hair streaming behind him, but then I would see it was just a white rabbit, though really it should have been brown, like the rest of the rabbits around here.

Well, that rabbit ducked into a cave back in the woods and I followed him all the way through. I knew better than to go in a cave. My grandfather told me once that those spaces are not to be entered lightly. He only ever tells a thing just one time. If it weren't important, he wouldn't bother saying it at all.

The cave got narrower and smaller. That rabbit disappeared out the end of the cave and I got down on my hands and knees and crawled out after him. When I came out the other end, there was a small village with houses that looked like they were built for someone my size, and instead of a rabbit, there was a small man squatting next to this round piece of boulder jutting out of the ground and covered in carvings. I had never seen anything like this rock, or this little man, though I had heard of them both. The man spoke Cherokee, but it sounded a little different than the way I am used to hearing it.

He called me over to him and offered me some food he had in a twined bag. I hadn't realized I was hungry until he held a peach out to me. I squatted next to him and he asked me about my troubles. He said he had heard me crying and wondered if he could help. Before I finished that peach, I had told him everything. He listened and began to smoke a small, finely carved pipe.

"Your people didn't leave this land by choice," he said. "I would hate it if you could not be spared this." He took another draw on the pipe.

"Camp here tonight while we think on this. We are going to

have a dance and you can come eat with us and listen to some of the stories your people are in danger of forgetting."

So that is what I did. I stayed and went to the dance. I listened to the stories told around the fire that night and saw clearly what I would lose if I went to the white schools back East. I wanted to stay with my people and live in our way, in our community. Even though my grandfather was a preacher, he believed in the old ways. Grandmother had left Indian Territory rather than watch my grandfather grow more Cherokee every day.

That night I slept happy.

Imagine how sad I was when the next morning the man came to wake me and walk me back home. He told me to remember all the stories I had heard the night before, but made me promise not to speak of my visit for seven years. I understood what he meant, for to break a promise like that is certain death. Then he handed me a thick blanket and told me to stay warm. I smiled but didn't openly laugh. The summer had been hot and wet when I crawled through the cave the day before. Still, I wrapped the blanket tight around my shoulders, and crawled back through the hole, into the small cavern, and out the other end. Overnight the weather back home had turned.

My lips chattered and I walked as fast as I could.

I didn't look forward to facing my Grandmother after spending a night away without her permission. I heard the chopping of wood and the crying of a baby. As I got closer to the wood lot near the church, the chopping stopped, and the baby no longer cried. In the distance, I saw a man holding a baby and singing softly, while a dark-haired woman held an ax near a stack of wood.

"Eduda!" I yelled. I began to run and my grandfather turned and stared at me. Etlogi Ama leaned the ax against the stump of a tree.

I ran to him and hugged him around the waist. "I don't want to leave, Eduda," I cried. "I want to stay here. I want to stay with you."

My aunt took my little sister from my grandfather. He kneeled down and looked me in the face. "Edgar?"

"Yes, Grandfather. I don't want to go away to school."

My grandfather hugged me tight.

"We've been looking for you for four months. Your grandmother gave up and left a week ago and took Charles with her. Your Etlogi Ama just came back this morning."

I didn't speak for a long time after that. When people asked me where I'd been, I'd just shrug. Grandfather and Ama didn't ask me any questions, though. When we got home, Grandfather took the blanket I was wearing and looked at it for a long time. It has been on my bed ever since.

That was ten years ago, and this is the first time I have told this story. I hope I live long enough to tell it again. It's dark now. It is no longer time to speak of these things.

# Hell Hound in No Man's Land

Wilbur Spears, Jess King
Duninhdi 31, 1919
10/31/1919

RIFLES AND BAYONETS OF WWI

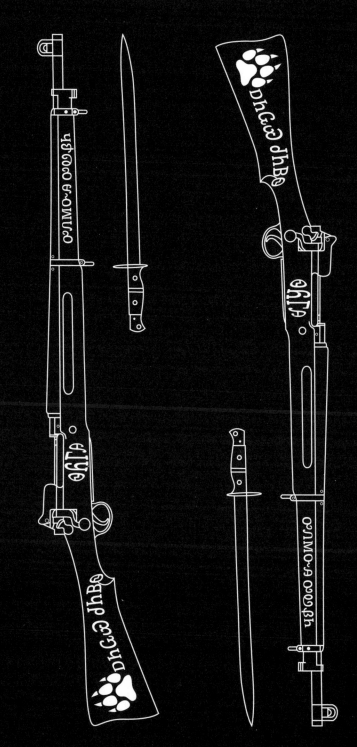

U.S. Rifle, Caliber .30, 1917 Model

U.S. Rifle, Caliber .30, 1917 Model

S pecial report to the *Tulsa Specter* by news special service
Raven's Hollow, Oklahoma—Oct 31, 1919

There is more evidence the "Hound of Mons" was not a legend but a true terror in No Man's Land, according to stories heard around town. Wilbur Spears, son of Cherokee preacher Edgar Spears, Jr., recently returned with an unusual war story that was confirmed by his cousin, fellow soldier Jess King, son of local ranchers Billy and Georgia King.

According to sources, the two men, who only speak Indian, were in charge of taking care of the horses with the 13th Infantry at the Meuse-Argonne Offensive. Sergeant Jones, also from Oklahoma, was well-liked and unfortunately killed soon after the men reached their assignment in France. He was quickly replaced by a Sergeant White who showed up in the middle of one of the bloodiest battles these Cherokee boys would ever see.

There was a full moon on the rise on that dark and stormy night. Privates Spears and King had returned several horses to a barn far from the fighting when a barrage of gunfire cut them off from their troop in the trenches. Mindful of their duty, they took care of the various injuries of the horses and then bedded down for the night. They had just lain down when the howl of a wolf was heard close by. The horses erupted in fear and the men secured the barn, latching the sliding door just in time as they heard the sound of animal nails on wood.

Neither man nor horse got any sleep as they listened to a large creature stalk the barn, pawing at its timbers. King and Spears sat back to back, pistols ready. Eventually, the creature began to scrabble at the mud beneath the door, digging feverishly. King unsheathed his bayonet and stabbed at the huge paw, until he pinned it to the ground. The creature wailed and yanked its paw back, cutting it nearly in two with the blade. The creature then hurled its whole body against the barn door. The men considered shooting through the door, but thought it wise to wait until they could see the beast. This went on for hours, covered by the noise of the rain and the front. The men slept not a wink as the assault would randomly begin and end. Finally, as the sun began to rise and the machine gunfire on the front abated, the attack by the creature stopped. When the horses were no longer unnerved, they knew it was over. The two men stayed put until two other soldiers showed up to take over the watch.

Outside, the barn was covered in large bloody paw prints. The exhausted privates, Spears and King, returned to camp. Passing the hospital tent, they saw Sergeant White, looking haggard and having his right hand bandaged. He was loaded into an ambulance with other wounded men for a more substantial hospital.

There is no record of a Sergeant White ever transferring into or out of the 13th Infantry.

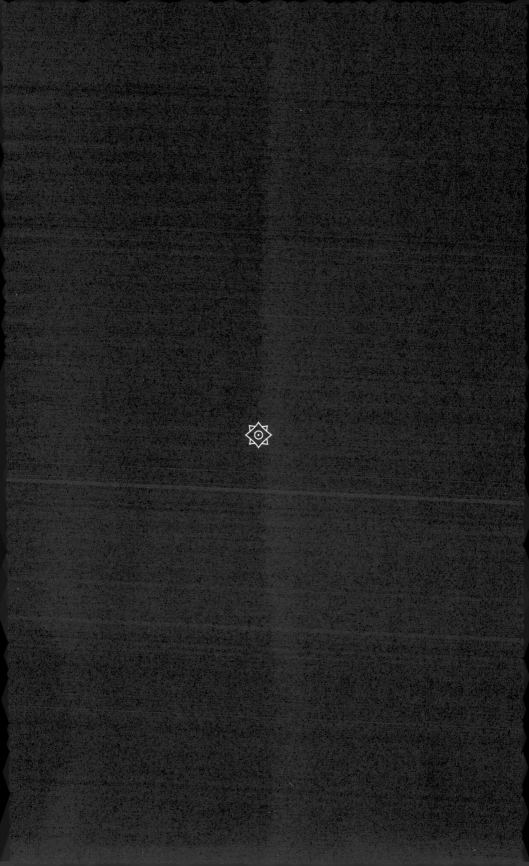

# Homecoming

Rabbit Wilson

Anisgvti 26, 1945

05/26/1945

**B**eing roused by the smell of bacon and coffee was Rabbit Wilson's favorite way to wake up. It was better than having icy spring water poured on his head by his little brother, Pug. It was better than the wet odor of oatmeal his oldest brother, Joseph, said filled the boarding school. On the stove, beans and grape dumplings simmered for tomorrow's celebration, too. It would be a good feast to honor his oldest brother's return from the war.

For the two years Joseph had been in the army, Rabbit's mother had worried. A month ago, she saw in her tea leaves he was on his way home. The Wilson family knew Joseph was returning before it was announced on the radio during the broadcast from *The Grand Ole Opry*. Soon after, a letter arrived saying Joseph was being discharged. He would come back with other surviving and wounded Cherokee boys.

In this part of Oklahoma, most eligible Indians had enlisted to fight. Some even lied about their age so they could go. Joseph had been the first Wilson to go to war since his edudu, Robert Wilson. Joseph quit training for a minor-league ball team so he could join up.

Etlogi Dolly arrived with her two sons, Ujets and Yona, later that morning. One boy was called Ujets because he was always grinning like a possum. His brother was called Yona, which means "bear." The name suited the younger boy, strong and husky. Etlogi Dolly's oldest son, Jackie Lee, who would always be twelve, had hung himself outside the boarding school dorms in Wyandotte just before Christmas a year earlier. With Joseph and Jackie Lee gone, Rabbit was the oldest at thirteen.

Etlogi Dolly and his mother were going to cook all day. The four boys were banned from the house, otherwise the women would never get ahead of the boys' appetites. More aunts, uncles, and cousins would be showing up all weekend.

Rabbit and the other boys spent the first part of the day doing chores. They cut and hauled firewood from the woods where the pecan trees grew. They chased and killed snakes. They gigged crawdads and boiled them over a fire for lunch. Rabbit had learned everything he knew about hunting and fishing from Joseph. He was trying to train up the younger boys.

Two years earlier, on Joseph's last night at home, he had taken Jackie Lee and Rabbit out to spend the night gigging frogs, crawdads, and fish. It had started to rain. Joseph was packing up their catch so far, a burlap bag full of big carp and catfish. It was Jackie Lee's turn to shine the light into the water, kicking at the weeds to frighten the fish and crawdads out to be caught. Joseph stabbed the water with the fork-shaped gig, the wooden pole it was attached to as long as both boys put together. They were about to give up when Jackie Lee hollered he had spotted an eel. He and Rabbit gave chase running upstream. From behind, Joseph hollered, "Hlesdi!"

Suddenly, the creature swam straight out of the water into a bush. Not thinking, Jackie Lee reached in and grabbed it. Fortunately, he got his hand just behind the back of the water moccasin's head. The snake opened its mouth wide, his fangs at the ready. Both boys screamed, their mouths as wide as the snake's. Jackie Lee flung the viper as far from them as he could. The boys turned and ran back to where Joseph stood shaking his head. "Dang," he said in English, "you threw that snake like it was a baby Uktena."

Their grandmother, Nelly, had been allotted 160 acres when the Cherokee Nation was forced to accept the breaking up of their reservation. This meant the Indian Nations would have to give up more land that the Federal Government would then sell cheap or give away to settlers. Their allotment was somewhat intact, though prime grazing land adjoining the white neighbors on either side had been chiseled away in criminally cheap leases.

Directly behind the backyard was the small family cemetery. Cherokee words were carved into its sandstone markers. The occupants were mostly young children, babies, and toddlers who never made it past three. Some had died in a smallpox epidemic, others in the 1918 flu. Would-be aunts or uncles who hadn't survived the accidents and illnesses that came with growing up on a farm. No one was supposed to play in the cemetery.

Rabbit, Pug, Yona, and Ujets spent the rest of the day horsing around. Between the chicken coop and the house was enough space to play baseball. When Joseph had been home, he never let the boys sit still. Joseph could hit the ball farther than anyone in the county. But when he pitched, he always threw the ball so the younger boys could hit it. That afternoon the boys played baseball until twilight, when a pop fly caught Pug above his left eye. He staggered into the house, leaving only three of them.

Rabbit declared the front porch base and hollered, "Not it!"

The boys dashed over rocks, around pecan trees, and dove out of each other's reach. Rabbit hid beneath a mimosa tree with low-hanging branches. His cousin, Ujets, struck him from behind, then dashed back away, leaving him sprawled on the ground. Yona ran by and then disappeared into the house.

From where Rabbit lay, he saw a boy dash out of the grave-yard. From this distance, Rabbit couldn't tell who it was. Pug must have recovered enough to come back out to play. That ball had shaken up his brains, though. He'd get it if his mother caught him playing on the graves. She'd do a lot more than holler "Hlesdi!"

Rabbit jumped up and ran toward him. The boy turned and disappeared back over the tall grass that ringed the burial yard. Instead of giving chase, Rabbit cut back around the house. He just barely missed his cousin Ujets as he made it to the safety of the front porch. Both boys stood looking at each other, bent half-way over with their hands on their knees, breathing hard. Rabbit's mother hollered from the back door that dinner was ready. Ujets grinned at him and then disappeared into the house.

A noise in the backyard caught Rabbit's attention and he ran toward it. When he rounded the corner of the house, a dark shadow was cutting back toward the front yard. Rabbit's running was slower now as he chased the boy. Just ahead of him, the boy cut backward, making for the cemetery once more. Rabbit reached his hand out. He could have sworn he'd made contact with the boy's shoulder, but he only grabbed air.

Rabbit slowed to a walk. It was true dark now. The squares of light on the grass from the kerosene lamps in the kitchen glowed yellow. His mother stepped out of the back door and ordered Rabbit to get cleaned up and come eat. As he stepped inside the dark well-house, she turned and went back inside. Rabbit pulled up some of the icy-cold spring water. He poured it into a tin cup and drank. He filled and emptied the cup twice. Then he washed his face in the freezing water.

When he felt the shadow run past the well-house door, he ignored it. He'd had enough. Beans and fried pork called him. Instead of chasing the shadow, he walked up the stone steps and into the kitchen. At the top step he hollered, "Chooch, c'mon. Let's eat."

The smells of biscuits and sausage greeted Rabbit. He filled his plate and told his mother and aunt, "He's still outside." The room got quiet.

"Who's still outside?" demanded his mother.

Rabbit looked around. Ujets and Yona were refilling their plates. Rabbit poked his head into the front room. His wounded younger brother, Pug, sat in a chair and held a wet rag to his head. Rabbit returned to the kitchen.

"Outside. There was another boy running from me outside."

His mother laughed. "Chooch," she said, "I told you not to play out there after dark. You've been chasing a skilly."

Rabbit sat down at the kitchen table. He leaned over his plate and thanked Unelanvhi for the food. He thought of the cousins and uncles who never got to grow up. What kind of man had his brother Joseph become? Rabbit decided that when it was time for him to go to boarding school, he would run away. He would live in the cabin his Eduda had built back in the hills. He would hunt for deer and grow corn and raise chickens. When it was time for Pug to go to school, he could come live with Rabbit.

Rabbit sopped his biscuit in the gravy. He chewed slowly, savoring the bread and gravy with its bits of sausage. His mother refilled his plate before he was done. Being alive tasted good.

The evening was cooler than usual. Firewood was brought in. Quilts were placed all around the floor. Rabbit's mother came in and sat down in front of the fireplace with an iron poker in her hand, watching the fire. Rabbit's blanket was directly behind her chair in front of the fire. Ujets plopped down behind him and was soon snoring. He watched the fire burn on the other side of her chair. He was just drifting off when the first snake fell from high in the chimney into the flames.

*Thwack*. His mother stood and struck quickly.

Rabbit sat up. It was a good-sized snake, dark skin and coppery in the flames. She struck it again and fished it out of the fire. The smell of damp burning filled the air. She dropped it in the ash bucket next to the fireplace. The other boys slept through her quiet killing. Rabbit was good and awake now, listening for the sound of snakes falling into the fire. In the distance, out by the road, he heard two crows bickering.

*Thwack*.

Rabbit sat up again.

"Where there's one, there's two," his mother said. "At least."

Rabbit watched the fire a few more minutes.

"Chooch, go to sleep."

Rabbit turned away from the fire and squeezed his eyes tight. He thought he heard footsteps on the front porch.

"Etsi."

"Go to sleep, Chooch."

"I heard something."

They both listened and heard the soft cry of the screen door.

His mother got up and went to the front window and pulled the curtain back.

"Who is it, Mom?"

Rabbit's mother opened the door and went outside. She closed it behind her. Rabbit stood up, not sure whether to watch the fire or the front door.

He went to the window and peeked outside. A tall man was standing on the porch, his hands in his pockets. His mother was talking quietly to him. The man leaned down and picked up a large duffel bag and they turned to come inside.

Rabbit scrambled to open the door.

The man stepped into the house, an army-green hat on his head, taller and skinnier than Rabbit remembered him.

"Siyo, Joseph."

Joseph nodded and set his bag quietly next to the door. The bridge of the hat covered his eyes, while the firelight danced across the rest of his face.

It was midnight and the world was asleep.

Joseph reached up and took his hat off, folding it up in his hands. Still, his eyes seemed to be in shadows.

Their mother led Joseph to the chair in front of the fire. He sat down and she handed him the iron poker and told him in Cherokee to watch for snakes. As he passed him, Rabbit noticed Joseph smelled like dust and sweat, like he'd walked all day. Rabbit rolled back up in his quilt behind the chair and watched his brother's unmoving legs and the fire.

In the kitchen, his mother warmed food and filled a plate. Soon the smell of beans was covering the grit of dust from Joseph's long walk home. He put the poker down next to the fire and took the plate of food from his mother. She got another chair from the kitchen and brought it in to sit next to him.

She sat next to Joseph's still form for a long time. She stood up and took the bucket with the snakes outside. Before she left, she grabbed the ax they kept next to the fireplace. Rabbit heard a few thwacks and then she returned to sit vigil.

"Son, eat," she commanded.

They all waited. She put another log on the fire and stabbed it toward the back with the iron poker. Sparks flew up and out onto the hearth.

Rabbit watched his brother's still form through exhausted eyes. He fell asleep listening to the spoon scrape the bottom of the bowl.

# Maria Most Likely

*J*

Mary/Maria Spears Henry

Dehaluyi 11, 1968

06/11/1968

J esus rolled slowly between Maria's fingers.
INRI
Italy
INRI
Italy
INRI
Black beads, tarnished silver chain, charm-sized Mary and baby Jesus, beads, beads, beads, hail Mary full of grace, beads, beads, beads, Iesus Nazarenus Rex Iudaeorum died for your sins. She clutched the rosary tightly in her left hand while she filled in the ovals on the mandatory CAP form.

Maria, blue ribbon for penmanship, second grade. Yearbook editor. Member of the National Honor Society. Girl Scout. Girl most likely to succeed. Ask anyone. Maria was a good girl.

"Maria, my lady of sorrows," Joseph had teased her this morning. He had tiptoed into the bedroom home from work early and found her curled up on the bed, weeping.

"You have a bandit to thank for this, you know? I get held up at gunpoint, again, and the boss lets me 'clock out early.'" He sat down on the edge of the bed and ran his rough hands through Maria's shiny black hair. "Is the honeymoon over, baby?"

In response, she reached over to put her arm around his waist, but he gently pushed her arm away and stood up. He leaned over and kissed her on the forehead, mumbling, "Got to have a bath first, baby. Go back to sleep."

Maria had rolled back over and stared into darkness. She had swallowed back the ever-present sour taste in her mouth, the nausea tickling the base of her throat.

Six hours later she was using a lead pencil to fill in an answer sheet. She was stumbling on "Full legal birth name" because she hadn't gone by it for years. She had been named Mary Spears after a woman she had never met, the sister of her grandfather Wilbur Spears. But on the first day of school, Joseph had christened her Maria, and the name had stuck. It made life easier, the assumptions that went with a name like Maria. If your skin was not quite "white" and your name was Maria, no one asked you how much Indian you were or if you practiced your Native religion. Passing was easy. The only people she knew of who had made money from being a Cherokee Indian, weren't.

She filled the dots in quickly and couldn't have said later what answers she had chosen. She read the instructions at the end of the page: "Please sign and date. Upon completion, dial six."

She picked up the phone's heavy black handset and dialed. A ringing began and it seemed very far away. It was followed by a click and the quiet white noise of a taped message whirring to life. "Hello, and welcome to the CAP Brief Therapy Program. Please place your paperwork in the drawer on the right side of the desk. Then dial zero."

The answer sheet. Her identity. Race. Level of education. Zip code. Be completely honest. This process is completely confidential. Information is compiled only for statistical purposes. Her breath left her in a sigh that crushed her womb as she dropped the paperwork into the empty drawer. When she dialed zero, the phone began to ring once more. She imagined God on a faraway cloud looking down at the earth, down at her, the phone summoning him to his desk, a prayer of the penitent necessitating that God direct Michael to run the show, God picking up the phone, a warm voice saying,

"Hello, Mary."

Startled, she hastily hung up the phone and looked around the room frantically. She hadn't put Mary on the form. There were two doors, and she couldn't remember which one she had come in. In the empty foyer, she had been preoccupied and entered as soon as she was buzzed in, staring ahead and seeing nothing. She had gone straight to the desk without looking around the room. It was nondescript, furnished like every other doctor's office she had ever been in at the Indian Hospital she had gone to as a child. She hadn't a clue which solid wood door was the exit.

Maria tried to open the drawer and retrieve the form, but found it locked. Flight was not an option. She sat down at the desk and placed her chin on top of her closed fists. She tried to slow her shallow breathing.

She picked the heavy black receiver up again. Once more she dialed zero. The ringing resumed. Perhaps Jesus would be left in charge this time, she hoped rather dizzily, twisting the hand that still clutched her rosary into the folds of her out-of-season wool skirt.

Once more the voice, cold and metallic she realized now, spoke: "Hello, Maria. Welcome to Confession, Absolution, and Penance."

"Hello," she whispered, her voice shakier than she expected. Had she misheard?

"Shall we begin?"

Maria was breathing shallowly again. "I'm not sure"—her throaty whisper was barely audible—"maybe this was a bad idea."

The other line was empty.

Maria waited. She heard a whirring, and then, "You're in a lot of pain, aren't you, Maria?"

Maria only nodded.

"Why don't you tell your story, and we can proceed from there?"

Maria took a deep breath and exhaled. How many times had she told this story to herself, not daring to even write it down, not daring to speak the words in the confessional? When she thought them, she knew them to be true and the words escaped before she could edit them. "I've done something that would kill my husband if he ever found out."

For a moment there was silence and then once more the mechanical voice said, "Please, go on when you're ready."

She thought of Joe, catching up on his sleep, six hours earlier facing a drug addict with a gun in a cold 7-Eleven before being forced to walk into a freezer. If he awoke in their apartment now, he would assume she was in class. Always supportive of his promising Maria. Proud and happy to be with "the girl most likely to . . ."

She started again, "If Joe finds out . . ."

"You'll have to start at what you believe to be the beginning."

She sighed. She wished her story didn't have to be told. Silent confession would be better. Especially when you had to buy forgiveness.

The beginning. When you make a bad choice, when you do something that will break the heart of the one person who loves you most in all the world, when is the beginning? When he held your hand in kindergarten? When you went on your first date?

When you looked wistfully at the world where you always felt like an outsider? She decided to start with the evening it happened.

"I went to a party after graduation. I was salutatorian so I got to introduce the valedictorian." She felt a creeping blush. Would one brag to God about being high school salutatorian? "Joe dropped me off at this party afterward. He had to go to work and this girl I know promised to drive me home." She stopped. There were no windows in the small office she was in, and it seemed as if the lights had dimmed. She closed her eyes for a moment and then opened them. Still, it seemed dark. No matter. The darker the better, Maria thought, as she clutched the black plastic handset too tightly, her fingers beginning to feel numb.

"Joe and I have known each other forever. Since we were kids. He's older and he takes care of me. I mean, he's the one working and I'm just going to school." She stopped again, waiting. "Even when Mom was alive, she never had any extra money or love." She paused, ashamed of her whining, her excuses, blaming a dead woman for my mistakes, she thought. Her tale was caught in her throat.

She wound her fingers through the phone's black cord.

"So, I was sitting alone and watching everyone. It seemed like everybody there was getting drunk, and the music was loud, and the house was nice. It belonged to some rich kid whose parents were out of town. And I felt free for the first time ever. I didn't have a paper to turn in or a project or a date with Joe and I was just watching things, watching everyone the way I always do. It felt kind of lonely. Like I wasn't connected to anything or anyone anymore." She paused thoughtfully, as if in saying it aloud she had reached both an inevitable and surprising conclusion. "And then from across the room Lucas started talking to me . . ."

✼

"Congratulations, beautiful Maria." An olive-skinned boy with dark shaggy hair and the black eyes of a doe was speaking to her.

Maria was sitting on the couch, drinking a soda and thumbing through her copy of the yearbook. Without looking up she recognized Lucas's cool, soft voice. Lucas the artist-poet. Deeply talented, deeply sad.

She smiled. "I hear you're off to art school."

He shrugged. "I'm off, anyway. What about you? What do you want to do?"

Maria began to tell him about the partial scholarship she had to become an English teacher, but he shook his head.

"Is that what you want to do? Or what you think you should do, you know, to be a productive member of society?" He rolled his eyes as he finished. He glanced around at the house and the drunk students to make it clear his meaning was exactly the opposite of what he said.

"I like reading," she stammered. Books, she thought, I want a world of books. I want to write a world that I want to exist. She thought about this all the time, but no one ever asked the question that would force her to put it into words. Books were the reason she had taken the job as a clerk at the library. A job where they wouldn't even let you shelve books or check out customers if you got pregnant. What a world. She changed the subject awkwardly, "Want to sign my yearbook?"

For the first time since she had known him, he smiled. Coming over to the couch, he sat next to her, strangely familiar, oddly comfortable. She handed over the yearbook and the silver pen Joe had given her that evening as a graduation gift.

"Can I sign yours?" she asked.

Lucas laughed and shook his head.

He took the pen from her. "What would be the point of me

having a yearbook? So people could write, 'You'd be so handsome if you smiled more?' I don't think so."

He flipped the pages until he reached the section for the seniors, some people they had both been in classes with for the last twelve years. "Let's tell the future instead."

Maria laughed.

Lucas didn't.

"Monica Beal"—a pretty cheerleader—"goes to college and graduates from Marijuana to Heroin."

"Don't write that." She reached for the pen, but Lucas pulled it away.

"Not poetic enough?"

"Someone might read that."

"You'll never see these people again. They'll write, 'Stay beautiful,'—he paused and looked at her—"'you sweet girl' and 'call me sometime.' But you just try it."

Maria frowned. "So, you have a gift, do you? Is this your precognition?"

He fixed her with his black eyes. "You never really saw these people before."

Maria flushed.

"Bob Ewing, fat boy turns frat boy."

"Stop," Maria forced a laugh she didn't mean. "I'm serious." She leaned closer toward him, reaching for the pen. He didn't pull away this time as she wrapped her fingers around it.

"Joseph," he whispered, as she pulled the pen away. "Dumb, lucky bastard."

A couple tumbled onto the couch next to Lucas, pressing him momentarily into her. She stared into his eyes and wondered whether they were bottomless, or completely empty.

Lucas stood up without breaking his gaze and said, "Let's go outside." He put his hand out, and when she touched his cold fingers, they wrapped tightly around her wrist. He pulled her up from the couch without effort. His strength surprised her. She followed him to the quiet outside. The sliding-glass door closed behind them, trapping the noise inside.

They walked past the quietly drunk smokers on the patio, their random loud laughs and burning embers punctuating the night.

Lucas and Maria crossed the thick lawn to a rock-retaining wall and then climbed up to the terrace. Lucas reached out to steady her and guide her up the rock walk, but he didn't let go once she stood beside him. They walked farther up the hill, to a spot that allowed them to see Tulsa's skyline, a spot to see from and not be seen upon.

"Let's sit here," he said, pulling off his leather jacket and tossing it onto the grass. She sat down on it, her legs stretched out and crossed at the ankles. He sat down beside her, not looking at her but staring into the darkest part of the early evening sky. The edges of the clouds became white as they drifted in front of the moon; the deepest part of the cloud was black and blocked the moon's light.

"And God said, 'Let there be light,' and there was light. And God saw that the light was beautiful, and God chose light over darkness," Lucas muttered sadly.

The silent black sky stretched forever. Maria leaned her chin on her hand and stared into dark space. Her smallness, her tiny existence in comparison to the vast blackness, seemed to shrink in upon itself.

As if sensing her impending existential crisis, Lucas touched her waist and pulled her gently into a position where she now leaned against him. She shuddered involuntarily and he asked if she was cold. She shook her head lightly.

He reached forward and took her hand. "Shall I tell your future then?"

Maria hesitated. "I don't know. After the things you said in the house . . ."

"I can't change the future, my dear. Que sera, sera," he whispered. Then he said, in an uncharacteristically light tone, "C'mon, give me your pen and your palm."

"Hmm," she muttered, "a poet, a philosopher, and a prognosticator. How very Byron."

He laughed. "Well, we do share a birthday." He took her hand and turned it palm side up. The moon reflected off its whiteness, the valleys faintly visible as shadowed lines.

With her pen he traced the crease in the middle of her hand, and she reflexively jerked. "Don't"—she laughed—"that tickles."

Lucas cradled her wrist. "You shall have a long life."

She tried to appear relaxed. "They always say that."

"You will have many children."

Maria laughed again. "How many?"

Lucas shrugged. "Twenty or thirty." He paused. "You're about to get married for stability, not love."

Maria laughed without mirth. Marriage was not on the horizon.

With the pen Lucas traced a line from her palm on to her wrist. "What line are you reading now?"

He ended the line in a flower design over her light blue veins and leaned closer to her. "My heart line," he whispered.

Goose bumps spread from her arm across her shoulders. She reached for the pen and set it on the damp ground. With a fingertip Lucas traced the flower he had drawn. He continued to outline a pattern of invisible vines, flowers, and leaves. Slowly, his finger wound up her arm and over the sleeve of her shirt, across her throat and up to her cheek.

"You are chosen, Mary," he whispered.

"You will be the beginning of great things," he kissed her chin softly, his impossibly long lashes brushing her face, a wave of exhaustion rolling over her.

The sky was like an ocean, an ocean she had never dreamed of, but imagined.

The stars seemed to vibrate.

Maria could feel the earth slowly turning beneath them, Lucas had stretched back out.

She moved to lay her head on his chest. The blood thudded in her ear, the sound of a sea shell.

"Great things are impossible without hope," his voice seemed to come from very far away. For a moment she wondered if someone had drugged her soda. The last thing she thought she heard was, "Children are the hope of the world."

On the phone line in the doctor's office, all was silence. A tear trickled down Maria's cheek. She checked her watch. Joe was probably still in bed. If she had gone to the university that morning, she would have had another hour of lectures to sit through. She was conscious of the empty hollow feeling in her stomach. Her period three weeks overdue. Her very Catholic marriage two weeks old. Too terrified to wait and make the trip to the Indian Hospital to find out if the rabbit might die.

"Is that all you remember?"

She felt as if she was speaking to a whispering robot. "Yes," she whispered back. Maria's heart thudded heavily, her cheeks burned, her eyes hurt. Still, there was no absolution forthcoming. The silence threatened to last forever, emptying Maria of tears, and she rushed to fill its vacuum.

"Except for the dream," she offered.

"Tell me about the dream," the metallic voice clipped.

"I dreamt of an angel."

"What did the angel do?"

She thought for a moment. "The angel said, 'Mother is the name for God in the lips and hearts of little children.'"

The connection hummed with static for a moment, then Maria heard the voice chuckle softly. "The angel quoted William Makepeace Thackeray."

Maria felt a blush start beneath her ears. She heard a clicking and the sound of a tape being rewound at high speed, then the voice for the last time: "Hang up the phone and a technician will be in momentarily."

Maria nodded and placed the receiver into the handset. She wondered what magic could clean her soul. How did you erase a feeling? Badness, guilt, the desire to cry all the time, your first big lie. "My last," she promised herself aloud.

The door opened and a woman in a white nursing outfit came in pushing a cart. She plugged in a small chrome box that had Absolver 2000 written on the side and four curled wires coming out of it. She smiled vacantly at Maria. "I'll have to have you make your donation before we begin. Will you need change?"

"Oh," Maria stuttered, "the money."

She dropped her rosary into one pocket and fished her money out of the other. The tech kept babbling. "You know, they're experimenting with the CAP program and abused children."

"Oh, really," Maria said, as she began to hand the five twenty-dollar bills and four tens over to the technician. It was the money she had saved up for textbooks. The scholarship she was terrified she would lose wouldn't cover those. The woman gestured toward the drawer with her paperwork in it. "Drop it in there, please."

Maria was startled to find the drawer opened easily and she dropped the money on top of her form.

The technician continued: "They're finding this is much quicker and cheaper than therapy."

"Really?"

"Oh, yes," she nodded. "Now, you'll need to hold on to these, please." She placed two small silver rods in Maria's hands. The other two wires the technician attached to Maria's forehead with adhesive. "You'll feel a slight tingling and you may have a coppery taste in your mouth. There may also be a slight twitching in the muscles of your face. It's nothing to be alarmed about."

Maria nodded.

"Any questions?"

"Do I need to think of anything in particular?"

The technician smiled broadly. "You'll never need to think about it again, dear. The Absolver 2000 uses a memory map and only those bits of memory will be erased."

Maria felt her chest swell with panic. "Only memory bits?"

"Don't worry dear. You'll be completely clean. Just like you were before this terrible thing happened to you."

It sounded like a rehearsed speech. Never tailored to a specific event. The technician nonjudgmental and comforting. Better absolution through science.

"Now, just close your eyes, dear. This will only hurt for a moment."

Maria's eyes flicked back open. "But what about the baby?"

The technician smiled blankly. "What baby, dear?" she said, and flipped the machine on.

Maria's eyes slammed shut. A tiny muscular twitch began over her left eye and crossed over her skull, then back down across her shoulder through her right arm until the pulse ended in her hand. Pennies in her mouth. The Absolver 2000 doing what all her prayers and tears could not. A slight twitch, a small menstrual cramp, a night beginning at dawn and ending at dusk. An innocent conversation with a boy from school. Maria falling asleep on a couch, alone. A girl from class waking her up to drive her home. Joe Henry waking her with a phone call and a proposal. Her eager, "Yes, why not?" And once more all is right with the world. Maria the happy, blushing, virginal bride. Maria most likely to . . .

Maria was surprised by how quiet it all was, only the taste of money in her mouth. The doctor's office was astoundingly white and sharp in focus when she opened her eyes.

The technician was removing the adhesive from her forehead with a cold, alcohol-soaked cotton ball.

"Migraine gone, dear?"

"Migraine?" She rolled the word over on her tongue. "Yes," she said, "no migraine." She stood to go. A large cramp began to shudder across her left side and she pressed her left palm against her belly.

The technician was rolling the cart out of the room and called back to Maria. "Isn't science a wonderful thing?"

# Me &
# My Monster

Gina Wilson
Gogi 1968
Summer 1968

He's a monster," Gina Wilson whispered. Her grandmother, the widow of Robert Wilson, a man who Gina had never met, sipped her medicine.

"All boys are monsters, sweetie. I've been telling you that since you were no taller than a ditch lily."

Gina wrote a letter to the *Fort Worth Star-Telegram*, where daily monster updates ran accompanied by blurry photos. Gina, however, knew the "Goat Man." She had held his hoof while they watched the moon rise over the lake from a secluded bluff. She left that detail out of her letter.

Dear Mr. Editor,
The "Lake Worth Monster" is no monster. He is a perfect gentleman. If he threw a tire at someone, they had it coming.

I was talked into going to the lake to look for the monster. Moments after we parked, my date had his hands all over me. I got out of the car, and he followed. Knocked me to the ground. I screamed for help. It immediately arrived in the form of what one of your readers is calling the "Goat Man." He towered over us, and my terrified date fled. The Goat Man gave chase. My date drove away, leaving me behind.

I curled into a ball. When I looked up and saw those beautiful, red-rimmed, baby-blue eyes staring at me from several yards away, I got up and dusted myself off. I walked in the direction of the highway. He stayed a ways behind me, following me slowly. When I turned back to see if he was still there, he waved at me shyly. Once I got to the road, I flagged down a nice Baptist couple on their way home from choir practice. As I turned to look back, he gave me one more long wave.

Lady in Distress

Class of 1969

What Gina hadn't said was (1) the monster was much too young to be called a Goat Man; and (2) she had surreptitiously watched Goat Boy turn away as soon as she was safely in the car, his shoulders stooping low, as if he didn't want to be his full height of seven feet, as if he were the loneliest boy she had ever seen. Lonelier than she was, a girl who wanted only to have someone to hold her hand now and then. She didn't say she had returned later that week to thank Goat Boy for saving her from the jerk who was now ignoring her in the halls and whispering about her behind her back. She christened the one everyone called the Lake Worth Monster "Matt." She offered him a plate of fresh chocolate chip cookies. Their first visit was interrupted by jeering onlookers from below the bluff. Matt rolled a tire in their general direction. Embarrassed, she got into her car and drove away, turning to take the long route and avoiding the Goat Man hunters.

Matt was goatish, but the fishiness was an exaggeration. He was tall, but there hadn't been a fish scale on him as multiple lovers' lane witnesses had reported. His black horns curled a little forward, then back, like a pompadour on Johnny Cash. The lake smelled of dead fish in several places, so perhaps this accounted for the misperception. Gina kept a scrapbook of all the Lake Worth Monster articles and was thrilled to see her letter to the editor when it was published. She cropped out the introduction, though she still remembered every word. They wrote that her "fictional account" had given the newsroom such a big laugh they felt they owed it to their readers to spread the mirth.

She drove back out to see him on the night of the new moon. Her heart thundered. When she had to slam on her brakes to avoid hitting two rabbits dashing across the unlit road, she considered turning around. As her dad's Oldsmobile climbed the dark roads toward the bluff, Gina wondered whether there were worse things than asking yourself what-if? and refusing to hear the answer. When she parked, Matt was soon next to the car, as if he had been waiting for her.

Gina had salvaged a torn pair of jeans from the laundromat and handily patched the ripped knee. She took a shirt of her father's, much too small for Matt and missing several buttons. As soon as she got out of the car, she handed him the folded material. He sniffed at the cloth, and she had to stop him from biting down as he took a tentative nibble. She unfolded the shirt and held it up against Matt's muscular chest. The color set off his electric-azure eyes. She helped him slip it on, noticing the warmth radiating from his furry skin. Handing him the jeans she gestured toward the bushes. Matt disappeared as she turned back to the car, popping open the trunk where she had packed a picnic. She spread a blanket in their spot and set out her cookies and peaches from the tree in their backyard. Mosquitoes buzzed and she covered the food back up with foil while she waited.

When Matt finally stepped out of the brush, he cradled a bouquet of wildflowers in browns and yellows and purples but held the jeans up with his other hoof. Other people would have laughed. She jumped up and took the gift.

"No one's ever brought me flowers," she said.

Matt's shirt still hung open, the buttons impossible for his hooves. Gina set the wildflowers on the blanket. Drawing him closer, she began to button his shirt, starting at the collar. Next time she would bring a shirt with snaps, a blue Western shirt with short sleeves that would show off his biceps. As she stood close, she sensed something that felt like fear emanating from him as he leaned down toward her from his greater height. She spoke to him quietly. "It's always nice to dress up a bit for a date," she instructed. "It makes a girl feel nice when a boy makes an effort." She smiled shyly into his eyes.

Matt ate all of the peaches and the cookies. The cold fried chicken sat on the plate, untouched. He curled up on the blanket, unable to hide his sudden drowsiness. Gina patted her lap, letting him lay his head on her thigh. He smelled of sweetness and heat. She stroked his brow as he napped lightly. She tried to remember what stars made up the constellation Capricorn. She talked about the stories she knew about the heavenly bodies while Matt snored gently. He startled when she spoke his name a little more loudly. He sat up next to her and stared into her eyes. "I'll undo these for you," she said, as she began to carefully unbutton his shirt. "Next time I'll bring you a belt." Matt looked over at the plate covered with peach pits. "And more peaches."

As Gina backed the car into the dirt road and drove away, Matt stood next to a tree, his sad eyes watching her leave.

✸

Inevitably, it was a star-crossed romance beset with challenges.

First, she didn't own a car. Borrowing Edoda Rabbit Wilson's Oldsmobile required a complicated chain of deceit.

Second, Gina quickly realized she would not be getting any love poems from him. And he immediately attempted to eat whatever notes she proffered. She had to remind Matt to put the outfit on each time she came to see him.

Third, his romantic gestures ran to gifts of prickly-pear-cactus fruit and bleated love songs.

Fourth, she was set to go to Bacone Indian College in Muskogee, Oklahoma, soon. While it was obvious to her that her cloven-footed boyfriend was no demon, she wondered if her love for him would survive four years of a Baptist education.

The evening before she was to leave for school, she borrowed her father's car once more. She wanted to discuss their future. Gina found Matt sitting on a log wearing his jeans and unbuttoned-up shirt. From somewhere he had obtained a tie and wrapped it haphazardly around his throat. He absentmindedly chewed on its short end as she drove up.

She sat next to him and took his cloven hoof into her hands. She talked. He quickly became agitated and withdrew his foot. He made a short, angry bleat, stood up, stepped out of the jeans, and then dropped to all fours. His head swiveled back and forth as he struggled with the removal of the tie. Eventually, it fell to the ground, and Matt trampled on it while dragging the cuffs of the shirt over the rocky, sandy soil. Without ever looking back, he disappeared into the scrubby growth between the parkway and the lake.

There would be no salvaging that shirt, Gina thought, as she stood watching him disappear into the dark. She heard a splash and soon saw the moon glinting off his back as he swam toward Goat Island. Tears ran down her cheeks as the distance between them grew. The night he had saved her, she felt like an invisible thread had bound her to him. Tonight, she had cleaved it in two.

Dating teenage boys had been more dangerous than she had expected, more dangerous than being courted by the Lake Worth Monster. But in the end, long-distance relationships were too difficult.

Unsurprisingly, Matt was a strong swimmer, but Gina held her breath until he crawled onto the cluttered shore. He stood up on the shore of the island, his silhouette white, then gray, then disappearing into the dark, scrubby growth. What would become of him, she wondered? From the island she heard a cry, the wail of a motherless creature, baa-ing into the night. She got into the car and rolled up the window to block out the sound of Matt's grief.

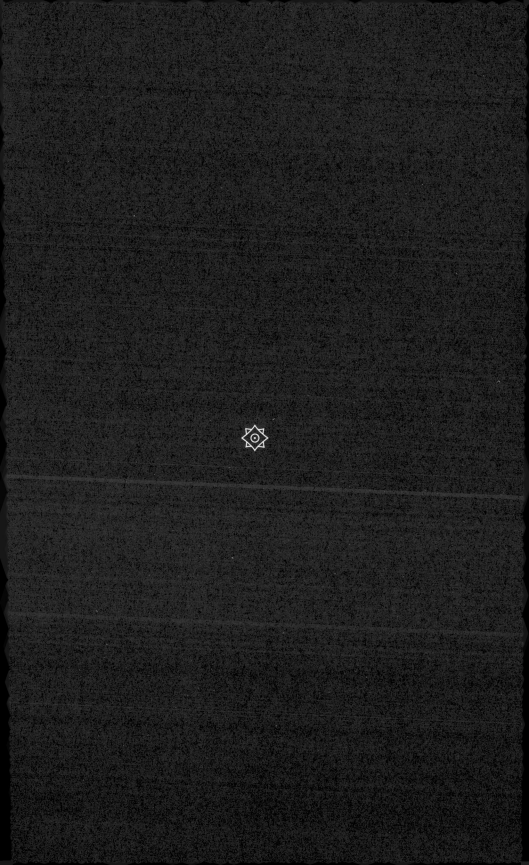

# Shame on the Moon

Jimmy and Janie King
Duninhdi 16, 1969
10/16/1969

As I stepped out of the bright lights of the movie theater's lobby, I had two things on my mind: Lon Chaney Jr., and a cheeseburger. I had just seen Chaney in *Johnny Reno*, but I was thinking about all the yak hair Jack Pierce glued onto him when he made him up as the Wolf Man. I was wondering what I looked like when I changed. Did I still look like a greaser? A bad boy from the wrong side of the tracks? Did my hair stay swirled up in the front like Ricky Nelson's? But I was also thinking about a cheeseburger, because it was one day until the full moon. Every day, I grew hungrier and hungrier.

I hoped that I looked more like a rock-and-roll star and less like a hairy, prehistoric man. But anyone who has seen me can't exactly bear witness. Not many people see a werewolf and live to tell about it.

I made my way toward the diner. I could have closed my eyes and followed the smell of grease and fries and hamburgers. It was Thursday, and I would catch hell tomorrow when Coach found out I was out late the night before the big game, but I didn't care. I should have. It had taken him a year to forgive me for missing out on the game last year, getting an infection from getting "dog bit" and all. When my sister was still alive, I cared a little about what people thought. If I hadn't, well hell, she'd still be dead.

I'd seen another kind of monster in Tulsa a couple of months ago. He was coming back with his team to play against us for Homecoming. He was a pale rich kid in prep-school clothes, a nouveau riche kid in a wave of Madras and deck shoes. I smelled him before I saw him. Normally, vampires smell clean. They don't sweat or defecate and age so slowly eighteen lasts one hundred years. They feed though. They seduce and destroy and deceive, and then they feed.

The diner had a jukebox and someone put on Glen Campbell's "Wichita Lineman." Like being thrown through time, I was inexorably back a year earlier when that song came out, when my sister was still alive, when I learned there were all kinds of real monsters in the world.

My sister was beautiful and smart. Smarter than me. We're Cherokee and the white boys didn't let her forget it. She ignored most of them with their Pocahontas fantasies and their yen to go to a powwow or a stomp dance, but somehow Mark got to her. She told me once that he was the only boy who acted like he didn't even notice she was Indian; he only saw that she was brilliant and beautiful.

I'd said, "You mean the only white boy."

"No," she said. "Indian boys don't let me forget I'm Indian, either."

I can see now how that might have been appealing, to be the prettiest, smartest anything without some kind of ethnic label. Like Jim Thorpe—he was a great athlete, but people always have to stick Indian in front of it, like an asterisk. Don't even mention that he's Sak and Fox Nation, just Indian, like we're all alike.

I don't fault her for that. She had no idea Mark was a wealthy vampire boy, a perfect predator. I didn't see it either. I just saw a rich white kid trying to make time with my sister.

Janie had worked at the only diner in Pryor. Just like then, I waved at the cook in the back. He started on my cheeseburgers immediately. However, a year ago, I didn't ask him to leave them dripping with blood, barely hot, as rare as you could socially eat them when surrounded by teammates and cheerleaders. Janie had been a senior, but still worked until close every night. She didn't have time to date, but I had seen Mark hanging around too close and too secretly to have any good intentions. I figured I had control of the situation, though, since our mom insisted I give Janie a ride home every night, and when I wasn't eating, I was lifting weights and running and boxing. When Etsi went to work in a plane factory in Tulsa, she made Janie and I promise to watch out for each other.

I messed that one up.

Janie was killed the week of Homecoming last year. Earlier in that week Mark and our neighbor, Walt Rock, another greaser like me, had gotten into a shoving match at the local gas station. By the time the fight was broken up, there was a dent in the side of Mark's red Mustang. Walt had longish hair and lived in the rent house across from us. He'd been in the army and come back with an eye patch over his left eye. Most people assumed Vietnam, but Janie and I knew he'd done his tour in Germany. Walt and I were friendly, but I was pretty sure he was only watching out for me on Janie's behalf.

I was thinking about that the night it happened, while eating my french fries and gravy, when Janie's auburn-haired coworker Carol showed up next to our table.

"Hey, Chief."

I lifted my eyes and frowned. I went back to dipping my fries in the white-peppered gravy.

"I'm just messing with you, handsome. Your sister said you hate it when people call you Chief. You try being called Red all the time." At this, I stared hard into her blue eyes, her red curls framing her face. Carol reached out and helped herself to one extremely long fry, dipped it in gravy, then held it out to me.

"You know," she said, leaning close to me, "I'm part Indian, too."

In order to not get pasted with gravy, I bit the fry she held.

"Your sister asked me to take her shift tonight. She said you have to be in bed early on account of the big game."

This was news to me. Janie and I hadn't talked about this arrangement, but I merely said, "Yup, big game tomorrow."

"Christ, don't I know it," she replied, rolling her eyes at my teammates and their girls that surrounded me. They were eating burgers and ice cream as if it were the only sport they were truly good at, as if winning the big Homecoming game would be determined by how much food they consumed. The diner was also hopping with alumni, people whose school spirit had led them to come home to cheer on the Tigers, relive their high school glory days.

I picked up a fry and offered it to her.

"No, thanks," she said, shaking her head. "I hate the food here."

I dropped it. I glanced back up at her as she leaned in.

"I offered to walk her home myself and tuck you in, but she

wouldn't hear of it. So then I said I would take her shift since you're so darn good-looking." At this, she squeezed my biceps and leaned into me, whispering, "See you in my dreams, kemosabe," before walking away.

Within moments, Janie was at my table whispering, "What did Carol want?"

"What does Carol always want?" I observed nonchalantly.

At this Janie growled and then stomped away.

I drove home and hung out until almost eight. Then I went out to start the car. I was going to show up early whether she wanted me there or not, but for the first time since I had been driving, the old Bel Air wouldn't start. Pryor is a small town. The drive to the diner is five minutes tops. I turned the key several times, but nothing happened.

Walt Rock was smoking a cigarette and watching me from his porch. He headed over as I tried to start the car again. Walt is a big guy, bigger than any of us playing football. He was six foot two and about two hundred pounds. And yeah, I might compare him with Jim Thorpe, but Walt wouldn't even play a pickup game with us. He'd just take a drag on his cigarette and say, "Nah, if I played someone would probably die." He said it real serious though, never ever laughed, until I'd start laughing, and then he'd just grin.

I got out of the Bel Air and popped the hood. Walt turned and went back to his own car and retrieved his jumper cables.

"Where you going, Jimmy?" he drawled around his cigarette.

"Got to pick up Janie."

"I thought she worked until close." Everyone knew everyone else's business in this town. But that bit of knowledge sounded pretty specific.

"Carol said Janie wanted to come home early."

I felt, rather than saw his immediate recognition. "Got it." He tossed the cables in the back of my car. "Forget it. Let's take my car."

We climbed into the black T-Bird and headed for the diner. It was 8:05.

Janie was already gone by the time we got there. Walt got out of the car and walked around to the back of the restaurant. He came back and hopped into the driver's seat. "She headed west."

He ignored my puzzled look.

We drove toward the darkening horizon. Overhead, the moon was a waning crescent that kept disappearing behind the October clouds. The Illinois River lay in the same direction in which we were driving. Walt stopped a few times and got out of the car. Each time he hopped onto the road, he seemed to be sniffing at the air, tilting his head up, his black greasy hair longer than any school would allow. He had his back to me, but I could have sworn he was lifting his eye patch as he stared into the dark. The third time he returned, he said, "A car picked her up here."

Walt turned onto a gravel road that ran toward a bridge, but then we parked. It was dark. Our headlights lit up the dirt road and beneath the bridge was Mark's red convertible. I walked down to the empty car. Janie's shoes and white uniform from Danny's Diner glowed in the back seat. I felt angry and sick. I was going to beat the hell out of Mark when I found them. Walt walked into the dark of the overgrown woods.

By the time we caught sight of them, Janie was limp in Mark's arms. I reached them before Walt. Mark was biting Janie's neck. He never heard us. I shoved Mark away from her and he stood up, baring his fangs at me. From behind me I heard a growl and I turned to Walt rushing toward us. But Walt wasn't quite Walt anymore. His teeth were different, long, sharp canines bared. Where the patch had come off, his eye wasn't missing, so much as it was wolfish. When Walt crashed into both of us, I fell on top of Mark. Pain spread through my right arm where one of Walt's fangs caught me.

I freed my arm from between the two fighters. I pressed down on my wrist to slow the bleeding and rushed to Janie. Next to her was some medical tubing that ran to a plastic blood bag. The blood around the tear in her throat was crusty and dry. I placed my hand on her carotid artery and felt nothing. I put pressure on the rip in her neck, but there was no blood flow to stanch. My other hand searched her chest for a heartbeat. There was none. But there was a cross cut over her heart.

As I held my hand over the hole in Janie's throat, the bite mark in my hand began to throb. It burned. It reminded me of the time I tried to pull two dogs apart in the middle of a fight over a food bowl. They had no idea they had bitten me and just kept trying to kill each other. Now the pain was turning into an itch. I tried to ignore it and turned my attention back to Janie, remembering something I had seen a guy do once when one of my teammates collapsed.

I laid Janie out flat and begin to press rhythmically on her chest, but suddenly blood shot out of the wound on her neck.

"Walt!" I screamed.

In a moment the Walt I knew was standing between me and the crescent moon. Except when I looked closer I saw his eye still wasn't quite right. It was wolfy, not human. What I had imagined under that leather eye patch was anything but. In Walt's hand he held the silver Indian head knife he had picked up in Germany. The knife was red from tip to hilt.

"She's gone," he snarled. "He drained her."

"Mark?"

"The vampire."

"The vampire?" I stammered. "He was no vampire. He's just a psycho."

"He's a dead vampire and a psycho," Walt replied. He leaned over and placed his hands on his knees. "Look, I have to get out of here. No one's going to believe he killed Janie, even if they find him with her. And when they find them both, it's me they'll come for."

"Walt, what are you? What happened to you?"

"Jimmy, if you didn't believe your own eyes, I can't explain it."

I lifted up my wrist. It was swelling, redness spreading up my arm.

"Oh, man . . ." He reached out and grabbed my hand.

"What . . . ?"

Then Walt turned from me to Janie. Suddenly, the big man was holding my sister and whispering into her neck. The words I made out were "Sorry . . . tried to look out for him. O . . ."

I stood up and walked over to the water. I stepped in and washed my hands and my face. Seven times I dove under. The clouds parted and the sliver of moon reflected off the white stones and fish beneath the water's surface. It was beautiful. It was the most beautiful thing I had ever seen. Still, I had a feeling that these ablutions weren't going to change what had happened, weren't going to set things right. I had a feeling that that was going to be up to me.

When Walt was able to think and talk, we made a plan. Walt took Janie's body to the river and cleaned her up, re-dressing her carefully. He wrapped her in a blanket and laid her in the back seat of Mark's car, leaving it parked beneath the bridge. Mark we left on the bank.

Walt was going to drive as far away as he could that night. Said he knew a guy who could help him become someone else.

Maybe get him a job playing steel guitar in a band. "California," he said. "Janie wanted to go out to California."

I didn't say anything for a moment. "Yeah," I said, "she wanted to write for the movies."

Walt reached out and put his large hand on my shoulder. "I'm afraid you're going to become someone else in about three weeks, as well. And I'm real sorry about that." With his chin he pointed toward the sky. "Next full moon, you need to be locked up somewhere. Maybe your grandparents' cellar? Maybe take a goat down in there with you. No point in going hungry."

I stared at him.

"I'm serious, Jimmy. It's going to be a while before you can control it like I do. You'll need to find a cellar and hide. Handcuff yourself to the pipes. I wish I could stick around and help you. Your sister would have wanted that at least . . ." His voice was wavery, but then he continued: "I mean, no one showed me How to Win Friends and Influence Monsters. That's just kind how life is for people like us." He let this sink in for a moment. "I'm sorry about your sister."

I still can't control it the way Walt can. But tonight, as I sit in the diner, I know where I need to be on the night of the full moon. I have a date with a vampire.

I finished the burgers and gave my fries to an old guy sitting at the counter, drinking cup after cup of coffee. Potatoes weren't really my thing anymore. I decided to go back and see Janie's grave. I wasn't normally sentimental. Survival doesn't give you time for that. But as I approached the one-year mark and listened to that Glen Campbell song, I felt the pull of my old life.

Etsi came home long enough to get Janie buried in the family graveyard at the back of my grandparents' 160 acres. She went back to Tulsa after. Before they had passed my grandparents built a pantry inside the house and had stopped using the root cellar. In spite of the occasional snake, that was my refuge the first time I turned during the full moon. I spent the next seven weeks building a soundproof cell in there.

Trying to control the change has been an afterthought each time since, though. I plan now how I will give in to the hunger. I choose my victims carefully and far from where I live. I mark my territory to keep others like me away and only hunt in ranges that were not recently marked. Since that night, I have hunted a few young vampires, destroying them easily as they feed. A vampire loses all outside perception when it focuses on killing and feeding. They only hear the slowing heart of their prey. I cover myself in smoke, so they sense me as nothing more than the burning cedar of bonfires.

I stopped my car a mile from the turn into the land and walked the rest of the way slowly. I hopped the barbed-wire fence closest to the back of the family plot. I hadn't been in the cemetery since we buried Janie, but I had been to others. After I changed, I could smell the sting of the chemicals the embalmers had traded for blood. It was an acrid, bitter scent that seeped up through the ground for years after the soil covered the coffin. But I didn't smell it at Janie's grave. Instead, I smelled a smell like ice. Frost and old clothing and the air of the cellar. I turned and looked into the woods. I heard an owl hoot in alarm. I turned back and followed the smell, jumping back over the fence and running until I found myself at the sandstone-lined hole behind my grandparents' house.

I pulled the root cellar's heavy door open. It no longer creaked, just glided silently on its hinges. I noticed a large new bolt on the inside of the door. It was black iron, about two inches in diameter, and sharp where it slid into the wood frame of the cellar. It had been installed since my brief stint underground. The shelves that held old mason jars of food no one would dare eat had been rearranged to obscure the back corner. I moved as silently as possible into the corner, but I could smell the books and paper and blankets before I saw them. I quickly confirmed with my eyes what I scented. The last place I wanted to be cornered was a stone cellar underground. But that's what had happened.

I turned to go back up the stairs but Janie and Mark blocked the way. Janie's skin glowed unnaturally in the moonlight. Her long black hair was the only soft thing about her. Her features seemed sharp and chiseled. There was no flicker of recognition or warmth in her eyes. Mark looked like the same jerk I'd watched Walt kill a year earlier. He reached forward and pushed me. I fell backward down the stairs on to the root cellar's sandstone floor. As I stood up, he tackled me and thrust me back into the shelves. The wooden boards cracked apart, the glass jars smashing to the floor. The smell of old blackberries, persimmons, corn, and green beans made me feel sick. Shards of glass scattered across the stone floor. From behind Mark, I heard the cellar door slam shut and the wrenching of the thick iron bolt.

Mark grabbed me and flung me into the stone wall and I dropped to the floor. For a second, I lay there stunned. My brain and body were on fire, but my strength would be no match for his for another two nights. He dropped down next to me, placing his right elbow on my chest, both of his hands at my throat. His nails became like claws as he bared his fangs. In the dark I could see Janie standing behind him. Mark noticed my expression, and as he let go of me, I rolled out from underneath him. Janie lifted the iron bar over her head and then thrust it through his back over the left side of his cable-knit sweater. It was buried six inches deep in the dry ground. Mark screamed. It was an awful sound, like the death cry of a rabbit through an amplifier. Janie spoke to me for the first time.

"Go get the ax."

When I returned, we finished the job quickly.

Janie put Mark's head in a bag and told me to carry the body. She followed behind me with a shovel as we walked toward the old corral that still smelled of dry horse manure.

We took turns digging a hole large enough for the body, putting him deeper than normal. Before we covered it with dirt, Janie spit into the dark earth.

I laughed. "Any last words?"

"I hate those stupid preppy kids," Janie said.

"Yeah, me too."

We went back to work covering him quietly.

"You're going to have to burn this when you burn those clothes. I hope you have something to cover your car seats." Janie handed me the heavy bag. "You can't stick around."

"Janie?"

She looked at me. "There are others like Mark. Older than Mark. Older than America." She paused. "It's complicated. Mark violated a treaty by changing me. I don't know if you'll be safe here. Go to Texas—they won't follow you. They're not allowed. At least, not for now."

For the first time in a year, I felt empty. The desire for revenge had kept me full. The need to hunt had allowed me not to think about my life. Going somewhere else just meant more days of solitude and lies and hunger and blood, but not much else.

She smiled sadly. "I'm sorry. Go live a life. Go play football. Go eat bloody steak at diners. Come see me before you go and I'll help you figure things out. Tell you the rest of what I know. You can stay with our cousin, Gina, and her family in Fort Worth for a little bit." She smiled. "Maybe I'll come to one of your night games there."

She reached up and touched my pomaded hair. She grabbed the longer piece in the front and twirled it around her finger, wrapping it into a bouncy curl. I had forgotten that she was shorter than me. "Enjoy what you can of life." She stood up on her toes and kissed me on the forehead. I smelled her cold skin and her empty gut that smelled of death. "Enjoy the sun."

It was still dark enough to build a fire deep in the woods. I walked back to my car for jeans and a white T-shirt. One of the rules of being a werewolf is, always have a change of clothes. The can of fire accelerant in my car was a lucky bonus. I carried the clothes, the gasoline, and the weighted bag to the creek. The night creatures talked about me as I passed. I looked like a man, but beneath the blood, I smelled like the earth. I made a pile of dry cedar and covered it in gasoline. Flames shot into the sky. I took the head from the burlap bag and dropped it onto the fire. I thought vampires were supposed to turn to bone when you killed them, but Mark's head was heavy with his evil brain. It wasn't like the movies at all. I didn't relish the thought of watching him burn while I bathed. So, I soaked the burlap bag and my dirty clothes with gasoline, and threw it over his head.

I walked into the spring-fed part of the creek and scrubbed the blood away with sand. As I watched the fire burn, I didn't even notice how cold the water ran. As the sun started to lighten the sky in the east, I realized my skin had begun to wrinkle and I climbed out. I knelt beside the fire to get dry and fed it more wood. I was going to be there a long time. I got dressed and pushed the skull around the fire so that its empty eye sockets were staring into the sunrise. It was going to be a beautiful day. I needed to sleep.

The temporary life I had lived had distracted me from the world I'd lost. But now my home was lost to me, too. I didn't blame Walt. The accident was caused by a predator I hadn't been able to protect my sister from. And I hadn't appreciated my old life and our land until I was denied it. No more stomp dances in Texas, no Hog Fries, no street signs in Cherokee, no running into other Cherokees while night gigging on Lake Eucha, no going to water in our land.

That night would be my last in the Cherokee Nation for a long time. Tomorrow the Pryor Tigers were going to play against that vampire from the rich, white high school in Tulsa. They had beaten us every year. All season Coach had told us all he wanted was to beat the Dutchmen. He told us about the vacations those kids went on and the cars they drove and the universities they would go to that none of us could ever afford. Earlier in the week a parade of Vettes and Mustangs had cruised through town and, before the local law did anything, the drivers and their passengers vandalized a statue of Sequoyah in front of the high school, spray-painting "Kill the Indians" across the base in red. I had gotten distracted, but now I could focus, and once I was rested, I was going to be ready for the big game.

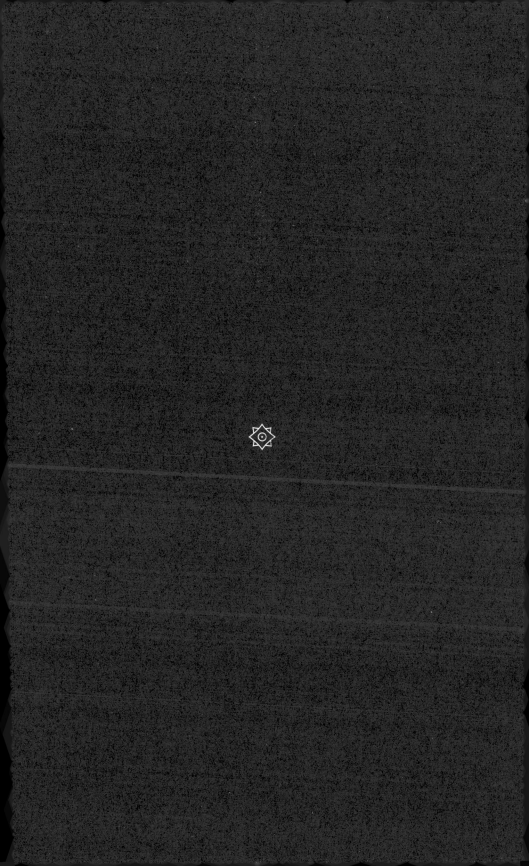

# Snow Day

Audrey "Sissy" Henry & Sarah "Jisdu" Henry
Unolvtana 1979
1/1979

The girls across the street say a man hung himself in my parents' bedroom before they bought the house. My parents say those girls are liars. Mama says this house isn't haunted, but of course it is, or I wouldn't be telling you this story.

When I was younger, we used to hear things a thump upstairs, footsteps crossing the carpeted master bedroom, the door opening and closing.

The first time I saw a ghost in this house, I was still in elementary, during one of Tulsa's rare snow days. The snow had started after school began that morning. Our school was brand-new and we rode a bus to it, in a rough part of town. Each morning we sat in my dad's car until the bus came, and in the afternoons, unless one of our parents was waiting for us at the morning stop, we got off a mile farther from the house to hang out at the public library until our parents came to pick us up after work. We behaved ourselves and never gave the librarians any trouble. I helped out by putting books away when I finished with my homework. We'd sit at the tables reading until I saw my mother or father pull up in front of the building.

At school there were no windows to watch the uncharacteristic blizzard that day, but we were all excited anyway. Word made it around that all the Tulsa public schools would dismiss early, and the buses were back by lunchtime. They herded us to the cafeteria to feed us and then called us to the front of the building by bus number.

"I can't wait to play in the snow," I said to Dorice, a girl in my class who rode the same bus I did. She nodded in agreement. Dorice often wore outfits she designed herself. Her mother helped her sew them; they were beautiful. I had only recently begun to notice other people's clothes. A few days earlier in reading group, two of the Southside girls told me how much they liked my shirt, while our teacher was out of the room.

"Where did you get it?" Amy asked.

I smiled, "K-mart."

I heard a giggle from another girl.

"I'll have to ask my mom to take me to Kmart to get one," Amy replied cloyingly.

Being one of the only two poor brown kids in our gifted and talented class was not a great time. I put the shirt in my closet. I went back to the regular hand-me-downs.

Now, while Dorice and I talked about snow over lunch, Amy turned and looked at us. "This isn't like the snow in Colorado. When we go skiing, now that's snow." She went back to her conversation with the girl she carpooled with from the Southside.

Dorice and I looked at each other. She rolled her eyes. I smiled. But when we heard them laugh, we both flinched.

When our bus number was called, I waited for my sister, Sarah, at the doorway. She was wearing her nice shiny black shoes and white socks. Neither one of us had snow boots, but her shoes were more slippery in the slush than my Keds. She ran up to me and yelled, "Gutiha!" She was always running, even when it was not a good idea. I grabbed her hand.

"Yup. Did you bring any gloves?" I asked.

She shook her head.

"You can have mine," I said, and gave her my black knitted gloves. I started to put them on her hands, but she grabbed them and pulled her hand out of mine.

"I want to go sit with my friends."

"Okay, but don't run."

She walked away quickly.

Parents had been picking kids up early all morning. Dorice sat down with me even though there were a few empty seats. She would spend the bus ride sketching or reading fashion magazines before she got off at the first stop. I, usually, read. I pulled my copy of *The Ghost Next Door* out of my drawstring bag, but then only stared out the window, watching a real genuine snowstorm outside. The flakes were large and sticky and had already collected in the corners of the windows by the time we got on the bus. Three seats ahead of me a window was stuck open about an inch. Occasionally, the snowflakes blasted through the gap. I reached up to catch one, but it was instantly a cold, wet dot in my hand.

"Uyvdla," I said, when Dorice looked up at me.

"What's that mean?"

I shrugged, "It's cold." I didn't know much Cherokee. My grandparents had gone to boarding school and lost it.

"Uyvdla," she repeated. "We're either Choctaw or Seminole," she said. "And Black, obviously." She smiled. It didn't surprise me. There were a lot of Black people in Oklahoma who were also Indigenous, whether they were recognized by their tribes or not. Probably everywhere.

The bus was stopping and Dorice stood to go. "Donadago-hvi," she said.

"Hawa," I said back.

Behind me, my sister chattered happily about whatever fourth graders talk about.

I hoped our parents hadn't taken off work early and looked forward to sitting in the window seat at the library, watching the snow fill the courtyard garden. The librarians would have it locked due to bad weather, so the snow would be clean and deep and untrodden, a perfect garden in varying shades of white and gray. At the stop closer to the house, we looked out the window to see if one of our parents was waiting, but no one was, so we rode on to the stop near the library.

As we neared it, I put my book away and slipped my jacket back on. It matched my sister in style though it was a different color, hand-me-downs from a family at church, neither really adequate for the snow. A bone-chilling cold was rare enough that a really well-insulated coat would just end up getting left behind on the playground or bus anyway. But not that day.

I grabbed my book bag and my cold fingers struggled with the large brown buttons on my jacket as I exited the bus. Once off, we began to race each other to the door of the library, running through the iced-over wet and muddy grass because the sidewalk was already slippery. We didn't notice how dark the library was until we made it to the locked door. My sister made her hands into goggles and peered in. We had never found the library closed before. It would be a surprise to our parents, too.

I shifted the drawstring bag I carried from one shoulder to the other, reached out and took my sister's left hand in my very cold right. My parents had the kind of blue collar jobs where they couldn't listen to the radio and things like library closures.

We were on our own. We turned and began to walk up the hill that would lead us behind the shopping center.

We didn't hold hands for long since our pockets were warmer places. We had to cross 21st Street and there was no crosswalk to help us get across. It was always dangerous, but it felt especially so in whiteout conditions, in a city where drivers freaked out at the slightest bit of rain. It was hard to tell how fast or slow the cars were going and we watched as some cars tried to stop, but skidded into the intersection.

I thought about the time my dad had gone to jail for being Indian and sliding through a patch of ice at a stop sign. The officer didn't believe he hadn't been drinking. Dad was the only one working at the time and bail was a luxury my parents couldn't afford, not to mention we were too poor to own a phone. My dad spent his only night in jail and had to start going to church by order of a judge to avoid more time. There was never any booze in our house after that. I hoped my dad wouldn't have any trouble getting home from work that night. I knew the ice made him nervous.

It made me nervous, too, and as we dashed across the street, cars honked at us going either direction.

"My feet hurt," my sister said. I was thinking the same thing.

It was the kind of pain that was part cold and wet, and part a rubbing that wouldn't go away until you could take your shoes off and get warm and dry. I just shrugged and said, "It'll be okay when we get home."

My sister looked ready to cry and I felt guilty for not being able to fix things. There was nothing to do but keep walking.

We went to school with kids from all over Tulsa. My class was all honors kids, mostly white and pretty well-off money-wise.

The girl with the locker right next to me carried an L.L. Bean backpack and had taken her bright red snow boots out when we were getting ready to walk to the bus. I wondered what it was like to have enough money to always be prepared for things like freak snowstorms.

There were no sidewalks on our street, so we meandered between the grass and the curb. The places where cars had driven were freezing puddles of dirty snow and cold water. The grass was two inches of fluffy snow tall enough to edge into our shoes. Neither choice was good, but when we tired of the tortures of one, we shifted to the other.

At home the door was locked and we peered through the front window of our house just like my little sister had done at the library. In truth my mother would probably be later instead of earlier that night, since she was a letter carrier and bad weather meant a longer day for her than usual. Our dad would be home shortly after five. He worked for the gas company. When it was cold, they were busier than normal. That meant we had four hours or more of waiting. We turned and looked up and down the street. We knew there were several retirees home, but none who were friendly. In our old neighborhood, the more run-down one, Nana our next-door neighbor would have let us in and maybe even made us peanut butter cookies. We would have sat and watched the daytime soaps with her. But in this neighborhood, there was no one like that.

We went around to the garage door, but it was locked as well. So then we went to our side yard. There was no gate, so we gathered some concrete blocks and built a stand to put an over-turned, empty five-gallon paint bucket on. I stood balancing on that and hanging on to the gray fence panels as my little sister climbed over me like I was a ladder. On the other side, she hung by my gloves, afraid to drop the three or four feet, and then suddenly one glove disappeared while the other hung on and I heard an *oof* and a cry.

"Are you okay?" I hollered, as I peered through the wooden slats. I heard a sniffle and a quiet "I think so" and another sniffle. I stretched up and retrieved the sodden glove that had snagged on the fence. There was a small tear on one finger and bits of ice all over. I shoved it into a pocket and then went back to the garage door.

I stood on my tiptoes and saw my little sister in silhouette in the garage. She turned on the overhead fluorescent lights and they flickered and reflected off the top of my uncle's gold-colored Impala. It had belonged to my cousin and he had brought it over shortly after she died. My parents told us he just couldn't bear to look at it or sell it, yet. She had bought it herself with the money she saved up through high school. She had called me Sissy, and my sister, Jisdu, which means "Rabbit" in Cherokee. My sister and I had an agreement not to let anyone at school know our nicknames. Etsi said if the other kids found out, we'd be Jisdu and Sissy forever, not just with our Cherokee family. At least at school, I got to be Audrey. I didn't even know my cousin's real name until we went to the funeral; everyone had called her Gigage because she once tried to bleach her hair blond. The peroxide had made it orange. Somehow that turned into everyone calling her Red, but in Cherokee. Maybe the uncle who started calling her Red didn't know the word for orange.

I heard my sister try to turn the handle that kept the garage door shut, but it didn't move. "There's a lock," I said, "turn the lock."

A few seconds later I heard a click, then she easily turned the handle. I reached down and pulled the door up. I stepped into the garage, pulling the door back down behind me. I stood up and breathed a sigh of relief, but my breath was a cloud of steam in the freezing air.

"Well, it's a little bit warmer," I shrugged.

"The door to the house is locked, too," she sniffled. She was having trouble not crying.

"Let's get in the car," I said.

The car was unlocked and the keys jangled as we slid in. Inside the car was a blanket, and we wrapped up in it, cuddled together in the front seat.

"Should we take our shoes off?" My sister was shaking with the cold. I wondered if her asthma would kick in.

"Yeah, those shoes aren't very warm anyway," I said.

We took off our shoes and threw them in the back seat, then wrapped back up in the blanket. We were both shivering pretty hard now.

"Will we freeze to death?" my sister asked.

I didn't know. I had never been this cold before. If it was this cold you were supposed to wear the right kind of clothes, and not get soaking wet and sit in a garage where buckets of water could freeze solid. I thought about my elisi having her legs amputated, not because of frostbite, but because of diabetes, and I shuddered.

Then I had an idea.

"Let's see if the heater works." I stretched out my legs and pumped the gas pedal like I did on my Grandpa Henry's tractor. I turned the key in the ignition.

My sister leaned forward and turned the heater on full blast. She stretched her feet under the dash where the warm air would eventually start blasting out, but then she yanked them back in. "It's like air-conditioning!" she squealed.

I laughed. "Give it time to warm up."

We stayed bundled up a few more minutes while the air warmed up, then both of us stretched our bare feet under the dashboard and our hands in front of the air vents.

"Ohhhh, that feels good," I said.

"Yeah, it does." My sister leaned back on the seat and closed her eyes. "I'm sleepy," she said.

"Maybe if we sleep, Mom and Dad will be home faster," I suggested.

My sister didn't answer. She leaned her head toward me and stretched her legs out a bit more. I reached around and brushed her black bangs out of her face. She was a cute kid. She sure looked sweet when she was asleep.

I glanced in the mirror and saw my cousin sitting in the back seat. For a moment her face was a blue black and I should have been terrified, but I felt funny. She leaned over and climbed out of the car without opening the back door, then came and stood next to the driver's side door. When she leaned down, she was pretty again, her black hair feathered back like a Cherokee Farrah Fawcett. She gestured for me to roll down the window, so I did.

"Hey, Sissy."

"Hey, Gigage."

"Do me a favor, Sis. See if the horn works."

"What?" I wasn't feeling well. My head was starting to hurt and I felt a little nauseous.

"See if the horn works."

"But Jees is sleeping," I said.

"It's okay. Do it for me, please." Gigage leaned down and tousled my hair. I remembered how she always brought us ice cream from her work when she came by. We were always happy to see her.

I reached out and hit the horn.

"Real long," my cousin said. "Don't stop."

I nodded and held the horn down. The blast hurt my ears and I looked at my cousin and she smiled. My sister didn't move, her lips parted, almost snoring.

My hand started to hurt, so I switched hands. Then I got up

on my knees and pressed with both hands. The horn was the loudest car horn I ever heard. I never heard the garage door open. I barely noticed when they reached in and took my sister out.

I didn't stop pressing down on the horn until I vomited all over the steering wheel and dashboard and they pulled me from the car.

Sometimes, I wake up at night and hear that horn. Whenever that happens, I get up and go across the hall to check on my sister no matter what time it is. If she's not in bed, I get in the car and I drive and drive until I find her and I don't go home until I know she's okay.

# Ama's Boys

*law*

Ama Wilson

Gogi 1990

Summer 1990

**M**ost teenage boys are easy. I generally target the socially inept, book-smart boys, the cute and girlfriendless. They get my companionship for a while, I teach them some social skills, I satisfy a few of their less serious physical longings, and while they sleep, I feed. I play at being a rebellious teen girl, though I was able to pull off sixteen for one hundred and fifty years. Passing for that young is getting harder. Going to have to switch it up soon. There were years I bobbed my hair and seasons when I shaved my head. For now, it's long and straight again, as I began. Long enough, men think they can grab it. I have traveled the world. I have wandered Indian Territory, which is now Oklahoma. I have placed flowers on my father's overgrown grave in the small Wilson family cemetery. I have gone to the place where Chief Bowles was executed and mourned him and the other friends and family massacred on their exodus from Texas. I have learned to drive a car and play Schubert's Fantasie in F Minor, both parts, on the piano.

I have returned to this part of the United States because it's warm and, can be, clean. The homeland of the Comanche, the

Apache, the Caddo and, for a time, Cherokees. I like the immaculate, neat streets where the boys I hunt live. I like the houses their mothers pay to keep clean and historically accurate and the yards their fathers pay yardmen to manicure. I love their saltwater pools where we swim at night in the hottest part of the year, tasting of tears and blood, leaving their skin brined and damp.

I don't often make a mistake in choosing the boys. I almost never have to kill one. Yet, to every rule, there are exceptions.

Like Fred. I met Fred at a Con. He didn't dress up, but he didn't dress well either. He dressed like his mother dressed him or he wore his father's hand-me-down clothes that were ten years old. I fixed that. His mother was sorry she ever invited me in.

Instead, I hung about, leaving enough clues to make it obvious I had been there. The long black hairs in her bathroom, the wet towels we left on the floor after sneaking out to swim at midnight, items moved around in his closet and beneath his bed that led her to think I hid there when she checked on him. I didn't. I simply showed up when she was in a deep sleep and left before she awoke.

As Fred began to look better due to my tutelage, he began to drop hints that he was receiving attention from other girls. He also pressured me to "give myself to him." Again, it amused me that he expected a normal response—jealousy, possessiveness, a desire to keep him in exchange for my virtue—rather than the weariness I felt. Usually, I was the first attractive girl to listen to them, and the boys fell hard for me. I expected that. His growing hubris annoyed me.

With all the boys, the pattern was the same. On most nights, we curled up together, he fell asleep, and then I fed, taking as much blood as I needed to live, always careful not to infect him. As I grew bored, I made up fathers with job losses. I gave them one photo, one that I told them was shot in Silver Dollar City with me dressed in Victorian costume. In reality, it was shot in 1852, shortly after I became the monster I am now, before I knew all the abominable things the last one hundred and fifty years has taught me. I had it taken after I found the monster who made me. I try not to think too hard about what I have had to do to survive. When genocide is what you're up against, you regret nothing.

On the night I planned to break up with him, Fred's mom stayed up later than usual. I waited in the darkness of their backyard trying to choose my next city. San Antonio and Austin had waiting lists. Since blood hunters are always cold, we like to live in warm places. I had been grandfathered into Texas, and now West Texas was calling me.

Years ago, limits were put on migrating. Too many hunting in one area stops looking like a heroin epidemic and starts looking like a serial killer. The young hunters learn quickly to abide by the rules and eagerly fill out the applications to relocate to popular areas, places they wanted to live before they were bitten. South of the border is off limits currently. You don't want to get caught immigrating illegally to the warmer climates, and the legal routes can take years.

Fred's mom finished her bottle of wine and turned off the home improvement channel. Fifteen minutes after she had gone upstairs, Fred came out to their back deck. Gone was the shy posture he'd had when I met him. His swagger almost kept me from stepping out of the shadows.

"I'm moving," I said.

"When?" his brow creased with annoyance.

"Next weekend. But I won't be able to get away after tonight."

He didn't even pretend to be interested. Then I saw it register with him that he was being rude. As he realized I might not even go with him to his bedroom, his entire demeanor changed.

"I have something for you." Now he spoke sweetly. "I was hoping tonight would be our night." He stepped closer toward me, reaching out to pull me toward him. "Since you're leaving, I think it's more important than ever."

His lips lingered at my ear, "I'll die if I can't be with you tonight." He pressed his hips toward me and the smell of the blood beneath his skin caused my teeth to ache.

"Let me carry your bag," he said, reaching for my gear.

My bag is a weird old carpetbag. It has a change of clothes and everything I need to get cash and change my identity. It also has my works. If anyone ever opens it, they'll think I'm a heroin addict myself. It contains an artificial leech, a piece of antique medical equipment I have vastly improved upon. Once upon a time, bleeding was an acceptable medical treatment. A line of medical tubing could run blood straight into my veins without wasting a drop.

"I got it," I said, grabbing my valise.

Just one last time, I told myself.

We made our way to his room through the dark house. My vision allowed me to avoid obstacles in the dark, and I tried not to laugh as he ran into things in his own home. Once in his room, I produced the mythical father with the layoff, but it was obvious he was unconcerned.

We lay on his bed, watching *Near Dark* on his television. Fred pressured me more than usual.

"I think the first time, it should be with someone you really love," he lied into my neck. "If it's not you, it will be a long time before I love someone else."

I turned my head, kissing him back dispassionately. I summed my options up in my head. I was becoming angry he was going to force me to stop playing the role the way I enjoyed it. I was annoyed he wouldn't let me watch the film.

I sat up and took off my jacket.

He sat up and pulled a ring from his pocket. "Real gold," he said, as he slid it onto my ring finger. "It will be like we're married."

"I think I should go," I said.

Fred grabbed me and pushed me playfully back to the bed.

"Enough," I said strongly.

Fred grinned and instead dropped on top of me.

I feigned average strength for a teenage girl, warning him to get off me.

Instead, he leaned down, attempting to force his tongue into my mouth, while he shoved a hand beneath my skirt.

"No," I said.

He ignored me, continuing to kiss my face. I turned my head ever so slightly and darted my tongue out to taste his salty skin.

"That's it, baby," he said. I turned my head away, sensing another presence in the room. There was someone else nearby I hadn't noticed before. A second heart beat frantically, muffled by the doors of Fred's walk-in closet. While I was distracted, Fred shoved his tongue into my mouth. It tasted of old food.

For a moment I relaxed. Fred's attacking hands shifted to his own clothing, but he kept kissing me forcefully. With my sharp teeth, I bit down, catching the end of his tongue and spitting it out onto the carpet.

Fred went white. A low moan began in his throat. I grabbed him with all my strength and flipped him off the bed onto his back, banging his head on the wooden floor. I heard a clattering in the closet, but I ignored it. From my bag I grabbed the leech and stabbed it into his throat. The other end I shoved into the soft skin of my elbow's interior. I drained him until he was still.

I could hear light crying behind the wardrobe's doors. I pulled the already partially open door completely ajar. Inside sat one of Fred's friends, holding a video camera. I held out my hand, "Show me. And if you make a noise, I will kill you."

He had trouble operating the camera, but he finally got the digital display on and handed it to me.

I put the camera in my bag. I sat down on the floor next to the boy. I stroked his blond hair. I preferred the taste of blood tempered with lust, not fear.

"Come," I said, finally, when his heart rate returned close to normal. I stood and went to Fred's dresser and threw a pair of his trunks to his friend. The boy looked embarrassed to be changing with me in the room.

I took his hand and led him through the dark house, never letting him stumble into anything. When we stepped into the warm salt water, I knew where I wanted to go. The ocean was calling. I pulled the boy to me and kissed his salty face. I followed the dripping water down to his neck. The waves of the ocean are like a heartbeat. Like a heartbeat that never stops.

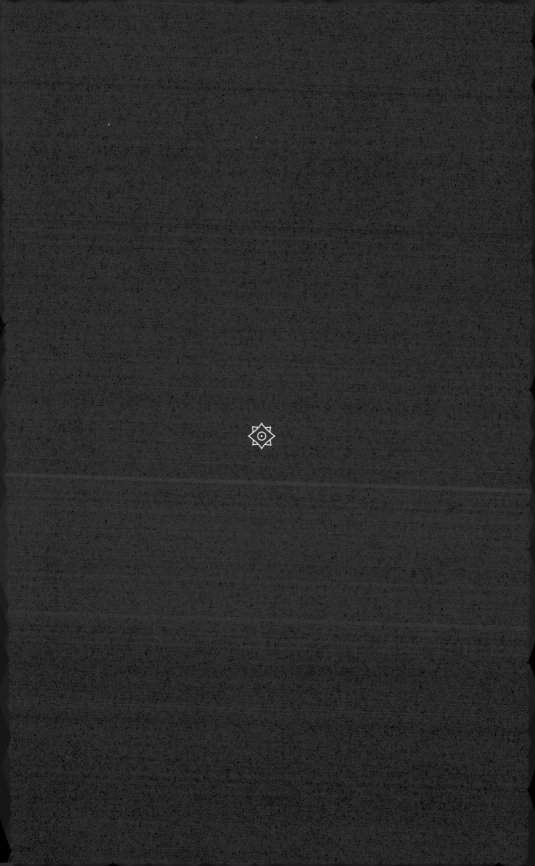

# American Predators

Darla King

Nvdadegwa 8, 1997

11/08/1997

"Which poor choice got you here, Jamie Shore?" you ask yourself. Once more you have fallen asleep on top of a motel's cheap polyester bedcover. The itchy fibers reek of smoke. The whole room stinks of smoke, but the bed has undertones of an odor you would rather not discern. It has seeped up into the sports bra and boxer shorts you fell asleep in.

It occurs to you that it may not have been one bad choice, but a combination of wrong turns that led to the hovel of self-hatred in which you now reside. Once a girl you had a crush on told you she believed in fate, that it was like math, that there were lots of different ways to get the one answer—but it would always be the same.

You follow the route in your nineteen-year demise backward, as if figuring out where you went wrong could redraw your current landscape, where you're working on a sizzler reel for national television in hopes of catapulting a local celebrity and his sidekick into fame and fortune. The show is supposed to be like *Antiques Roadshow*, but instead of appraising old stuff that belonged to someone's great-great and making them happy, the hosts are treasure hunters. Tentatively called *American Scavengers,* the premise is two guys drive around the country talking people into selling them things like vintage motorcycle signs and collectible cars at super-low prices. They turn around and make a huge profit off the items, making the original sellers look like fools.

Your most recent wrong turn was getting kicked out of the state university and letting your father make a phone call to get you this job. It is a gig he reminded you that as a girl your age with no degree you were lucky to get. Reminds you at every chance he's got. In fact, he was able to remind you of this fact without ever saying a word. That father of yours is talented. You had at last agreed with him (in a period of guilt and depression) that maybe college wasn't for you. Your father made the phone call because he had given up on you. Was tired of writing checks for classes you had been too hungover to attend. Dad traffics in guilt and shame as well as the fire-and-brimstone preacher who once convinced you you're going to hell since you first tried to kiss a girl at Vacation Bible School summer camp. Nope. Can't go there.

The backward trek takes a different route, but continues nonetheless. Things might have been different if you had gone to class more your freshmen year and partied less. If you had paid attention in the French class in high school and then aced French 1101 your GPA might have been high enough to get you onto academic probation, rather than outright expulsion.

If you hadn't spent years living in the television station your father ran, learning everything, not quite through osmosis, but almost. He was right though. You could do this and you didn't need a degree. It didn't matter that this wasn't what you wanted to do. What mattered is that you didn't know what you wanted to do. But you knew other things. You knew what it took to run a television studio, edit video, shoot footage, write a script, run a soundboard, coddle the talent.

So here you are, your life happening to you, dragging you along as if you are merely the occupant of a hamster ball someone pushed down the side of a dirt hill. You rub your eyes and hope it is not as late as you think it is. Motel clocks are often wrong, yeah?

You are throwing all the horror novels you brought with you back into your gym bag when the phone rings. In the room's quiet, it's like a scream. This is bad. This means you are really late and the talent, Whit and Billy, are sitting in the lobby of a slightly nicer hotel than the one you're housed in and they are tired of waiting for you. Whit is the taller, better-looking one. He likes having Billy as a sidekick because Billy makes Whit seem even taller, better-looking, and smarter.

Showering is pointless, you reason, as Whit will smoke next to you in the van, sometimes with the window down, but only if the weather is nice. And according to the news, it looks like rain. But you have to change into a clean bra and underwear, so you do it as quickly as possible.

After you fill the van with gas you pull up and see Whit on a payphone, checking his watch and shaking his head. This means you'll get a phone call from your father tonight.

Whit gestures for you to pull up next to where he is standing. He keeps talking on the phone while you load his suitcase into the van. In his hand he is holding a calendar featuring pictures of sepia-toned Indians by Edward Curtis. In order to fit his suitcase all the video equipment has to come out first. Billy comes out of the hotel, shoves his suitcase in, and jumps into the van's second row. Whit hangs up the phone and gets into the passenger seat. They both leave you to reload the cameras, battery packs, lighting equipment, sound gear. Yeah, sure, maybe it's your job, but still.

As you slip into the driver's seat neither guy speaks to you. You thought only girlfriends and relatives used the silent treatment to punish. You learn something new about being an adult every day. Whit has slipped on his glasses and is looking through the calendar. You want to rest your forehead on the steering wheel. It's not even seven o'clock in the morning.

"You know," he says, turning to Billy, "if we could just find a few rare photos, we could make so much on licensing. Licensing is where it's at. Calendars, art prints, posters, books . . ."

"Yup" is all Billy says. He's studying the map and marking it before he hands it up to you.

"So," Whit says, glancing at you over his lenses, "did you have a big night last night, Shore?"

You consider your answer carefully. On the one hand, you're single and nineteen, and the guys like to remind you of that often. "Free as a bird," Billy sets up Whit. And Whit adds some variation of "Not the best-looking bird, but still free." Often, they liken you to a stork or an emu—some gangly bird that's skinny and graceless, never a swan or even a chick, maybe an ugly duckling when you're not around. Though they claim to envy your unattached status, you're fairly sure that neither one of them is a faithful husband. You also know that from your lips to Dad's ears is where any information you give them will go, so you don't even lie to impress. Plus, they seem to have assumed that you're straight, though they have made it clear that given their druthers, you're not their type, at least when they're hanging out together and sober.

So, you don't mention the six pack of beer you were able to get at the corner store, but everything else you say is true. "Just stayed up late watching horror movies."

"Yeah"—this interests Billy, or maybe he's testing you—"which one?"

"*The Hunger.*" This is true. In fact you watched it early in the evening and stayed up late reading *Wolfen* so you could watch it again. You fell asleep watching it.

"Well, Billy and I had a bigger night than you," Whit says. And you think for a minute this was just his way of bragging about hooking up with someone impressed by his lean national television résumé. But then he adds: "But we still managed to get up and make it to work on time."

Billy laughs.

Whit turns to him, "You probably should have stayed in and watched *The Hunger*, though. Sounds like your kind of film." Whit blows out his cheeks. You hate when Whit makes you feel sorry for Billy.

Still, Billy doesn't laugh, but you do. You are very sure that it is not a film for Billy or Whit. In this way, what passes for balance is restored.

Less than an hour into the drive, Whit decides that he likes the light and the landscape. He wants you to shoot some footage. It's the kind of stuff that is picturesque and can be used over and over again if the show is picked up for national broadcast. These scenes could maybe even go in the title credits. Heck, the station can use this stuff over and over. You stop and get the camera out of the back. You trade places with Billy. You film bits of the Llano Estacado, a herd of antelope, some oil rigs, what you can see of an adobe ghost town, truck beds full of brown kids, grazing sheep, a sky full of rain with lightning that seems to slice through the nearly indigo striations to touch the mesas. When it starts to rain, you shoot a little longer. When you have enough you pull the van door closed and sit back, enjoying having the back seat to yourself. You pre-edit the footage in your head as you play it back through the camera. You imagine the films you could make, if only you found the right story.

The rain stops and Whit tells you he wants you to film the

billboards for a well-known travel stop you are driving toward. The large signs advertise soft-serve ice cream and Indian moccasins and other genuine "Indian-made crafts." From the passenger seat, Billy hollers, "Whoo-wooo-wooo-wooo!" while he slaps at his lips with his right hand. You remember why you hate Billy.

"Save it for the set," Whit says.

When you pull in just outside of Santa Fe, the guys go in to check out the large travel station. You've been drinking soda all morning and your teeth begin to ache knowing this is the bathroom stop, the way a dog jumps when he sees a leash. Usually one of you stays with the van to keep an eye on all the equipment. When you can't stand it any longer, you make sure all the doors are locked and park right in front of an entrance. When you walk in you see Whit talking to a guy who radiates that he is in charge of the place. You catch Whit's eye and nod toward the back of the building, where you assume the bathrooms are located. You're sure he sees you, but Whit doesn't acknowledge you.

When you come out of the bathroom, you see an automaton, an animatronic fortune teller. This one, in keeping with the Southwest Indian theme that seems to draw in the tourists and make this place a lot of money, is an Indian. His upper torso sits inside a cabinet, the area surrounding his trunk littered with dream catchers, feathers, miniature drums, a painted pot, and a bundle of sage. Across the glass the machine announces, "Medicine Man Speaks—50 Cents." He wears a headdress and a cheap costume breastplate over a black shirt. Now and then a recording whirs to life playing drums. There are screams you imagine to be war cries, then the recorded drums become fainter. It's gross. A joke.

This is exactly the sort of thing Whit loves.

You buy another soda and go out to the van to wait. You pull out your copy of *The Stand*. When a guy walks by and sneezes the kind of full-body sneeze that creates a fountain of spray in the air, you put the book away. Yeah, the killer flu is scary, but the people in the book, they're the monsters.

As Billy walks out, Whit leans from the doorway and hollers at you both to grab the gear and come on into the restaurant. You had planned to tell him about the mockery of a Medicine Man, but you hadn't wanted a whole shoot. Just maybe some footage to splice in. Billy doesn't look thrilled, either, but he grabs the lights and returns the way he came.

In the restaurant, Whit has already grabbed a large round table in the corner and is making notes.

As you set the cases down, he says, "This place is great. I got permission to do some shooting."

"Did you see the fortune teller in the back?" you ask. "It's by the bathrooms."

Billy sets a case down. He and Whit go to have another look around.

The attached restaurant is a Dairy Queen. The hotel Billy and Whit stayed in had a breakfast option. You've been living on peanut M&Ms and Coke. You get up to order some lunch. You finish before they return, so you pull out your copy of *The Shining* you were too scared to read alone in your room the night before. You like horror. You just like it better in the daylight.

"Good call on the red man," Whit says when he sits down.

"This one's going to write itself," Billy says, joining him, blocking you in between the two of them on the circular bench.

"You wish," Whit says. "Billy's going to go order me and him some lunch, since eating is his talent. You go shoot some footage of the quirkier items here. Make sure you get those taxidermied frogs playing guitars and all that made-in-China American Indian stuff."

"Don't forget the stuffed buffalo head," Billy says, getting up so you can get out.

"The manager says the foot traffic will slow down later tonight. We'll do the shoot inside then."

You grab the camera and wander around. You're tall, so many of the people who see you never look up at the camera. You like that about being tall; it makes you feel less like you're in the wrong body. Some people never look up past their eye level.

Whit sends you to book a hotel nearby. There's an old motor lodge that's been restored. Even though it doesn't have a bar, which will irk Whit, you book three rooms. Whit's and Billy's next to each other, yours as far from them as possible. The place seems familiar, and you're already booked before you realize it reminds you of the Bates Motel. Luckily, there's no Addams Family house towering over the rooms, and the retired couple running the place seem nice. They are very into historic preservation. There are no taxidermied animals anywhere. You hope the vintage car out front will charm Whit. *Charm* is a word you would rarely use in relation to Whit, though.

When you get back, Billy and Whit have their script written. They like it to appear unrehearsed and off-the-cuff, as if their banter is naturally quick, knowledgeable, and witty. This means you're going back to the motel to practice. First, though, Whit wants you to shoot the episode's introduction as the sun is dropping behind the Llano Estacado west of the travel center.

Whit's right, the sunset is beautiful. It's hard to light right, though. You have lens flare to contend with and you have to light the talent properly, but still try to get the colors behind them. You're a professional, though. You have skills beyond your years. You set up the camera and Whit and Billy step in front of it. You slip on your headphones to monitor the sound from the wireless mics.

"Here we are at the Four Corners Travel Center. You can buy a lot of interesting things here, including genuine Indian-made crafts."

Billy repeats his line from in the van, "That's Indian whoo-woo-woo!" He exaggeratedly slaps at his lips like a kindergartner.

Whit gives him the look that says, bless your heart, before responding, "I don't know, Billy. Let's go see."

About eight, they order a pizza and have you go over the production notes with them. What shots they need you to get. The manager told Whit to come back about ten to film inside.

You walk in at ten on the dot.

He was right, it's less crowded. Still, you don't know if it's the dark or the neon and fluorescent lighting, but you would swear that 60 percent of the people now are a little bit sketchier—even some of the families, the little kids even. When you walk in with the equipment cases you get suspicious looks. You hope nothing gets stolen. It would piss off your dad, and no matter what, the theft would somehow be your fault.

Whit and Billy meet the staff that are now on duty. The manager introduces his seventeen-year-old daughter. He tells Whit he thought maybe he could find a spot for Lacy in the shoot. She's pretty, so of course Whit can. It's another one of his talents. She goes over some facts about the moccasins a whole small-room-sized area is devoted to.

Whit finds an expensive pair of boots with fringe in his size. "How about if Lacy helps me on with these, while you film."

Billy catches my eyes and rolls his, but he doesn't exactly walk away.

Lacy glances around for her dad, but he's not there. I pull out the camera and start filming. This is the kind of stuff Whit has me shoot that he has no intention of using. Makes the pretty girls think they might end up on television, might go somewhere, somewhere not here.

She kneels carefully in her skirt that just barely hits her knees. Even though she's wearing a brand-new ironed Four Corners blouse, you doubt she even works here.

While Lacy is tying the top string of his boot, Whit says, "These moccasins are awfully comfy. I wouldn't mind walking a mile in these babies."

And that's it. Whit leans down and extends a hand to Lacy, who is shaky in her heels. He stands up and leans in a lot longer than necessary, whispering something that makes her blush. I hear him ask her to stick around to watch, might learn a thing or two that will help her with a future career. She nods and offers to go get him a soda before disappearing.

"We're going to have to add some stuff in about the company's history making moccasins. How they started in travel centers and tourist shops in the forties. Downplay the part about all the Indian shoes being made in the Dominican Republic and China now."

Billy nods. He rarely takes notes.

We move to shoot right in front of the neon sign that guides customers to the restroom.

This time Billy speaks first, setting Whit up for the joke.

"Hey, Whit, I want to show you something back this way."

Whit raises his eyebrows, "I promised our producer to never take the camera into the bathroom, Billy."

"No, no, no. This is just outside the bathroom."

With the camera, you follow the two men to the large glass case with the gaudy Indian in it. It reminds you of a case at a zoo, a diorama at a museum. The last of the Mohicans appearing nightly for your viewing pleasure.

Whit acts as if it's the first time he's seen the thing, all little-boy-excited: "Hey, Billy, loan me fifty cents!"

Billy reaches into his pocket. "I think you still owe me fifty cents from our last visit with a 'fortune teller.'"

Whit switches to a slightly conspiratorial pitch, "That was more like fifty dollars, and Madame Lola did a little more than tell fortunes. Let's see what Chief Red in the Face can do."

Billy hands him two quarters and Whit drops them into the machine.

Whit switches back into his antique-expert voice, "This seems fortuitous."

"A good sign?" Billy queries.

"You don't see a lot of these coin-operated fortune tellers anymore. This Medicine Man is in fabulous condition."

As the machine kicks to life, you zoom in on the red-brown plastic face framed with long black synthetic braids. Drums can be heard and the recorded *Wooo-wooo!* starts. The headphones you monitor the audio with are making it sound like the machine is in your head. In editing, you'll flip the image around to a dis-orienting angle, reminiscent of crazy scenes in a fun house.

In a mock-serious voice, Whit intones, "Chief Four Corners Truck Stop Medicine Man, are we on the trail of something special?"

More drums are heard. Almost too quickly, a card slightly smaller than a business card pops out of the machine, but you fail to catch the shot. Annoyed, Whit feeds two more quarters in, and you catch it the second time.

"I think he speaks," Billy says, as the card pops out.

"I hope it's good news."

"What does it say?"

Here, Whit has you focus the camera in tight on the words. Whit reads in a serious monotone, "'It is certain.'"

You step back and shoot a wide angle of the two men jumping up and down in front of the automaton. "Woo-hoo!" They high-five each other.

After they stop jumping, Whit remarks, "My Magic-Eight Ball said the same thing this morning."

"And it didn't cost me fifty cents."

You back away farther and pan across the back of the truck stop. The fortune teller, the claw machine game where people fail to pick up a toy with a crane, the entrances to the bathrooms where people who are real characters are ducking in and out. Finally, you end on the huge stuffed buffalo head like Billy told you to. You zoom in and wonder if his fake black eyes are plastic or glass.

Back at the motel by 2:00 a.m., you go right to sleep even though you're sober. You don't sleep well, though. You blame it on reading *The Stand* off and on all day, then you wish you hadn't even thought about the book in the dark like that. When you wake up again it's six o'clock. You get up and walk across the street to the diner. You have already decided not to shower until the sun is up.

From New Mexico you wander across Texas, not really stopping but shooting the expected footage through the open van door. You film cotton fields, windmills, and more oil derricks. The show's next appointment is really in Arkansas, but you are shooting footage in Oklahoma as you drive through. You capture golden fields and a herd of buffalo. The sun is high in the hazy yellow sky. Eventually you capture scenes of vacant storefronts, abandoned oil field equipment, liquor stores with busy parking lots, and empty houses with boarded-up windows. Billy asks someone where to get a good meal and you end up in downtown Tahlequah.

Unfortunately, the restaurant shares a parking lot with a pawn shop. For Whit and Billy, a pawnshop is like a library, a great place to do research, but someplace where they will never spend any money.

On the front door of the pawn shop is a poster of "The Cherokee Outlaw Ned Christie."

"See," Whit says, "that's what I'm talking about. And we, Billy boy, have a better chance of making bank off something like that because we're always looking."

The glass cases are full of beaded items, jewelry, rattles, and some (according to the label) old Cherokee double-walled baskets. You know next to nothing about Indians. Your ignorance makes you feel stupid and hungry at the same time. A tall girl stands behind the counter. She is still and quiet. Most women don't want to date someone shorter than them, so you always think statistically you have a better shot with an unusually tall woman, though so far, you've been 100 percent wrong. You assume this one is Indian since you are in the Cherokee capital. She has long, straight black hair and she looks shyly (or is it angrily) away when she realizes you have turned the camera toward her. She finally gives the camera (or is it you) a long, hard look, then disappears into the back.

Whit and Billy and the pawnshop owner, who is an older white guy, are looking in a case. Whit directs you to come over and film while they talk.

"Tell me about these gigging rods," Whit says.

"These were forged by hand. They're used to hunt crawdads. You see how they are shaped like a fork? You stab at the upper part of the crawdad's body, because you're going to eat the tail.

You have to catch a lot of them to make a meal. Crawdad gigging is a good way to spend the night around here. These were made by an old Cherokee man. He's passed now. They're worth quite a bit now that he's gone."

Billy responds to the set-up, "Well, I guess he's not making any more of them."

Whit reaches down and picks up a bent stick wrapped with leather. "What's this?"

"Darla!" the old white man yells. He picks up the other stick and a leather-wrapped ball and continues talking. "This is a stickball ball and stick. It's made out of bent hickory wood and tied with sinew. The ball probably has a rock in it and is wrapped in leather."

Darla comes out of the back. She is frowning.

"Didn't your Grandfather Wilson teach your dad how to make these?"

Darla nods.

"These are made the traditional way. No power tools. All by hand. That's why they're so expensive."

Billy pipes up to try to prompt for more information. "Stickball, isn't that like lacrosse?"

"In the Cherokee game of stickball, the men played with sticks, but the women played using their hands."

Whit looks over at Billy, "Since we only have two sticks, I guess you'll have to play with your hands, Billy."

The host and the pawnshop owner laugh hysterically while Billy looks embarrassed.

Darla speaks up. Her voice is strong and clear: "The women are fierce. They often draw blood. People used to die during these games. More often than they do now."

All of you are quiet. You have turned the camera toward Darla, but she is not seeing you.

Whit is not pleased. "You might be a little too serious for this shoot, sweetheart. I think we better shoot that again without Pocahontas."

Darla turns and disappears into the back room and you hear a door slam. The scene is reshot. This time at the end, Billy manages to look cinematically emasculated as he fails to catch the leather ball and the two other men play an embarrassingly long game of "Monkey in the Middle."

Eventually, you shut the camera off, but Whit is still picking up beaded moccasins and asking about prices. He hasn't collected Native American items previously because he is not unaware of his vast amount of ignorance. Still, he's obviously intrigued. You remember the calendar with the Curtis photos. It occurs to you that this is the kind of town where someone might find something like that.

You go out to the van and put the camera away. On a hunch you grab Whit's cigarettes and your copy of *The Howling*. You walk toward the back of the building. Darla is there, but she's not smoking. Instead, she's reading a battered copy of *The Hunger*. You shove the cigarettes into your jacket pocket before she looks up.

"That's a great book," you say, even though you have never read it. You have only watched the movie and are still thinking about it.

She looks up and shrugs, "We'll see. It's pretty different from the film." She looks at your copy of *The Howling*. "That one's not very realistic."

"Well, yeah, it's about werewolves. But it's still a great book."

Darla shrugs again and goes back to reading.

Nervous, and with no reason to be there other than to talk with her, you blather on, "My boss is kind of a jerk."

At this, Darla smiles.

You continue, "I mean, obviously, you're more of a Tiger Lily than a Pocahontas." You think you're flirting. You think this because you're an idiot. You realize this when her eyes turn sharp and unblinking.

"I'm sorry," you stumble. "I've been trapped in the van with those jerks too long. Losing my social skills," you lie. This is why you don't talk much. That way you don't prove what an idiot you can be.

Yet, you can't be stopped. You have this feeling, this idea, this notion that maybe you can find treasure. You wonder if this is what people who gamble feel sometimes. That sense that this is the night, the moment, that everything has aligned, that your fate is not really what you thought it was, but this, this new thing that is about to happen to you and change your life. So, you start talking about photographs and calendars and licensing and money.

Whit listens to you and you see he's excited. He has a monologue ready before you have the camera set up.

"That thing on, yet?" he demands. You nod and he turns to the camera. "So, our camera gal, Jamie, traded some cigarettes to Pocahontas for some information. It seems her grandfather has a whole stash of those stickball sticks back at his place and she thinks he might let them go for a song. Some of them are at least a hundred years old." He stops. "Okay, let's reshoot that and this time I'm going to mention the photos, that way if it doesn't pan out, we can still use the first one."

It's the first time he has mentioned your name on camera, and you like it. In the next run-through, he adds, "Her grandfather may also have some old photos of the Cherokees playing stickball with the same sticks he might be willing to sell. Those photos might be worth something, too, especially if he can identify the Indians in those photos. There is no shortage of famous

Indians around here that people would like pictures of. The money's in the ownership and licensing. You can turn old photos of famous people into calendars and T-shirts and make some cash. Maybe Ned Christie is in one of them . . ."

You take the guys to eat all the catfish they can eat and then you follow the map Darla has given you to her grandparents' home. It's dirt and gravel roads all the way there. When you pull into the driveway, she is waiting for you. She has you pull up behind the barn, behind a convertible that used to be cherry red when it was first made in the sixties. You glance at Whit, and you see he is calculating how difficult it would be to haul that Mustang back to Cincinnati.

You park. Your dad is going to be pissed about the dings in the paint and on the undercarriage of the van.

You pop on your headphones and grab the camera and lights and walk toward the house. Darla comes from inside and says her grandparents don't want to be filmed. Whit orders you to leave the camera on and film him going to the door and trying to sweet-talk the grandparents.

From where you are, it's just a closed, black screen in front of a dark green door with cracking paint. You keep shooting while Whit tries to talk his way past it. Finally, the interior door closes and the host stomps off the porch, visibly angry.

"Man, did you see that couple? Straight out of the movies. Wouldn't take any reasonable amount to appear on camera. Said his way of making things wasn't for sale." Whit is practically spitting. "He shut the door in my face." Then he turns on you, "Can you turn that off for a minute?"

You tilt your camera toward the sky. It's getting late. You were all supposed to sleep in Fayetteville, Arkansas, tonight. "Looks like a full moon tonight," you say to no one in particular.

"I need a smoke," Whit mutters.

Darla materializes from the dark. "How about if I show you his studio? I know how to make the sticks, too. Plus, his photos are in the cellar workshop."

Whit shifts back into a good mood quickly.

In the cellar, Darla pulls out an album of old photos of men playing stickball, lined up in teams. There are handwritten words labeling the people in the photos.

Whit has pulled a magnifying glass from his pocket and is asking questions faster than Darla can answer them. "Are any of these guys famous outlaws?" He turns the page while Darla is still pointing out names of stickball players to him. "What are these pictures? Why is he holding that beaded belt up?"

Darla leans over, "Let me see," she says. She takes the album from him. "I can't remember," she continues, stepping toward the cellar door. "Let me go ask my grandfather."

She takes the album and heads up the stairs. As she leaves the cellar, she closes the door behind her. It slams to a close with a heavy thud. A moment later, you hear the sound of heavy metal sliding and then the clink of a lock.

Billy looks at you and Whit. "If I didn't know better, I'd say she just locked us in here."

Whit and Billy laugh and then you sit down on the cellar stairs. You film Whit and Billy while they pick up the stickball sticks on the worktable.

Finally, Whit turns and looks at you. "What the heck is taking so long?"

You move out of the way as he stomps up the stairs and tries the door. He pushes at it. It lifts up slightly and then hits resistance. "She really did lock us in here," he shouts. "What the hell? Billy, come help me with this."

You back away, still filming. You have already turned the

Frezzi light on the top of your camera because the one light bulb hanging from the cellar ceiling is worthless as far as lighting goes.

Finally, Whit turns and yells at you, "Are you in on this? Is this some kind of joke? If I were you, I would put that camera down and help us try to open this door."

You set the camera on the worktable and point it toward the cellar door. You crowd beneath the door on the wooden steps and help Whit and Billy press against it.

Billy freezes, "Stop. Stop a minute. Did you hear that?"

"What?"

"It sounded like a chain. It's coming from that back room." Billy gestures toward a dark corner of the cellar. The sound of a chain being dragged across the floor is clearly audible once there is silence. Then, there is a long, haunting howl.

To no one in particular, Whit mutters, "This isn't funny."

It is clear by the look of terror on your own face that you agree.

It sounds like a very large animal is at the end of a chain, stretching it. It clinks as it bangs. A growl is heard over the sound of the stretching chain. The men turn and start banging at the door.

"What was that girl's name?"

But you are already screaming, "Darla!"

The other two men finally hear you and scream with you.

There is another long wolf howl. It is the eeriest thing you have ever heard through your earphones. You all become silent. You notice that the camera is still pointed toward you. There is the sound of metal straining and then clinking as it comes loose and bounces to the floor. Something steps out of the back room.

You are all trying to get back up the stairs—get as close to the exit as possible.

The creature is hairy and tall, with claws. He's not shiny like the American Werewolf in London, but you tell yourself this can't be real, even while you see the individual hairs extending from each pore. His head brushes the single light bulb in the center of the room. Then he is a blur as he grabs Billy and drags him down the stairs. They disappear from view into the back of the cellar. For the next several minutes, you know Billy is still alive, because he is still screaming. You have to turn the volume down on your headphones so as not to be deafened by Billy's screams.

Whit runs to the worktable and grabs a hammer.

"Jamie, get something to help me break this door." Whit is striking the door when the screams end. Whit stops and listens. Now you know how the crunching of human bone sounds through a wireless microphone. Whit is striking the door. You pick up the camera. Whit is hitting the door and screaming for help, and you're filming him. He doesn't even notice when the creature's heavy breathing returns. Whit is taking another swing at the door's hinges when the creature grips him by the back of the neck and hauls him back him down the wooden steps.

You back toward the cellar door, your camera pointed toward the dark corner of the cellar into which Whit and the creature have now disappeared. You sit down on the stairs listening to Billy's wails as they become softer. The camera is on your right shoulder, and with your left hand you reach absentmindedly into your pocket as if you are looking for a cigarette. Of course, they are still there from when you borrowed them as a prop earlier. Tears start to trickle down your cheeks. You set the camera on the workbench, opening the lens up so it will capture the whole room, and it is still filming, though you are not touching it, merely standing next to it, like it's none of your concern. The Frezzi light is pointed toward the yawning black hole that is the back of the cellar. You go and sit on the wooden steps again.

When Whit stops moaning, there is only your heavy breathing. The creature steps into the light and snarls. His front paws and legs are covered in blood. He is a huge, carmine wolf, but you can't imagine he is still hungry. The fur of the creature's muzzle is, also, covered in blood. He is glaring into the camera's bright light. He steps towards it. You take the lighter and lift it to the end of a cigarette. It flares as you place it to the tip. The creature's eyes turn towards you, transfixed. You draw figure eights in the air.

"You know," you tell the creature, "this footage is priceless. Someone is going to make so much money—"

The lighter starts to burn the tip of your finger. You let it go, and there is only the burning ember of the cigarette between you and the monster. The giant wolfman turns away and stalks back into the dark of the cellar. You inhale the tobacco deeply. When the werewolf hits you in the chest, the cigarette falls to the ground. It sparks and then flares out, ground into the dirt. It occurs to you that maybe you didn't hate your life as much as you thought you did, as sharp teeth graze your arm.

# Manifesting Joy

Joy and Dylan Stone

Nvdadegwa 2000

11/2000

J oy, you only have one earring in," Joy's brother, Dylan, said, as they got into the back seat of their father's car. Their plane had been delayed and rerouted as they tried to return from their Grandma Stone's funeral, and it was nearly midnight. Joy reached up and found that the earring in her right ear was, indeed, missing. Without asking permission, she jumped out of the car and retraced her steps to the baggage carousel, then the bathroom. Her brother was standing at the bathroom door when she came back out. "TSA made Dad move the car. He has to swing back around. C'mon."

"They were the earrings that Grandma Stone made me."

Joy's fifteen-year-old brother grimaced and shook his head. Joy understood it as "sorry."

Joy had been misplacing little things since her grandmother had gone into hospice three weeks ago. She had known something was wrong when her grandmother hadn't texted to say, "Good morning." Known so strongly something was wrong she hadn't wanted school to end, to see her parents and be told something had happened. Since then, she had misplaced a glove, a favorite pencil, and a science paper. Luckily, she had been able to reprint the paper moments before class started. But the first important and completely irreplaceable thing that she had lost was her journal. She had left it behind on the plane she and her mother and brother had taken to the funeral in Albuquerque, New Mexico. She had been so careful not to set the journal where her mother could read it, or her younger brother, for that matter. She had even chosen not to leave it at home, afraid that her father would find it.

It's not that she had written anything incriminating, but they were her private thoughts, some she had dashed down "in the heat of the moment" as they say, and she found she was not so proud of those entries when she reread them. She couldn't believe she had left her diary on the plane, and not noticed until she got to her grandparents' house. It was the closest thing she had to a best friend, and she had forgotten it. She got online and filed a lost-item claim with the airline, daring to hope, even before she went through her two bags over and over. There was no doubt it was missing.

All weekend she had worn the pair of blue-and-white-beaded earrings her grandmother had made her. She checked her phone constantly for the e-mail from the airlines that never came about her journal. She reached up regularly to check to make sure her earrings were still in her ears. She had meant to get some of those little plastic cylinders you could stick on earring hooks so that they were less likely to fall out, but she always forgot to buy them when she went to the kinds of stores that sold stuff like that. It had seemed important to wear them when she packed for the funeral. Now, she only had one sad earring. She took it out of her ear and put it in her purse's side zipper pocket.

In the front seat of the car, her mother was crying, and her father was trying to drive and comfort her at the same time. Joy swallowed her tears and pulled out her phone and filed a second lost-item claim with the airline. She uploaded a picture of her lone earring.

Once home, she slept fitfully. All day at school she obsessed on the journal and the earring. She vowed she would be more conscious, more present, convinced that she could cure herself of her carelessness. She was thinking about the jewelry when she opened up her locker after lunch and saw the remaining blue-and-white-beaded earring in it. How had it fallen out of her purse without her noticing?

The missing earring had been ever present in her thoughts, but she had also talked herself through all her actions, noting, "Now I am putting my favorite pen in my backpack." "Now I am taking my phone out of my pocket." "Now I am returning my phone to my pocket." All day she had been so careful with her things. Yet, there her last earring sat. She had never taken it out of the pocket of her purse the night they got home, though she had meant to. She had planned to treat it as the irreplaceable reminder of her grandmother it had become. But now, it lay in the bottom of her locker.

She pulled her purse from her backpack. The side pocket was still zipped. She turned the purse around in her hands to check for a hole the earring could have fallen out of, but it was untorn.

Curiouser, she thought. She unzipped the flawed side pocket. There jingled the other blue-and-white earring. "Curiouser still!" she said aloud.

She put both earrings in the pocket, zipped it up, and returned it to her backpack. Throughout the afternoon, she would take out her purse to make sure both earrings were still there.

When she got home that afternoon, she took the earrings out and hung them on the scarf above her dresser where she put all her favorite things.

She sat down at her desk and thought hard about her diary. Maybe her luck would extend to that. She checked her phone and was thrilled to see an email from the airline. However, when she opened it, it was simply updating her that the item's status remained unfound.

She heard her father call her brother downstairs to get his luggage. Dylan dragged it up the stairs, banging the wheels unnecessarily on each step. A few minutes later he hollered, "Joy, come here."

"What?" she yelled back.

"Just come here."

"Aaaargh," she groaned. Standing in his doorway, she asked, "What?"

"Guess what I found?"

Joy's stomach began to knot as she thought of the missing journal. She did not want Dylan to read the things she had written about him.

"Give it here!" she snapped, looking around his room. Had he had her journal all weekend?

He gave her a funny look. "Crazy much?"

"Give it to me!" She reached out her hand.

"Jeez, I thought you'd be happy nice, not psycho about it." He slapped something small and sharp into her hand. Joy was surprised to see her missing blue earring. Again.

The shock registered on her face. "Where did you find this?"

"It was in that weird pocket on the back of my carry-on. You must have dropped it after we went through the metal detectors." He paused. "What did you think I had?"

She held the earring up and turned it, examining it from every angle.

"Hey," he said, repeating, "what did you think I had?"

"Did you make this?" Joy said incredulously.

"What?"

"Did you make this? You know, to replace my earring so I wouldn't feel bad for losing the one Grandma made?"

"Joy, I haven't done beadwork since we made those tin cans covered in pony beads at camp, and I sucked at that. Now, you think that I spent the last eight hours making an earring to make you happy?"

Joy shrugged and made an I-don't-know noise. Then she turned and went back to her room. She took all three earrings to her desk. She examined them until she could tell which two earrings matched exactly.

She began thinking about her diary and her grandma. She wondered if her grandma would fit into her locker.

# Lens

Diane King
Kuyegwona 31, 2014
07/31/2014

The surgery won't cost you anything at all, Mrs. King. In fact, you'll get paid for your time and inconvenience," the doctor was talking to my mother, but leaning over me, his light shining into my mostly blind left eye. "And even though there are no guarantees she'll be able to see, it's unlikely to do any harm. Her brain has rewired itself to ignore this eye. So, as well as the lens being experimental, we'll have to work at rewiring the brain to pay attention to the messages coming from this eyeball."

"I'll have to talk to her father," my mother said.

What this meant was that she would decide what was best and then she and my father would argue about it. My father didn't trust anyone. Doctors especially. Indians can be like that. With good reason.

When I was four, a cousin shot me in the eye with a BB gun. My parents had been attending a funeral and when they came home, they found me screaming and inconsolable. The babysitter lied and told them I ran into the corner of a sewing machine drawer. Hence, trust didn't come easily for me either. I howled all the way home from Kansas City to Tulsa, insane and in pain, unable to tell them what really happened. I didn't stop crying until I fell asleep. By the time a doctor saw me, he said it was already healing and nothing could be done. A year later they removed the damaged lens and a thin white halo formed around the torn cornea. My vision was flat; I had no depth perception.

At sixteen, I was a candidate for a surgery to implant an experimental artificial lens. The tiny plastic computer chip would send messages from my left eye to my brain. The hope was that my brain would translate the reflected light into recognizable images. What could go wrong, yeah?

After my sister, Sali, and I went to bed, I heard my mother and father arguing. A door slammed, the familiar sound of my father leaving. Fifteen minutes later, I got up and found my mom smoking on the back steps. Fireflies danced in the middle of the yard. Their glow was yellow and fragile and cold.

"Well," my mother said.

I didn't say anything.

"Don't you want to be able to see out of both eyes?"

I shrugged.

She turned and looked at me, her cigarette glowing hot orange in her left hand.

"I can see okay."

She turned away and put her cigarette to her lips.

"Your father is worried they'll mess up your brain."

"Brains are kind of important."

Her laugh was derisive, "How the hell would your father know that?" She tossed the cigarette into the center of a cement block next to the stair. It glowed brilliantly as it fell, sparking when it hit the dirt. It landed on dry grass that caught and then flamed out. She lit a new cigarette, and I turned and went back into the house.

⊕

The surgery was a flight away from Oklahoma. Neither Mom nor I had ever been on a plane. Any place we'd gone previously we'd walked or drove. My twelve-year-old sister whined about how she never got to go anywhere, as if it were some great vacation we were going on. Finally, I offered to trade my blind eye for one of hers, and she shut up. From the airport we went straight to the hospital. Once we were on our way, Mom regretted not hustling for the luxury of an extra day or two. "Flying all the way to Seattle and we'll only see the ocean and mountains from a plane," she pined.

I had been enthralled with the view from the air and tried not to push her away as she leaned into me to see out my window. I tried not to think about the surgery going badly and never seeing anything afterward. I tried not to wonder if my first and only view of mountains and oceans would be from a thousand feet in the air.

Mom slept on a couch in my pre-op room and I watched DVD after DVD, as she snored. Nurses came in and checked on me. At two in the morning, I was still awake, and the floor was quiet. A dark-haired nurse came in and asked if I wanted something to help me sleep. I shook my head. On the screen, Bruce Willis watched his wife sadly.

The nurse turned and left. A few minutes later, she was back with a brush, and asked if she could braid my hair. My mother had given up on fixing my hair in kindergarten.

I nodded and watched the film, my face partially hidden by a rough blanket.

She adjusted the bed and I sat up. She neatly divided my hair, parting it down the middle. "Such pretty black hair," she chirped.

"Thank you," I whispered. I wondered if I was going to have to cut it for the surgery. If there would be a scar where they would cut into my brain. I suddenly wished I had said no.

"Are they going to cut my hair?" I asked the nurse, not taking my eyes off the screen.

"No, sweetie, I don't think so. They'll go in through a sinus passage."

On the screen a girl threw up, her face pale and terrifying.

I turned off the TV with the remote. I closed my eyes and felt the nurse drag the brush softly through my hair. Her fingers tugged gently, spreading my hair apart and then weaving it into plaits. I drifted off as she worked on the second braid.

A few hours later, I was hooked up to an IV drip, and this time, quickly out. Before I closed my eyes, I wondered if I would reopen them.

When I did, my mother was sitting next to the bed, reading a book. Books were her second addiction, the one that wouldn't give me cancer. I watched her. She was totally engrossed—lost in an interior life I didn't have a clue about. Behind her stood two little girls, one a toddler, the other five or six. They held hands and watched me. My left eye itched and I began to try to lift a hand to rub it. My hand was fastened to the bed rail and moving it caused a loud clanging. My mother jumped up and came to the bedside, saying, "Stop. They don't want you to rub your eye."

I closed my left eye, focusing on opening my right. There was only darkness. I panicked. "Why can't I see out of my right eye?"

My mother was pushing the call button. "They want you to use the left one. Retrain your brain to see out of the new lens, so they covered the right with a bandage."

"It hurts. It itches." I opened my left eye. The two little girls kept staring at me.

My mother stepped back out of the way as an orange-haired nurse came in. She gave me two pills and some water. She removed the bandage from my right eye, and her face suddenly seemed to wear two different expressions when I looked at her. She was smiling and frowning at the same time. I glanced over at the two little girls, and they were like gauze, watching the nurse fearfully. The nurse replaced the bandage with a clean one, covering my right eye. Her smiling face disappeared. I glanced over at the little girls, and they became solid. The older one walked up to the bed.

The nurse spoke cheerfully, "We're going to bandage this eye, too, but don't touch it. It has a lot of healing to do." She covered up my left eye. I felt the IV tube move and suddenly my arm grew colder with a rush of new fluids. I was suddenly sleepy. "It's best if you rest now," the nurse said, pleasantly.

I felt a small cold hand reach out and touch my arm. "Sometimes," the little girl whispered, "when she gives you drugs, you die. But you're going to be okay, so don't worry. Me and Bea are watching out for you."

I fell asleep feeling a second small hand patting me.

The bandage stayed on until the next day to keep me from scratching and clawing the new lens out. I could feel it, blood pulsing around it, swelling as if my eyeball might force the foreign object out. In the meantime, my brain had noticed whatever they had done in there and ached as if it, too, had a foreign object the size of a marble to push out. I begged them to let me sleep through it but dreaded the nightmare of the two dead-looking girls returning. They didn't visit my dreams again, though. My mother kept patting my arm when I would wake up moaning. At that point the pain had spread—my whole body sensitive—and I yelled at her to go sightseeing and leave me alone. I was grateful I couldn't see her reaction. I didn't know what I would do if she had the second cruel face I thought she might. Pain had made me a wild animal who wanted to crawl into its burrow and die alone.

The two dead girls only returned when the orange-haired nurse came back on duty in the evening. I felt their light, cool touch as the familiar voice warned me she was going to remove the bandages and place drops in my eyes. Her voice was suddenly sharp when I wouldn't open them, keeping them shut, nauseated at the idea of seeing the wan figures in my room.

"Do it," whispered the older girl right next to my ear. "If you're difficult, she'll hurt you." The girls had placed their little hands on my body and the pain seemed to channel to them and lessen.

I opened my eyes. The two-faced nurse was more horrifying than the dead girls on either side of me, watching me with concern.

"How's your vision?" the nurse queried. I heard a door open and glanced over to see the surgeon walk in. His face was one solid expression.

He held a small light. He asked me to follow it with my eyes. I did. I tried to avoid the nurse's frowning/blank face, as she stood behind the surgeon.

He placed his hands on my head, feeling for odd bumps and contusions. "How's the pain?" he finally asked.

A tear slid down my nose from my unimproved eye. "It hurts a lot," I whispered.

"Where?"

"Everywhere."

He nodded. "Perfectly normal. We'll keep you sedated so you don't hurt yourself touching that eye. Speaking of . . ." He held up a chart of letters of varying sizes. He covered my right eye with his hand.

"Read the fifth row, just above the green line." Behind the chart I saw only the nurse's grotesquely frowning face.

"Lie," I heard a man's voice whisper.

I pretended the line was as blurry as it would have been before the surgery, speaking like I was hazarding a guess. "They look like little black shapes. Boxes and circles."

The surgeon frowned. "Well, that's disappointing. What about the top line?"

"A large black box."

"Hmm, wonder if it's the lens or the brain not working. Look around the room. No, don't sit up yet."

Now, as I scanned the room, I saw a man in a uniform, his skin brown, his hair black, like mine, standing at the head of my bed, watching me. He smiled gently and placed a finger to his lips.

"How's your distance vision?" the doctor prompted. "Any clearer?"

The Indian man shook his head and I said, "No. Sorry."

The doctor sighed and turned to the nurse. "Well, we'll get her scanned." Then back to me, "Let's see what this brain is doing. I'm going to cover your eye again."

I nodded.

"Someone will be here shortly to take you to the X-ray room.

Nurse Stemmons, will you come with me? I need help with the next patient. And you're so good with children."

I shuddered as I heard her demure "Ah, thank you, Doc."

The door closed behind them.

"I hope I didn't frighten you."

I was afraid to speak, afraid to be heard.

"Smart girl," the man's voice was warm. It rolled with the sound of Oklahoma. Even if I hadn't seen him, I would have guessed he was Indian. A certain accent that spoke with the memory of another language. "Turn on the TV, so they won't hear you."

I extended my hand out, reaching for the remote. It came on lightly and I found the volume dial and turned it up, enough to cover my voice.

"You know you're an experiment. What you don't know is, you're not the first. They did this to me, and it drove me mad. Not seeing the ghosts, but seeing the living . . ."

"The evil?" I suggested.

"And if they know you can see me, and Bea and Kitty, you'll see more evil than you can stand. That nurse is just the beginning. And the really terrible thing will be the people that experiment on you who aren't evil."

"What do you mean?"

"I mean, there are people who are damaged and dangerous. But then there are people who don't feel anything. They're just doing their job. The kind of people that would have followed the law in Nazi Germany just because it was the law, not that they felt one way or the other."

"What should I do?" I whispered. "Should I pluck out my eye?"

The man let out a low whistle. "I tried that. When that didn't work, I ended the experiments in a more drastic fashion." We both were quiet a minute. "But, shoot, all you have to do is lie to them. And don't tell anyone else what you can see. They won't believe you about people like that nurse, anyway, and they'll fill you up with drugs to make it all go away."

I felt him place a warm hand over my left eye.

"You'd look cool in an eye patch," he suggested.

I considered this. Wearing a pirate patch in high school. The taunts. The name-calling. The alternative was madness, walking around high school, seeing. As if being a teenager wasn't hellish enough.

"This is a hard world for someone who sees clearly," I said.

"It's a hard world either way," he said.

"Who are you?" I asked quickly, feeling the warmth over my left eye subside. I reached out for the television remote and fumbled with the buttons, shouting, "Who are you?" I heard the door open and then close, quietly.

"Who's who, dear?" Nurse Stemmons demanded.

I froze.

"Who's who?" she repeated.

"I thought I heard someone," I whispered.

"You're not going to be any trouble, are you?"

I felt the light hands of Bea and Kitty touching me again. "No," I said. "I'm not going to be any trouble at all."

# Ghost Cat

Stephanie King
Dulisdi 17, 2016
09/17/2016

The week after my cousin and best friend Diane died and I decided calculus and life were too hard, my mother showed up to my dorm with her hair dyed red and a cardboard box in her arms. Covered with silhouettes of kittens, bunnies, and puppies, it was the kind of box the pet store gave you when you were willing to adopt an animal, but too cheap to spring for a real carrier. My roommate invited my mother into our suite, then left.

Mom found me underneath a too-thin comforter in my tiny dorm room. Except for trips to the bathroom, I had been in bed since my best friend's death. Mistakenly under the impression my mom was capable of providing some kind of comfort, my suitemate had gotten in touch with her.

Mom sat down in my desk chair with the slightly battered box in her lap. My mother is something else. She makes me crazy. She sat very still, but occasionally I could hear a noise. It was like the sound of someone methodically making tiny tears in the cardboard, patiently and minutely shredding it from the inside with an art knife.

"No cats in the dorm," I said, through the gap in my blanket of solitude.

Mom opened the box briefly and pointed its top at me.

"Do you see a cat?" she said.

I didn't respond. I didn't even try to guess what she was up to. It was best to keep your expectations low with people like my mother. I hadn't seen her in a year. Mom had once often repeated a story her grandmother had told her about a Blackfoot man coming to the door of their home on Ucluelet Island, claiming they were relatives. Her great-grandmother had no interest in Indians and ran him off, but Mom had gotten a lot of mileage claiming to be Indian. A year earlier, I'd asked her to stop, and we hadn't spoken since.

I heard the box land on my desk.

"You know, I cosigned some pretty big loans for you to go to this school. Do you know what I could do with an extra eighteen thousand dollars?"

I was well aware of what she could do with extra money. My father, David King, had moved back to Oklahoma to deal with his father, Jimmy, and had never been able to come back. Mom raised me in a house full of art and medicine cards. There was little food, even when there was extra money, since my mother had a weird definition of what constituted a necessity.

I rose to the bait: "I thought you always said money was less real than time. That it's just an illusion?"

She laughed. "Yes, but Sallie Mae is real. And she will really garnish my checks, if we aren't able to pay back your loans because you flunked out of school. It's a little late to decide calculus is too hard."

We were both quite for a moment.

"What's the formula for the reciprocation of unconditional love? The algorithm of secret keeping," I muttered.

My mother's laugh was harsh, like an ax chop. "I forgot the cat food," she said suddenly, standing up. "For the non-cat. And you haven't said anything about my hair."

I didn't have the energy to laugh, so I sighed. I communicated with Mom through sighs a lot. Even before Diane died. Even before Diane told me her doctor said she might die.

"I mean, I only drove all night. To New Mexico and back. And I've always had black hair. And I could use a nap, too. But I'll go get her some food."

She closed the room's door loudly as she left, but was kind enough to leave the lights off. I rolled over and saw the box still sitting on my desk. I closed my eyes. I wanted to go back to sleep.

Four days earlier, my doctor had prescribed some stuff for anxiety, and instead of worrying or thinking, I had spent those days slipping in and out of sleep. The pills were supposed to last a month, but I was halfway through them. I contemplated taking one from the bottle's hiding spot in the rolled-up socks in the girly combat boots beneath my bed. But, when I heard the shredding noise again, I sat up. I heard my *Game of Thrones* figure of the warrior-girl-too-good-for-the-world clatter down off the back of the desk. She landed in the nest of light and laptop cords.

The cat carrier went quiet. I got up to make sure it really was empty. I felt dizzy. That's what happens when you stop eating and stay in bed all the time. I walked over to the cardboard box. A hole the size of a pre-kindergartener's fist had been punched out from its inside.

"WTF?" I muttered.

I picked the box up and shook it. It was definitely empty.

In the bathroom I got a glass of water. I ferreted out my bottle of pills from under the bed and counted what was left. My best friend had gone into hospice two weeks ago while I kept going to class. She died drugged and afraid, I guess. I wasn't there.

I thought about taking all fourteen. The biggest problem I saw was screwing it up and ending up bedridden and at the mercy of my mother. With guardians like her, you couldn't afford to mess around.

Instead, I took one pill and a long drink of water and climbed back into bed. As I curled up around my pillow, I felt a weight on my shoulder. It draped there and I felt points of pressure across my upper arm.

"Diane?" I stupidly whispered.

I had done the same thing right after she died, called her name, while watching a tire swing move back and forth in the stillness of her backyard. I mused that she was hanging out, when of course the dead have better things to do than visit their old tree swings. Some Indians believe you're not supposed to speak the names of the dead in the year after they die, you're supposed to let them rest. If you call them, they might think they need to come back.

Over my cheek, the blanket pressed down. Heat of the lowest intensity spread from my arm to my elbow. I smelled kitten. Kitten smell is like newborn baby head. There is some weird chemical thing that happens to a lot of people when they breathe that scent in. Clean fur, fresh skin, warmth, milk. I felt my body relax involuntarily. I took another deep breath through my nose but tried not to move too much.

My mother had spent time in New Mexico before I was born. When I was little, she took me back to visit Aztec, the little town where she had spent a summer doing archaeology. As we walked through what the United States park service called Aztec Ruins National Monument, a historic site with a reconstructed kiva, she told me the story of an ex-boyfriend wandering through there in the middle of the night. "I warned him not to hop the fence," she whispered, her eyes wary of the park's interpretive guide. Her boyfriend had argued that his Native ancestors would have approved. Halfway there, a small cat began to follow him. When he got to the fence, the cat sidled between him and the fence and meowed insistently. He pushed the kitten away, placed a throw rug over the top of the fence, and climbed over. The cat was immediately beside him and walked adjacent to his route as he toured the site.

In the moonlight, he had wandered through what was left of the Puebloan structures. When he tried to climb down a ladder that led into what was left of a kiva, the cat blocked his path and meowed angrily. He suddenly felt he was being watched. In the shrub along the far side of the grounds he saw two red dots, like two small eyes. He thought better of descending. The cat followed him back to the fence. In his haste, he scraped his arm deeply on the prongs as he climbed over. The cat disappeared. As Mom and I walked through the ruins, I kept my eyes open, looking for a small, white cat. I was five.

I'd asked her, "What happened to him?"

She shrugged, saying she didn't know. She'd broken up with him soon after when his parents came to visit, and she found out he had lied about being Indian. Their relationship was too small for two wannabe Natives. She went to Oklahoma and married my Cherokee father, David King, soon after.

I heard the door open, and the smell of kitten was replaced with the smell of steamed buns and chili. I felt a light punch on my shoulder for a moment only, then weightless nothing. My mom stood in the doorway.

"I have Coneys and Pepsi and that popcorn ice you like."

I groaned.

"Please come to the living room. I don't want to eat lunch in here. Your bedroom stinks."

Reluctantly, I followed her into the front room. My body, the traitor, reacted to the smell of the hot dogs. I scooted into the corner of the love seat and Mom shoved the foam tray of Coneys into my lap.

Moments later she handed me a soda. I set it on the floor next to my foot.

"You guys will have to be careful about keeping the door shut or else she'll get out." She paused and sipped at her drink. "I mean, a cat like this, she has to agree to stay with you. No one owns a ghost cat. She has to choose you. Because eventually someone's going to leave a door open."

I looked out at her from underneath my longish black bangs. After I was born, she had started dyeing her dishwater-blond hair to match mine. It was a secret she didn't think I knew.

"What if my roommate is allergic?" As depressed as I was, I could still manage snide. It's my superpower.

She shrugged. "To an invisible cat?"

I reached out for the Pepsi and felt something sand itself across my knuckles. I yanked my hand back, knocking an unsee-able thing away.

My mother laughed. "That's not how you build relationships. You better pick up some catnip or something to make amends."

I looked directly at her. Her blue eyes glinted. She had these eyes that always seemed to be vibrating imperceptibly. She only blinked when her contacts were bothering her. It kept you off balance, if it didn't mesmerize you. Absentmindedly, I took a bite of my chili-cheese dog. Then I took a few more and suddenly my first Coney was gone. I set down the tray with the second Coney on the floor and picked up my soda. My mother raised an eyebrow at me.

"Once you've offered the food to Gris, you mustn't eat any of it," she said, gesturing with her chin toward the floor.

I glanced down at the tray. "I mustn't, mustn't I?"

Mother didn't respond.

"Why is he called Grease?"

"Not Grease. *Gris.* It's 'gray' in French. And it's a she."

We sat in silence. I felt something brush my ankle, sliding between me and the Coney. I stayed very still and tried to remember what the word was for a hallucination you could touch.

"It's not."

"Not what?" I said sharply.

"Not a tactile hallucination. She's a cat. And a ghost."

"Why the hell would a cat be a ghost?" She was starting to upset me now. "Does it have unfinished business? Is it seeking revenge?"

My mother got up. "Just not ready to move on, I guess. More stuff in the car. I'll be right back." She slipped out the front door.

I felt shaky. Diane had been my anchor. We created art and wrote for each other before we shared our work with anyone else. I could tell her anything and now I had nothing to say to anyone. I wanted to believe in ghosts, because that meant death wasn't the end. I didn't know if I wanted to believe in reincarnation. If death was the end, did that mean living was pointless? Eat, sleep, go to class, repeat? A life of meaninglessness loomed, a life where the people you loved died on you. And people who were supposed to love you kept disappointing you.

When Mom returned, she was carrying a litter box.

I stared at her. "Am I seriously going to have to clean up ghost-cat poop?"

Mom shrugged. "Maybe. Just fake it and see if that works out. You'll just have to learn what she likes. I wouldn't know. No *Ghost Cats for Dummies* at the pet shop. Maybe that should be your next book."

Diane and I had been trying to write books since we were in the second grade. When I used to trust her, I naively told Mom all my ideas. I guess snide is also my mom's superpower.

She walked toward my bedroom door and opened it. She stopped, turning as if waiting for someone to follow her in, then closed the door behind them.

I cleared our trash from lunch. Even when I wanted to die, I tried to be as good a roommate as I could manage. As I kneeled down, I caught a whiff of sour tears and sweat wafting off my T-shirt. Suddenly, I wanted a shower. I found my bedroom door locked and had to knock.

"What?" my mom called.

"I'm going to take a shower."

A few minutes later my mom opened the door and handed me my robe, a towel, and my shower caddy. "Got you some new shampoo."

In the shower, I let the water run into my closed eyes. Diane was really gone. Her family had buried the body she once animated, and they were all as brokenhearted and in shock as I was.

"Death, death, stupid effing death," I muttered.

Mom had bought me the unnecessary and expensive shampoo I loved. It smelled like heaven but burned the hell out of my eyes. How could she get everything else so wrong, but get little things right?

Once out of the shower I brushed my tangled hair for the first time in a week. I pulled it back in a ponytail. I kept a stash of razor blades in a drawer. I took one out and chopped at the top of the ponytail and my hair dropped around my face in an inverted bob. I wondered if anyone would accept the eleven inches of hair as a donation. I wished I had cut my hair when Diane lost hers. I wished she had seen me when it mattered.

Back in my room, my mom snored in my bed. She had set up a clean cat box underneath it and moved my boots. I rolled my eyes. Behind me, the door hadn't quite shut. I sat down on the floor next to the foot of my bed, my back against the wall, my legs crisscrossed. My mother had pulled the blinds up, but outside it was gray. I wanted to go back to sleep and not think. Thinking hurt. Everything hurt. Her snores taunted me.

I reached for my boots. The socks were gone. So were my pills. My mother had already found them, which probably explained her sudden deep sleep.

I found my breath syncing up with hers as I leaned back into the wall. I began to daydream about hanging out with Diane at her house late at night. It was one of those daydreams that starts out as a memory, where you watch yourself. I was revisiting one of our last sleepovers at the beginning of her illness, before not dying became everything for her and her family. We had stayed up until dawn watching scary movies. In the kitchen we created recipes and spells that would make us famous novelists, bring us true love, allow us to live forever, cure her.

I felt myself slide into the memory, shift into my own body as I stretched out on her family's black couch. In the reliving I saw something new, a wisp of white smoke, curled up against Diane's leg. I watched as she talked passionately but reached her hand down absentmindedly to pet the cat who wasn't there.

It was the only conversation we had ever had about her diagnosis.

"Are you scared?"

"What do you think? I'm friggin' terrified."

"I just keep thinking why you? Why now?"

Diane smirked at me, the face she made when she mocked the orange-faced guy running for President, and then shrugged. "Sad."

Then she laughed, and the gray, wispy cat climbed into her lap.

"How long is long enough?" she said.

I looked at her.

"A life? What's the algorithm for a death that's not a tragedy?"

"But you have things to do. Books to write."

"You're right. There should be more time." She stared into the eyes of the increasingly visible gray cat. "But there isn't. Can you imagine what it would be like if you knew exactly how much time you had? Would you do anything? Would you try to do everything? Think of the things people would never do . . ." Diane seemed lost in thought. "Why me? Why not me?"

In Diane's year of dying, I hadn't spoken to my mother. Her life was only slightly more of a mystery to me than it had always been. My maintenance had moored her life until I graduated from high school, but I had stopped being her best friend by third grade. Her internal life was something I had never understood. She told lies to make herself more interesting to strangers, to people who would pay her to read their medicine cards, to people who don't understand the word *Indian*, to absolve herself of a guilt she should have used to make the world better.

Kindness and self-preservation necessitate secrets between mothers and daughters, lovers and spouses. When Diane died, my secrets died with her. The future yawned before me, a world without, a world where I might or might not write the books Diane and I had talked about. Other than me, no one would care.

On my leg, a weight the diameter of a nickel pressed, and I froze. Then a second weight pressed and both weights punched into my thighs. Prickles, like tiny claws, poked and retracted, shoved and gave, and suddenly the weight of smoke landed in my lap. I inhaled the smell of kitten. I exhaled slowly. I drifted my hand slightly over edges of fur that wasn't there. A warmth spread up and through me as the ghost cat settled in to sleep in my lap.

Moving into a future without my best friend felt untenable.

But I had a cat to take care of now.

And I guess that's something.

# Happily
# Ever After

Riley and Laura Wilson

Kagali 8, 2019

02/08/2019

**M**y older brother, Riley Wilson, is making me a new boyfriend. Well, not really making me a new one, but trying to
find me one online. He's no Mary Shelley. Or Victor Frankenstein.
My brother believes in true love and handsome princes who save
brown-skinned, dark-haired girls like me. My brother believes
that a seventeen-year-old girl with two black eyes can be saved.

Jordan and I have been dating for six months, which is about
five and half months too long. Long enough for him to display
more than one red flag. No friends. *Check.* Irrational jealousy.
*Check.* Planning all our dates/controlling the stereo. *Check.* It's
weird how red flags can look like attention at first. Or a bad vampire movie.

The violence, though, that was new.

Jordan had showed up at my house after school unannounced,
as had become usual since he lost his job two weeks earlier. Losing his job at the restaurant had something to do with his boss
being an unreasonable tyrant. Funny how often Jordan's stories
had this same plot device.

"I think we need to take a break," I said. We were downstairs on the couch. He had begun kissing my neck.

"What?" he said. He stood up, suddenly towering over me.

I started to stand up, too, but he pushed me back down.

"What do you mean we need to take a break? Are you breaking up with me?"

I looked up at him and started to speak. The words stopped when he struck me across my nose with the back of his right hand. Just as suddenly he was lifting me up and hugging me tight.

"Oh my god, Laura. Oh my god." He was crying. "I am so sorry," he wept.

The sound of his strike rang in my ears. Upstairs Edoda was asleep. Riley was listening to music on his headphones. Neither of them had heard the smack across my nose that would give me the black eyes. They also missed all the I'm-sorrys-but-I just-love-you-so-much.

Jordan knelt at my feet and put his head in my lap, declaring that: "If you leave me, I will die."

He promised to be a better boyfriend. He promised to never hit me again. He blamed his behavior on his mom leaving. He made it clear that he was not ready for me to break up with him. I was too stunned to push back. What do you do when someone won't be broken up with?

He begged and cajoled until I agreed to give him another chance. When Jordan pulled out of the driveway, I went upstairs and climbed into my bed. Riley knocked on my door. Then he ignored the fact that I didn't invite him in.

When he saw me, he flipped.

"Oh my god, Laura, what happened to your face?"

"I tried to break up with Jordan."

"Why didn't you holler for me?"

I shrugged. Tears were coming again.

Riley stood next to me, uncertain what to do. Then he went and got me some frozen peas to put on my swollen nose. He sat down on the bed and rubbed my back and said, "Laura Ann Wilson, either I go downstairs and wake Edoda up, tell him Jordan has been coming over after school, and he is going to kill him. Or you are going to tell Jordan that he can't come over anymore because your brother snitched. I am going to be the bad guy and I just hope he swings on me. I'm going to beat him so hard, Andrew Jackson is going to feel it."

To be clear, Jordan is white, but I don't think he's a direct descendant of Jackson any more than the average white guy. Also, Edoda works nights at the Bell Helicopter factory. He doesn't just lie around sleeping at all hours of the day. Well, there was that month after Etsi died, but that was pretty understandable.

I begged Riley not to tell Dad. I didn't want my dad to think I couldn't take care of myself. It was bad enough that Riley knew. I didn't want anyone else to know Jordan had hit me.

When Edoda got up and made dinner that evening, I stayed upstairs and texted him that I wasn't feeling good. I pretended I was asleep when he brought dinner upstairs. He left the food on my desk, picked up my hairbrush, and sat down on my bed anyway.

"You all right?" Edoda sometimes overreacts when we get sick. The illness of my etsi had started out looking like a stomach bug, so everything worries him.

I turned my head away, "Yeah, just stayed up too late doing homework."

Dad slid the rubber band off my messy braid. He started to brush my hair, separating it into three parts. "This would be easier, if you sat up."

"Hurts," I lied.

"What do you mean it hurts?" He was more concerned instead of less.

"Sinus pressure. Allergies, maybe?"

He decided to let it go. He continued braiding my hair. "You know, you should come back to kickboxing. Your brother has gotten really good. You should at least come watch him."

"That sounds fun," I lied again. Nothing sounded fun, really.

Edoda finished my braid real quick. More quick than I would have liked. It was tight. His braids always stayed in longer than when I did it myself. His own hair was long again. He did his own braids better than me or Riley could too. Our etsi died when I was in sixth grade. He cut it to his shoulders then. I don't know what tribe that tradition came from, but it seemed like the right thing to do. He had been growing it out since then. He was good-looking for an old dude. It was embarrassing.

He sat next to me in silence a bit longer. I noticed he was checking his phone. Facebook. Most of the Indians are on Facebook. Finally, he had to go get ready for work. "You text me if you feel worse. Promise?" I nodded. He leaned down and kissed the top of my head. I was lucky he didn't drag me to the after-hours clinic.

When I heard Edoda leave the house, I got up and went downstairs. Riley and I watched *Blood Quantum*. I had left my phone upstairs and let the battery die, so Dad texted Riley on his first break to check on me. For once, I didn't bother with my homework. When we were finished with Indigenous future horror we switched to the *Princess Bride*. God, Etsi loved that movie. She had loved fairy tales, children's stories. She ran a preschool, but longed to write children's books.

"Listen to this," Riley read from his phone. "Go on a date with a Handsome Prince. Fill in this questionnaire and meet the man of your dreams."

He handed me the phone. I scrolled through pictures of handsome men and beautiful women paired up with normal-looking people.

"Is this a dating site?" I said, handing him back his phone. "Sounds kind of dark webby."

"No. It's more *Blade Runner* or *Ex Machina*."

I wrinkled my nose. "Sounds suspish."

Riley shrugged and kept scrolling.

In the morning, my brother met me in the bathroom with some concealer and powder. He helped me hide the bruises around my eyes.

"Girl," he said, "you need a new man." He sponged the light brown concealer onto my face, wincing with me when the pressure hurt my bruised nose. He worked as gently as he could. He opened a compact and brushed powder over my nose and face until the color returned to something closer to "girl who is Cherokee, but never goes outside." Then he brushed a few colors of eye shadow on. When he was done, he had me turn and look into the mirror where our eyes met. I felt weepy again.

"Don't cry," he said. "It'll mess up all my work."

I half smiled.

"Honey, now you are almost as pretty as me." I laughed. Riley put an arm around me and squeezed, not letting go until he was sure I wasn't going to cry.

"Here," he handed the compact and tube of concealer to me. "You're going to have to touch that up all day."

At school I charged my phone. When I turned it on there were multiple messages from Jordan and my best friend, Kitty. I saw Kitty and told her my phone was dead, but I continued to ignore Jordan's messages all morning.

By noon he had stopped sending them. Jordan attended a different school from us, but, like Riley, he was a senior. Neither one of them took high school very seriously, even though it was only August. Throughout the day, Riley messaged me with seemingly random questions.

What color of eyes

wtf

Your new bf

Ur handsome af prince

Hazel?

blue-green

How tall

Close to my height. In case I need to lay him out.

Then you can't wear heels. So at least 6 ft

Are you signing me up for that dating site??????

After school, Kitty was waiting for me next to the Panther in our high school's front lobby. We had met in second grade. We were not terribly alike. The only thing we had in common was once upon a time we had been the two new girls at the old school, and we rode our bikes everywhere. Our mothers had been friends. They enrolled us in Bluebirds, choir, and photography club together. Right after Etsi died, Kitty's mom left town. Our moms had thrown us together, then when they were gone, that was still what we had in common. We just kept hanging out of habit, I guess. We would end up in the same classes and we would gravitate toward each other because making friends is hard. It was easier to be friends with Kitty now, than not. It seemed easier than being alone. Or maybe it was easier to be alone together. If I was honest, I hadn't missed Kitty when I stopped hanging out with her that one time. She wasn't the kind of friend who lifted me up or even gave me loving attention. I guess she wasn't really a friend at all, so much as someone who was bored and needed a follower. Or maybe she just needed a witness.

The same year my mom was dying, our school's PTA organized a sock hop and all the kids got to wear something from the Fifties the day of the dance. Neither Kitty or I had a poodle skirt, so on the phone the night before, Kitty suggested we go as boys in blue jeans and white T-shirts.

"Seriously," she said. "Let's grease back our hair. Draw heart tattoos that say Mom." I kind of liked the idea of getting a tattoo in honor of my mom, though of course mine would say Etsi. At first, I thought she was joking, but she persisted until I promised I would be Johnny to her Pony Boy. "Stay gold," she said, as we got off the phone.

Riley totally got into it. I borrowed some of his clothes and he styled my hair into a pompadour. He and Edoda took pictures so Mom could see later. I looked pretty great, but I was super nervous about showing up dressed as a boy with a candy cigarette box rolled into the sleeve of my white T-shirt, like a baby John Travolta from *Grease*. Riley was already at a junior high on another campus, so once I went to school I was on my own. My bus stop was the last on the route going to school. Normally, Edoda dropped me off with the other kids at my stop, but that day he stuck around until the bus got there. As soon as I got in line, the other kids from my stop started giving me a hard time. I'd looked forward to sitting on the bus with Kitty, knowing there would be safety in numbers, even if it was just our oddball pair, but Kitty wasn't there when I got on. In a panic I turned back. I squeezed in next to two first graders sitting right behind the driver. The two six-year-old girls giggled openly at me. I had brought some gum to round out my look and I traded a piece for the window seat and ducked low. I ignored the taunts of some of the other kids behind me. I dreaded the spit wads that would surely come toward the back of my pomaded head. I pulled out a book and pretended to read until we got to school.

Once at school, I hid in the bathroom waiting until it was time to go to class. I prayed that Kitty would come in. I sat on the toilet with my black Converse on the seat, balancing and hiding. For a moment I was relieved when I heard Kitty's voice as the door swung open. I stood up and peeked through the gap only to see her offering eyeliner to one of the popular girls. They were admiring each other's poodle skirts and sharing makeup. I backed up and sat back down on the toilet and waited for the bell to ring.

After they left, I went to the nurse's office and told her I didn't feel good and I had puked. It was noon before Edoda was able to pick me up. He took me straight to the doctor. Etsi was home in bed resting from chemo. Once I got the all clear, Edoda took me home and I crawled in bed with Etsi and told her what happened. At first I didn't notice she was crying, too. She let me stay home the next day and we watched movies together. I never wanted to go back to school.

A week later Kitty showed up at my house on her bike. She gave me a bell that matched hers. We rode to the mall where we saw her new friends hanging out with some older boys in the food court. They looked over at us but didn't come over or even wave at Kitty. Kitty said they were dumb and only cared about impressing boys. We never talked about Fifties Day.

I took a summer geometry course just to have something to do and that's where I met Jordan. He was repeating it because his father wanted him to graduate on time and move "the hell out." After class, Jordan offered to drive me home, but I told him I couldn't leave my bike. He said he'd throw it in the back of his El Camino and then he did. He played his music loudly, so we didn't talk. His sound equipment was worth more than his car and I felt the music in a way I never had before. He never asked if I liked what he put on. When he dropped me off, he told me he'd pick me up in the morning. The attention felt nice. I put my bike in the garage and forgot about it. We fell into a pattern. I mistook it for love.

Outside of my friendship with Kitty, Jordan was it. Kitty wasn't happy about it. Where once we had spent every weekend together, I hung out with her only when Jordan wasn't around. Nights that had once been sleepovers, became evenings where we worked on homework together, but ended when Jordan came to pick me up for dates.

"I guess he's hot," Kitty said, "if you like that sort of thing." She wrinkled up her face when she said it, which was funny. As far as I could tell, that was the only sort of thing Kitty was interested in.

When she claimed to miss me, I thought about the time she ditched me for the cooler girls. My absence now gave her enough time to be bored, so she got a job scooping ice cream after school. Every time someone quit the Cool Jerk, she begged me to apply for the opening.

"That name," I said. "Kids don't even know what a soda jerk was."

She shrugged. "We could get paid to hang out together and eat sundaes!" she insisted. "After I get my license, my dad is going to fix up my mom's old VW Rabbit for me. Then I can drive us to work, and you can pay for gas." Kitty always seemed to have a plan.

Things with Jordan hadn't been great. He seemed to expect me to be around when he wanted me around, without considering what I was interested in. He played his music loud. I wasn't sure if it was because he wanted the outside world to know how great his music taste was (it wasn't) or if he was avoiding having conversations. The one time he offered to let me control the music, he mocked the songs I picked. He said he didn't want people to think he was listening to "girl" music, rolling up his windows. I talked to Riley about breaking up with Jordan.

"Finally," Riley said.

A job seemed like a good way to start reclaiming some space of my own. A few weeks before I tried to break up with Jordan, I applied for the job Kitty had lobbied for me to get. Unfortunately, it turned out I was now going to my first day of work at the Cool Jerk with black eyes. I ignored Jordan's text messages all day.

Kitty didn't have a license or a car yet, so we were going to ride the city bus together. Fort Worth wasn't the kind of place where mass transit was cool. We were definitely not going to change into our pink-and-brown work uniforms until we had to. When I met up with Kitty after school, she was way too excited to be going to our minimum-wage vocation. "I'm so glad I got you this job. Your hot boyfriend is driving us to work tonight."

I swallowed hard. I couldn't say anything. We walked to the back of the school where Jordan sometimes waited for me when he skipped his afternoon classes, but his car wasn't there.

"What the hell?" Kitty muttered, while we waited. It was one of those Texas January days that once upon a time should have been cold like a normal winter, but not anymore. At least not that day. When both of our phones dinged, I didn't even look at my screen.

"He said to go out front."

Jordan had parked his beige El Camino in front of the school where everyone could see him. He stood next to the driver's side door. In one hand he held two red roses I was pretty sure he'd bought at the gas station, in the other a large bag of fast food. Well, I thought, at least he's not holding a boom box. I felt my cheeks begin to burn. I yanked my black hoodie forward over my face as far forward as it would go.

"Ah," Kitty said, teasingly to Jordan as we got to the car, "for me?"

"Actually, one for each of you. But you'll have to share the fries. The coupon only covered the burgers."

"Ahhh, how sweet," Kitty said this time, completely non-sarcastically.

Beneath my hoodie I rolled my eyes.

Jordan opened the door for me. I scooted into the front seat. He kept holding the door open and gestured for Kitty to get into the front seat as well. Kitty giggled as he handed her the food and roses. I only shifted over far enough for Kitty to climb in. I leaned my head back with my eyes closed and Kitty chatted mindlessly between bites of fries and burger. The scent of decaying roses and fast-food grease made me feel gross. Kitty forgot to offer me any fries, but then proffered the burger with an apologetic gesture. I shook my head and she passed it to Jordan. He drove carelessly while eating and I sat forward, looking for songs on my phone to crash to, disappearing into my headphones. Etsi had been a Swiftie, I guess, and I thought about how much I wished we could listen to some music together, how much I wished I could talk to her. We never had bad blood, but it was a good song to listen to sitting next to Jordan. I wished I could play it loud. I wished I could go home. Jordan turned the music up so loud I could barely hear my own headphones. But it was okay. I knew the words.

Jordan parked behind the Cool Jerk and stayed in the car. Kitty and I went in and changed clothes and our boss showed me the list of tasks he wanted us to work on when we didn't have customers. Then he entrusted me to Kitty for training. As soon as he left, Kitty texted Jordan to come into the shop and hang out. She was giving him a free sample of every single flavor, instead of training me, so I excused myself, saying I should go to the back and neaten up the storeroom like our boss asked. Instead, though, I went into the bathroom and checked my phone. Earlier I had turned it off in case Riley sent me any more messages. Around Jordan, a dinging phone could arouse suspicion and jealousy. A dinging phone could be dangerous.

There were several texts from Riley asking where I was.

work

can you talk

no

why

WORK

so

plus bf out front

oh.
accents?

what

Like scottish/english/irish/boston. Any preference

British?

You know that's really broad
That they colonized lots of places and those places are British

I know

So what kind?

¯\_(ツ)_/¯

Good cause so far you've been pretty picky
narrows the handsome prince playing field

I gotta go

I'm going with something Dr. Whoish.
Sending pic

On my phone was a picture of a man with longish brown hair. How come no one calls men brunettes? I wondered. His features were sharp, and he had hazel eyes. He had to be at least twenty-five.

How old is he?

Is he too old?

What'd you say my age was

Handsome-princes-made-2-order don't care how old you are.

should he be younger?

Because hs guys have gone sooo well

I heard someone in the storeroom and cleared all the messages. "You okay?" Kitty said through the door.

"Yeah," I said.

"We have customers," she singsonged.

I finished deleting the messages. The concealer was in the pocket of my brown apron. I touched up the skin around my eyes. I turned my phone off again and went back out to scoop ice cream. Jordan was eating a sundae Kitty had given him. He sat in the pink-and-brown chair watching me. His look was critical. I felt his eyes linger over my thin pink polo and I avoided looking into his eyes.

Part of selling ice cream is selling happy. For better or worse, I can be professional. I can compartmentalize. I was able to pretend nothing made me happier than marshmallow topping or sadder than running out of Rocky Road while I ignored the boy who gave me two black eyes. I wondered if that was just part of being an adult.

It bothered me that Kitty hadn't noticed that anything was amiss. It's not like I wore makeup very often and I hadn't said a word to Jordan all afternoon. Yet, as soon as the customers were gone, she went back to chatting and flirting with him, the new normal-Kitty mode.

I started wiping the counters and scraping ice cream bins.

A warm water bath was mounted on the back of the freezers. You dip the scoop into the water before spooning up the balls of ice cream or scraping the ice cream bins. That involved flattening the ice cream across the top of the three gallon tub and scraping it down the sides so it doesn't dry out in the freezer. It's an art. If you use too much water, it makes the ice cream icy instead of creamy, and if you don't do it, the ice cream on the sides gets gummy and is wasted. Dry ice cream sucks. I could feel the muscles in my right bicep start to burn and I began to sweat. Makeup ran into my left eye. Without thinking, I rubbed it and the concealer came off all over my hand, leaving an exposed purple bruise. I glanced up and caught Kitty staring at me.

"Jesus, Laura, what happened to you? You've got a black eye." Kitty said it as if it might be a surprise to me.

I dropped the ice cream scoop into the warm water bath and hurried into the back room, locking myself in the bathroom. I covered my cheek and lid with the concealer and, then, nervously checked my phone. This time there was a new photo of a handsome prince. At least this guy could pass for a college freshman. I deleted the photo and dropped the phone back into the pocket of my brown apron.

I wasn't ready to face Kitty and Jordan and stranger customers, but I couldn't stay in the bathroom all night. I heard the front door jingle as it opened and closed.

I took a deep breath before returning to the counter. Kitty was the only one in the shop. "You didn't tell me you were doing kickboxing again. I mean, obviously it didn't go well if you got two black eyes, but why didn't you tell me? Why do I have to hear about what my best friend's up to from her boyfriend? You never tell me anything anymore."

Jordan had left the store. He was sitting out in his El Camino reading a book. I guessed it was the same Stephen King novel he had been carrying around in his car for the last six months.

I shrugged. "I don't know. Pretty embarrassing, I guess."

"And I thought you were too busy for anything but Jordan . . ." she said, glaring at me.

I went back to wiping counters and scraping bins. "If you got time to lean . . ." I replied.

The rest of the week went pretty much the same way. Riley continued asking me questions he claimed were from handsomeprince made2order.com, and Jordan was on kindness overkill. Now and then I forgot he had blackened my eyes. On Friday, I was off work, but Jordan and I drove Kitty to the Cool Jerk anyway.

When we got there, he went in and got a free sundae from her as payment for the ride. He came back out to the car with only one spoon.

"Can I have my own spoon?" I asked.

"None for you," he said. "Ice cream will make you fat."

I wasn't exactly shocked, but it was the first time he had been mean to me since he hit me.

He checked the time and said, "Looks like we still have another two hours before Daddy gets up."

"The neighbor told him you've been coming by after school. He was pissed."

"Which neighbor?"

I froze. I didn't know what to say. Would Jordan do something to get back at one of my neighbors for imaginary snitching? "Um, I didn't ask. I was too embarrassed. He asked if I needed to get on the pill."

"Hell yeah, you do," Jordan snickered. He gunned the motor and as he entered the highway he threw the ice cream out the window.

I shrunk down in my seat. How could I date someone who littered? Who the hell was I, even?

"I have to go home and write a paper," I yelled over the wind roaring through the car's open windows.

"For what?"

"English."

Jordan ignored me.

"I need to go home," I said loudly.

"Are you still mad at me?" Jordan's voice was low and threatening.

"For what?" I asked.

Jordan didn't answer the question. "I don't want to fight."

"I don't either," I said.

Jordan kept driving. There was a lake nearby with a parking lot that was pretty empty most weekdays until five. Jordan backed the car into a spot facing the lake. Two guys were fishing off the dock area, keeping their catches despite the sign warning against consuming the lake's fish. They glanced back at us, but then went back to watching the lake.

Jordan leaned over and forcefully turned my face to his. He pulled me to him then kissed me hard. I held still. This is what he had done right after he hit me on the nose. His lips were wet and forceful. His teeth clicked against mine and bruised my lips.

"I've never hit a girl, before. I won't ever do it again. I told you it reminded me of when my mom left me with my asshole father. If you treat me like you don't love me, I can't control myself. I'm sorry."

I nodded.

"I'm only like that because I love you."

I nodded again. He took his hand from the side of my face, and I scooted away from him next to the car door. I thought about getting out, but I hated making a scene. Where would I go? Who would I call? Kitty didn't have a car. I didn't want to wake Edoda before he had to go work. If Jordan stuck around until Riley showed up, I was pretty sure Riley would kick the hell out of him. If the fishermen called the police it would be my brown brother who would be in danger of being arrested or killed. There was an unspoken rule against calling the police in my family. Too many times the people you called for help made things worse.

Jordan leaned over, unfastened his belt buckle, and pressed against me. I flattened myself lower into the seat and both hoped no one was going to wander up and that someone would wander up. I wished I had let Riley know.

The next time I worked, Riley and Edoda came in to see me after going to kickboxing. It was Kitty's evening off, so I was working with a girl named Brittany Clay. We had worked together before. She and I talked about movies and poetry all night between customers. We made plans to see the new *Candyman* together whenever it came out, both of us wondering who would be the director, worried that it would not be as good as the original. I introduced Edoda and Riley to my coworker. Brittany excused herself to go work in the backroom while I talked to my family. That's what's called a professional courtesy. I made Edoda a coffee shake.

When I handed it to him, he said, "We never see each other anymore."

It was true. I couldn't think of the last time my dad and I had hung out.

"Well, with school and work, I stay pretty busy," I said.

"Maybe this job isn't worth it. You seem kind of tired all the time."

I shrugged. I wanted to say the job wasn't the problem, but I also wanted to solve my problem myself.

"There's some really old records cheap at the antique store next door," Riley told Dad. "You should go check out the vintage vinyl booth."

I gave Riley a look, but Edoda could take a hint. He was trying to collect the records he loved in high school. Otherwise, he had stopped doing much other than going to work years ago. He said a graveyard-shift life, staying fit, and two children were all he could handle and do okay at. My brother was the closest thing he had to a friend. I was pretty sure Riley did kickboxing to give him and my dad something to do together, more than for himself.

As soon as he left Riley asked, "How much money do you have?"

"On me? About a dollar?"

"No, in savings."

"About three hundred. Why?"

"When do you get paid?"

"Next week. Why?"

"Because Handsome-princes-made-to-order isn't free."

"You're so not funny."

"Did you even look at the profile I sent you?"

"No, I didn't."

"When are you going to break up with that guy?"

I slammed the lid of the ice cream case down. I really didn't want to cry. I knew the minute the tears rolled, a customer or my coworker would walk in. What I wanted didn't really matter, though, because tears were definitely on the horizon.

"I'm sorry," Riley pleaded. "That was mean. It's just awful to watch you be so sad. You never wash your hair, you never smile. I think you've been wearing the same outfit to school for the last week. If you were doing it because it made you happy, that would be one thing. I just don't know if it will make him break up with you."

I laughed because I was pretty sure it would. The better I knew Jordan, the more I disliked him.

"I think for once you are giving Jordan way more credit than he deserves," I said. I stuck a pink spoon into the peanut-butter-fudge ice cream. Then I stuck it in my mouth.

"You're probably right about that," Riley said. He stared up at the menu on the back wall. We were quiet for a few minutes, until he finally spoke. "So, anyway, if you could just make that check out to handsomeprincemade2order.com, we can see how this is all going to play out."

"No," I said.

He shrugged. "Can I at least have a Coke float?"

"Absolutely."

When I got home, I looked at the latest profile Riley had sent me. According to the website, Victor was a law school student from a long line of royalty. His hair was long and dark brown. He had an English accent. When I clicked on the sound file, a tenor voice said, "Hello, Laura. I'm quite looking forward to meeting you."

"Riley!" I screamed.

My brother didn't respond. I got up and went to his room. He wasn't there. I went downstairs and found him in the office on our Dad's computer.

"What are you doing in here?" I asked. Normally, he did his schoolwork on his laptop, in his room.

"I might have pawned my laptop."

"What? When?"

"Yesterday. I was kind of hoping you'd loan me the money to get it out of the pawnshop when we came by this evening."

"Are you messing with me?"

Riley kept typing.

"Riley, you didn't seriously sell your laptop for a handsome prince, did you?"

"Well, they may have had a two-for-one special."

I stomped out of the office. I went back to my room. I ignored Riley's text messages. Apoplectic. I finally had a reason to use that word in real life. A BOGO handsome prince sale.

Kitty and I both had taken Sunday off. We were supposed to go to the stock show with Jordan. The week before it had been icy and cold, but that February day felt like spring in Texas. The brown of the redbud tree was jeweled with new scarlet buds. The idea of spending the day walking around the fairgrounds, spending too much money on rides that were too short, eating junk food and navigating Jordan's dangerous moods and Kitty's light banter, exhausted me before I got out of bed. I was done. I called Jordan to break up with him.

"Hey," Jordan sounded happier than usual. "You're on speaker. I already picked up Kitty."

"Hi, Laura!" Kitty said cheerfully.

"Oh, hey." Suddenly I remembered to cough.

"Are you ready for us to come get you?"

It struck me odd that they were hanging out together and not on their way. I rushed forward with my excuse. "I'm not feeling so hot. I think I have the flu."

"Oh," Jordan said. "Okay." In the background I heard Kitty giggle.

"I hope you feel better," Kitty hollered.

"Yeah, feel better," Jordan echoed half-heartedly. "Catch you later."

I was momentarily struck by the oddness of the exchange, but too relieved to really think too hard about it. I wandered downstairs and found Riley braiding Edoda's hair.

"What's going on?"

Edoda blushed. It was hard to see, but it was there. He was dressed up. Really dressed up. He was wearing a black Western shirt with pearl snaps, crisply ironed jeans, and the black cowboy boots Etsi spent too much money on one Christmas. Next to him was the matching black cowboy hat.

"Edoda has a hot d-a-t-e," Riley stage-whispered.

"Yeah?"

Edoda shrugged, "It's a one-time thing."

Now my curiosity was piqued. "Yeah?!"

"It's all I could afford," Riley whispered at me for real this time.

"Where are you going?"

"Wine tasting in Granbury," Riley answered.

"Oooh-la-la," I smiled.

On cue the doorbell rang. Edoda froze.

"She's here. You look good, Edoda," Riley said. "I'll get the door."

From the door we heard a woman with a French accent introduce herself as Vanessa. My edoda asked me if he looked okay in an unsure voice. I echoed Riley's compliment. Then I hugged him really hard. I didn't want to let him go. I was afraid nothing could be better than that moment of anticipation, that every moment after would be a disappointment. I whispered, "Have fun."

Once the door closed behind him I ran to the front window and watched as they walked to the car. A driver was waiting with the back door open. Dad's date could have played a woman in a James Bond film. I kind of thought maybe she had.

Riley put his arm around me. "You know, I think Edoda has been talking to someone he used to go to high school with in Tulsa. Another widow. Amanda something."

My heart began to thud in my chest. "I don't know how to feel about that."

Riley shrugged, "I see him smiling to himself and texting sometimes."

I tried to think of the last time I had smiled to myself about anything. For the last five years, Edoda had given us his full attention. When we needed him, he was there. But we weren't his friends. We could barely stand each other's music. If Dad wanted someone to listen to Def Leppard with, I got that. I had my own playlists to compose. Maybe one day to share.

When you love someone, you should want them to have more of what makes them smile, yeah?

I thought about the things that made me happy. Riley stood next to me and when they drove off, he turned quickly to me. "You're next. We have rodeo tickets. Go put on the black skirt and the red shirt with the pearl buttons. They're ironed and hanging in the laundry room. And your red boots!"

"I can't go. I told Jordan and Kitty I have the flu. What if we run into them?" My heart was thudding in my chest.

"You won't. Just Uber to the rodeo and Uber out."

I looked at Riley. "I'm only doing this because of what you did for dad."

He shrugged. "Whatever."

While I dressed, I realized my phone had been oddly silent all morning. Jordan could normally be trusted to text whenever bored, terrified of the yawning silences in his brain. And Kitty hadn't shared one selfie from the stock show. It was uncharacteristic. I checked my phone to see if maybe it was off, but no, just still.

The doorbell rang while Riley touched up my lipstick.

"Riley."

"I'll get the door. Don't squish your lips together. It will ruin everything."

Victor Wollstonecraft was over six foot tall and carried a black Stetson. Riley presented me with practiced aplomb. I curtsied. I don't even know where I learned to curtsy.

When Victor bowed, the diamonds in his hat band twinkled. His black pressed jeans, blue shirt with pearl snap buttons, and dyed blue ostrich skin boots beautifully contrasted the outfit Riley had so carefully put together for me.

Victor escorted me to the car where the driver held the back door open. I felt my phone tremble in my purse. On the screen was a text from Kitty.

I have to tell you something

I hesitated.
Then I didn't.

Yeah?

Jordan and me are in love
It's been a thing for awhile
I can't believe you didn't notice
I love you, but he and I can't be a part any longer

I took a deep breath. That sound of silence all morning had been two people who said they loved me, lying behind my back. Once more I thought of Etsi. It was convenient to think that life wouldn't have been as sad if my mother hadn't died, that if she lived I might have found a better friend than Kitty. Then again, maybe it was just time to break up with Kitty, too.

I looked over at Victor as he fastened his seat belt. He was taller than I had requested, with blue-green eyes that Riley might be wild about and a clipped English accent. But something wasn't quite right. At least not for me. Uncanny valley, I thought.

"Pardon?" Victor queried.

I got a little chill, as if maybe he could hear the thoughts in my head. Then I said to him, "I think you have the wrong date."

Victor raised his perfect eyebrow at me. He followed me out of the car. I explained myself. He smiled and nodded. Riley was standing at the door when I opened it. "What's wrong?"

"I want you to go."

Riley stepped back. "No. I want you to have a perfect date. With a prince. Someone who treats you the way you deserve to be treated. If you have that just once—"

"But that's what I want for you, too." Both of our voices shook. "Besides, he's not my type."

"Are you insane? He's perfect."

"He's lovely. Have fun."

"I have been needing an excuse to wear my vintage Nudie suit . . ." he said thoughtfully. "Tell him to give me a few."

Once he left, it felt good to be alone. I wandered around the house as if I had just moved in. In the garage my bike was hanging from its rack—ignored and forgotten. I had filled more than the emptiness of my life with Jordan. I had also replaced the things I loved that didn't interest him. I had ignored my family for a boy who didn't even like the same music I loved, who had no idea what novels I got lost in.

I changed into bike clothes and filled the neglected tires of my bike with air. In my backpack, I dropped a composition book, a pen, and a water bottle. I grabbed my headphones and queued up one of Mom's playlists. I wondered again if I would have handled the stuff with Jordan better if she were still around. I didn't know.

I walked my bike out of the garage and looked up and down the street before I mounted the seat. Then I rode. I stood on my pedals and pumped as I went up the hill that crested the highway. The muscles in my legs burned. I felt like I was moving back into my body. The wind felt like a gentle touch on the skin of my bare arms and face, waking me. I took a deep breath and smiled for real for the first time in years, as I dropped over the hill. This was flying. Once it stopped being easy, I didn't have to think. It was awesome.

Ten miles out I stopped at a place where the Trinity River crashed over a low water dam. The wind, which should have still been wintry cold, was edged with the scent of the warm Gulf. The earth's breath kissed my bare arms. On a trail on the opposite side of the river, there was a man on a horse. He saw me staring at the golden mare, her muscles rippling, mane loose and free. The man reached up and tipped his hat at me. I nodded back.

I sat on a bench. I made a list of the things I loved and wanted to do. I wrote a note to Riley telling him how glad I was that he was my brother. I wrote a note thanking my mom for all she did to take care of us. I wrote my dad a note saying how grateful I was he was my dad. I even wrote a note telling Kitty I was sorry about being a crap best friend, but we needed a break from each other. I didn't add, maybe forever. When I was done, I thought about throwing that one in the river, but I don't litter. I folded it up and put it in the pocket of my windbreaker. I'd probably burn it. I went ahead and texted Kitty, though. I told her that I didn't love Jordan and the truth about my black eyes. Then I blocked both her and Jordan's phone numbers. I texted my boss to let him know I quit. I put my headphones back on with "Old Town Road" on repeat. It was a glorious ride home.

I was surprised to find Dad already back when I got home. He was staring at a blank TV screen. "Uh, Edoda, are you okay?"

He looked startled but recovered fast.

"Yup," he said. "Osda."

"How was the wine tasting?"

Edoda shrugged. "It was all right," he said, "but you know," he quipped, quoting Bela Lugosi's Dracula, "I never drink . . . wine."

I laughed. It was funny because it was true. Suddenly, I realized he was crying when he reached up and brushed a tear away.

"Edoda?"

"I miss her."

I sat down next to him.

"True love. Happily ever after." He brushed away another tear. "Your etsi saved my life. I was kind of a mess when we met."

I looked at him. I didn't know if I wanted to know what he meant.

"Before you kids were born, I was wild. But your etsi, she . . ." He stopped. "She was gone before I could ever pay her back. That's why I haven't dated."

"I know, Edoda."

"Plus, y'all are a full-time job." He laughed.

We were both quiet. I had started crying, too.

Edoda reached out and pulled me close. "This morning Riley told me Jordan hit you."

I stopped breathing. I was both relieved and embarrassed.

"Relationships are work, no matter how much you love someone, but I just don't know if you can ever really get over something like that." He was looking at me intently. "Do you love Jordan?"

I shook my head. I was feeling pretty weepy myself by now. "He hit me because I tried to break up with him, Edoda."

Edoda squeezed me, but I heard him take a long deep breath before he spoke. "Laura, what do you need from me?" he said, before letting me go.

I thought about that. What did I need? I guessed Kitty hooking up with Jordan had solved my biggest problem.

"I need you to make some of your famous real-butter movie-style popcorn and watch *The Princess Bride* with me?"

"As you wish," he said, in his best Cary Elwes imitation.

"That's pretty cheesy, Edoda," I said, wiping my eyes and laughing at the same time.

I queued up the film. I heard a car pull into the driveway and got up to see who it was. It was the fancy car Riley had left in. The driver stepped out and opened the back. Riley got out quickly and backed away from the car, keeping his eyes on the back seat. He kept nodding and backing away toward the house. Finally, he saw me watching from the window and looked at me with eyes that said, "Help!"

I opened the front door.

Riley walked quickly toward the house now. "Hurry," he whispered, gesturing toward the door with his head, "get inside, get inside!"

We went inside, but peeked out the window to watch the car finally back out of the driveway.

"Good date?" I asked.

"Don't ask. We might have to move," Riley said, visibly shuddering. "What about you, what did you do today?"

I showed him the text messages from Kitty on my phone.

"You know," he said, "I never understood what you saw in either one of them."

I'd been thinking about that a lot, too. "Proximity," I said. "They picked me. I'm going to pick my own people from now on."

Riley sat down with Edoda and me to watch *The Princess Bride*. We all laughed at the film in the same places. We all teared up at the same time.

Handsome princes from the internet were an expensive fairy tale. There was no way to buy happiness or love. Romantic villains and toxic friends lurk everywhere. Love is kind attention, not empty words. Love is what you do. Love is as one does. For now, I was better off alone. There are worse feelings than lonely. Sitting between two people who truly loved me, I understood, for a little while at least, how it might feel to live happily ever after.

# Deer
# Women

ℓ

Sali King
Galohni 31, 2019
08/31/2019

While hiding underneath the table during another lock-down, I found the note. Before taking cover, I'd grabbed my phone and my sketch of Deer Woman (no horns) as my art teacher locked the door and shut off the lights. My heart hammered in my ears. The other kids in the class were quiet and rapidly texting the ones they loved in case this was goodbye.

My mom works in the office, so I texted her to see if this was a drill or the real deal. While I was waiting for her to respond, I looked up to see my art teacher squatting behind her desk with tears running down her face. Next to me my best friend, Quanah, noticed too.

We started texting each other. We liked Ms. M, but she was sometimes a lot. She got emotional and cared about so many things. We wondered how much longer she'd stay in teaching.

Should we check on her? I texted.

Maybe, Quanah texted back.

I did it last time, I shot back.

Noiselessly, Quanah crawled toward our teacher. Despite Ms. M's look of warning, Quanah leaned in and, I knew, asked what was going on. Ms. M showed her the screen on her phone and Quanah nodded, her face no less worried. It was the first month of my senior year and I wondered if we were going to make it through another year alive.

Several times a year we did active-shooter drills. Our teachers locked the doors and we moved away from the windows, hiding behind tables we sometimes flipped over, waiting for the telltale jiggle of the knob that we hoped meant it was only a drill and not a killer.

Our school is large and every few years there was at least one memorial set up along the fence next to the parking area. Usually, it was a kid who died from suicide or a car wreck. But our freshman year Quanah's cousin, Lilli, went missing. We posted flyers. I helped her family look for her when I could. My sister, Diane, wasn't well. She went into hospice around the same time. The authorities declared Lilli a runaway pretty quickly. We didn't believe it. Her car was never found. Her family had some suspects, including a few boys at school who the police never followed up on. Between that and the regular lockdowns and tornado drills, school never much felt like a safe space. The best thing that happened in our time there is they switched the name of the mascot from Redskins to Jackalopes. Plenty of people still kept crying around about it though.

Ms. M handed Quanah the glass-breaking emergency hammer she kept in her desk in case actual shots were fired in the building. More than once after a lockdown drill, Ms. M had said, "Damned if we're going to hang out and wait for the good guys with the guns while a bad guy with a gun tries to blow our house down." Ms. M likes to mix her metaphors. In the past when an all clear was announced, we went back to our desks, our drawings forgotten. Unable to just teach, Ms. M would remind us that if we heard shots in the building, out the shatterproof windows we were to go. Her class was the only one I had on the first floor, though. For the other six periods of the day, I'd be trapped on a second or third floor. She didn't need to remind us of Sandy Hook or Parkland, so she didn't. We'd grown up afraid that going to school would get us killed.

My mom, the school's parent liaison, texted back it was only a drill this time. I wished she would have given me a heads-up, but she always said that then I wouldn't take it seriously, or I'd tell an oginalii, or my tsunalii—specifically Quanah and Lisa, my ride-or-dies. Of course she was right, but so? If I wasn't in fear of death, I wouldn't be white-knuckling my sharpest pencil. I wouldn't want my friends to be afraid longer than they had to, either. That's why they're called tsunalii.

I noticed Quanah putting her arm around Ms. M. I texted my friend to let her know it was only a drill. Quanah surreptitiously checked her phone while Ms. M was texting someone on hers. Then she leaned over and conveyed the message to Ms. M, who glanced up at me and smiled. Quanah gave her back the emergency hammer. Quanah and I are both seniors. Otsitsalagi. Quanah is also a Cherokee and a descendant of Freedmen. She and I met Lisa through the American Indian Education program years ago. Art is the only class we three have ever been able to take together.

Death drill, how are you? I texted our friend, Lisa.

She usually sat with us, but hadn't come to school that day. I was more than a little concerned since I hadn't heard anything from her since the afternoon before. She gets hyperfocused on art projects though, which usually explains her silence. We were the only Indian girls in the class and we had started working on a project we called Deer Women that week. My mom is Cherokee and grew up here in Oklahoma, but she'd never heard the stories until she was twenty-five. A Cheyenne woman she was hanging out with at a Toadies concert told her about Deer Woman. Deer Woman's origin story is attributed to a variety of tribes according to the interwebz and may be a sign of fertility, or a woman looking for revenge against evil men. Indigenous women have been targets of male violence for a long time. As my mom says, there is nothing new under the sun. Or moon.

Over the weekend Quanah, Lisa, and I had driven to my grandparents' house in Snake, Oklahoma. We hiked through the woods and looked for and poured plaster casts of deer hoofprints. Though my mom was raised in Tulsa, when her parents retired, they moved back to Cherokee Nation and the house built on the allotment where her mother, my elisi, had grown up. Lisa took the casts home and spent the rest of the weekend trying to figure out how to strengthen them. We were going to attach them to our shoes and go all multimedia with this project. That was kind of as far as we had gotten with our ideas. Ms. M was encouraging us to think big, do a public art project. Something we could expand outside the classroom or online. We were thinking about expanding it into a larger Missing and Murdered Indigenous Women project. Deer Woman definitely lent herself to MMIW.

While waiting for Lisa to respond, I pulled my backpack over and leaned back on it and started drawing stars on the underside of the table. The surface was smattered with gum and graffiti from other lockdown drills so I considered my work an improvement. I noticed a triangle of paper wedged between the wood and the metal leg in the corner of the table. I reached up and slipped it out. It was shaped like a paper football. Ignoring the handwriting I didn't recognize that said "Read and die" on its outside, I peeled the triangle open slowly and smoothed it out on the floor. The writing was in two different hands, only one I recognized as Lisa's. The conversation between two people was filled with jargon from *A Clockwork Orange* and tiny drawings of antlers covered in red ink. At the end of the note a strange hand suggested meeting at midnight to look for Deer Woman. "Who are you?" Lisa had scrawled back in reply. I didn't like the way that made me feel. We knew students who used dating apps to meet people in real life after meeting online. It never sat well with me. Quanah, Lisa, and I had debated the merits and dangers of this world, with Quanah and I erring on the side of uber-caution. We worried about what adults would have considered Lisa's riskier behavior, meeting up with friends she had first met online, assuring us she used an abundance of caution. Lilli's disappearance had scarred us, I guess, but Lisa was three years younger. She hadn't been close to us then.

Lisa was always peppering our group chats with Nasdat, the language *A Clockwork Orange*'s author, Anthony Burgess, made up for the book that was a bit Russian and a bit British street. She begged us to watch Kubrick's film at my house one time, and neither Quanah or I really got it. Malcolm McDowell's makeup was pretty cool. To be honest, though, I felt kind of icky after watching it, the boys getting off on rape and "ultraviolence." Lisa made devotchka, horrorshow, and droogie a part of our regular chats, but Quanah and I pushed back with Cherokee words we had learned for the same things. Ageyutsa, osda, and oginalii. Okay, osda maybe doesn't mean horrorshow, more like "good" or "well-balanced." Close enough.

I glanced around and saw the other students were engrossed in their own phones while a few couples held each other tight. I took a photo of both sides of the note before returning it to its hiding spot. Lisa's behavior had been odd lately. Distracted. She smiled to herself at times when she checked her phone or wrote in her notebook. A few times we asked if she had a crush on someone, but she shook her head violently and frowned. It's a story I'm working on, she'd say. She's a writer. She has online friends all over the world. Quanah and I just let it go.

Finally, a prerecorded announcement over the intercom stated that it was all clear and we could return to learning. With only a few minutes left in the day, that wasn't going to happen. Lisa still hadn't returned my text. I asked Ms. M if I could go ahead and go to the office to see my mom. Our teacher was distracted, so she just said, "Sure, Sali." Quanah grabbed her stuff to come with me. My name is not really Sali, but it's Cherokee for "persimmon." Which is cool because Quanah is Cherokee for "peach." I once ate a beautiful golden wild persimmon in front of my uncles. They are beautiful when they're not ready to eat. An unripe persimmon will make you feel as if your mouth will be eternally puckered, but a ripe one is darker and bruised-looking. The taste is heaven. After that, they started calling me Sali.

As soon as Quanah and I left the art room, I said, "I want you to look at something," and sent her pictures of the note. Between the note and Lisa's silence in our group chat since the night before, it was starting to seem dangerously strange.

My mom had already left her office to go work bus duty, but there was a list of the day's absences in her plastic inbox. Students with more than three absences for that quarter were highlighted in yellow. One of Mom's jobs was to reach out to the parents to see if they needed resources or support in order to get their child to school. Lisa's name was there next to *unexcused*, but it wasn't highlighted. It was unusual for her to be out, and even more unusual for her to not let Quanah and I know what was going on. We would text each other on our death beds, I thought. I flipped through the two-page list and took a picture of each page. I was certain the name of Lisa's secret pen pal was there as well. I wished I could ask my mom about the other kids on the list, what kind of confidential stuff she might know, but she never gossiped about them or their families. Snooping was the only way to find anything out from that woman.

Quanah had finished looking over the note.

"Can you drive us to Lisa's?" I could drive, but Mom and I rode to school together. I wanted a car, but I didn't really want the job I would need to pay for one, not yet. I drove Mom and me to school in her car, borrowed either her or dad's when I needed one, but otherwise just caught rides with my friend.

Quanah agreed and I texted my mom to tell her we were going to Lisa's to work on our art project. When the bell rang for dismissal, we were on the road. I was grateful Quanah had air-conditioning. Etsi said when she was a kid she thought of September as the season of fall weather, but we were still in the low nineties and super humid. Etsi wouldn't have time to respond with a yes or no to my text message until after all the buses were cleared out. She wouldn't be happy about it, but I had a bad feeling I couldn't ignore. On the way to Lisa's house I texted her we were coming, just in case, but she still didn't respond.

Once there, no one answered the door. Quanah waited in the car while I went to the back door and let myself in with the hidden key. The house was empty, quieter than it had ever been when I was there before. Thank God her parents hadn't installed a doorbell camera or anything more secure than the alarm system, for which I knew the code. I went directly to Lisa's room and found her phone on the charger. I unlocked it and looked through the messages. Quanah and I had an "If I go missing" file we shared via the cloud. Our files were pretty dull. Addresses for places we frequently went, for cousins, people whose houses we went to, new people we met. Lisa wouldn't do that. As I scrolled through her messages, there were several from a number without a name, and I sent myself and Quanah a screenshot of it. The last one was after midnight. It asked whether Lisa was going to meet them or not. There was nothing about this I liked at all.

I jumped when a text came from Quanah: I think I know where she went. Let's go.

I grabbed Lisa's phone and ran out to the car. Quanah drove as quickly toward Skiatook as possible, without breaking the law. Being brown and stopped by the police wasn't going to help our friend.

"At your grandma's house, she was asking me about places Deer Woman had been spotted. I told her about the drain in the woods, behind the lake. Remember my cousin, Chooch? He and some of my older cousins went out there a few years ago and passed out from drinking too much beer. Chooch stayed awake longer than everyone else and he saw something he still won't talk about. But it made his hair grow out with that white streak."

I checked Lisa's email and then her deleted folder and found a receipt for a ride from around eight the evening before. She had been dropped off at the little restaurant on the lake. I opened my maps app and got walking directions to the area where the drain is on the other side.

"I bet she walked over," I said. "Would have taken about two hours to get there from Billy Simm's Barbecue. Let's park along the side of the road on that side of the lake."

"Who else is on the absentee list?" Quanah asked.

I started reading. No one really set off alarms until I got to the senior boys. The first one I read—"Richard Armstrong"— gave me goose bumps.

"He's the one who stayed home for a week after Lilli disappeared," Quanah said. "We could never find any connection between him and Lilli, though." Our school was large enough that I had never spoken to Armstrong, but I'd seen him in the halls. He was over six foot tall and nice-looking. He had one of the newer, more-expensive cars in the student parking lot. He was a favorite of teachers and administrators.

When we got closer to the lake I started using my phone to take pictures of the few cars parked along the side of the road. When we drove past the lake's parking area I filmed the cars there. Armstrong's car would have stuck out among the new trucks and the many older vehicles. I'd scroll through the videos later, if it was necessary. I hoped it wouldn't be. We drove down a few side roads until we found the one closest to the large drain pipe we were aiming for.

Quanah edged her car off the road. When Lilli had gone missing, Quanah and I went with her family members and just walked various places, sometimes based on leads. Sometimes based on feelings. Searching never stops when someone you care for disappears. When someone just disappears, hope can take a long time to die. I checked my watch. Etsi would be home soon and might call Lisa's mom or even drop by. I wasn't even sure why I had lied, at this point. Things just felt wrong. Lisa had kept a secret from us. If everything was really fine, violating her privacy to make sure she was okay would definitely damage our relationship. I needed to know she was okay first, though. Then I would worry about that.

"Have we been listening to too many true-crime podcasts?" I asked Quanah.

Quanah shrugged, "I hope so."

I checked my phone. There were two more hours of sunlight left.

The woods were quiet and dark, but it was still hot. The lake's humidity made the air saucy and thick. Parts of the woods were overgrown with briars and poison ivy. There were places where no sun seemed to reach down through the trees, which still had their leaves. The dark moist ground caught in our shoes in some places. In others, moss grew between chunks of sandstone.

When we reached the thinner trees at the edge of the woods, we stopped and eyeballed the long dark drain that led back into a mound on the east side of the lake. The opening was tall enough you could stand in the center. For the most part, the mouth of the drain was all in shadow, a dark maw that yawned. Dry grass, then a long stretch of mud, then concrete lay between us and the hole.

"Do you want to hold the pepper spray or the flashlight?" Quanah asked. I slid the flashlight app open on my phone and handed it to her. We walked shoulder to shoulder toward the entrance. For five feet between the brown grass and the cement, the ground was damp red clay. There was a pair of large footprints going into the drain, but none coming out.

We exchanged looks, then Quanah gestured to other prints. Large divots in the damp dirt bore evidence of one or several deer going into the drain. The skin on the back of my neck prickled like icy nails were tickling it. I leaned closer to Quanah.

"We're not going in there," I said, holding the pepper spray at the ready. Quanah pointed the flashlight toward the dark tunnel, but it barely illuminated the graffiti we could see that started at the tunnel's entrance. On the count of tsoi, we both hollered our friend's name.

Two baby fawns came running out of the dark. They were young, their gangly legs carrying them so fast they almost ran right into us. At the last minute, they dashed to either side of us. Then bounded together back into the woods. We briefly felt the heat and smelled the scent of their young warm bodies. We both thought of the Deer Woman stories we had read—the fawns lying down with women who had been assaulted, comforting them in their last moments. We were so shocked we hadn't screamed, just grabbed on to each other. That's how we were standing when Lisa stepped out of the tunnel.

"Hey," she said, her voice scratchy. "Don't come any closer."

She turned and moved awkwardly, as if she was sore, disappearing back into the darkness.

She was back with her backpack quickly. We watched as she walked toward us, her Doc Martens leaving hoofprints where they should have left boot tracks. The first few tracks were edged in dark brown.

"What happened?" I said, grabbing Lisa when she reached us.

"I just want to go home," was all she said.

We trudged through the woods. I hadn't noticed the mosquitoes earlier. Now my skin itched. I was sure there were ticks crawling up underneath my clothes, searching for a place to bite me. I figured they'd drown in my sweat. I tried to step around the poison ivy I'd raced through moments earlier. When we got closer to the road at the edge of the woods, Lisa took off her Docs. She slipped them into her backpack. Then she stripped down to a slightly dirty camisole and boxers and shoved her black jeans and long-sleeve T-shirt into the pack as well. Down-dressed, she suddenly began to shake and cry quietly. I put my arms around her. She stank of sweat, mud, and blood.

I asked Quanah to go start the car. "Honk the horn when it's clear."

While we waited, I held Lisa and patted her shaking shoulders.

From the road I could hear more traffic than earlier. People were driving home or rushing out to the lake for a few hours after work. When there was a brief lull, the car horn bleated. I grabbed

Lisa's hand and we ran for the car. Lisa climbed into the back seat. She pulled the old black-and-white Pendleton Quanah kept back there over herself in spite of the late summer heat. I got in the front.

"Where are we going?" Quanah asked.

"Drive to Sonic," I said. After that, none of us spoke for a long time. I looked back at Lisa. She stared out the window in silence. I wondered if she was in shock. Quanah ordered for all of us at the drive-in. Quanah and I had been hanging out together for ten years. We had known Lisa awhile, but she was younger. She had started hanging out with us two summers earlier during Cherokee Summer Camp. Our favorite fast-food orders were predictable. Before that day I wouldn't have guessed we kept any dangerous secrets from one another.

Lisa didn't speak again until she was holding a boat of cheese curds and a Dr Pepper. She handed the fried cheese back to me. "You can have these," she said. She took several long draws of her Dr Pepper before she spoke again. Then she said: "He was going to kill me."

Their correspondence had started a month earlier via the art room table and paper notes like the one I had found. Sometimes they chatted via a messaging app. Richard Armstrong was in art class during first period. He sat at the same table we shared at the end of the day. A big fan of *A Clockwork Orange*, he was fluent in Nasdat. That was how it had started. Lisa had made a small drawing of Deer Woman on the table, and he had complimented it. "That's real horrorshow, my droogie." And like that, because they had something oddball in common, she threw herself into correspondence with her anonymous pen pal. Eventually, they agreed to combine their first meeting with a vigil for Deer Woman. Lisa told her parents she was staying at my house, leaving her phone at home in case her mom decided to track her. Then Lisa hired a car and went to the lake four hours before their midnight meeting, not a little unwary.

She wore her Docs with the deer hoof casts. At twilight, she braved the drainpipe wearing her boots, a sharpened antler in her backpack, a flashlight in hand. She hid as far back in the drainpipe as she dared go. Armstrong had shown up an hour early, armed with a hammer and carrying a plastic tarp. From where she hid in the dark, she watched him spread out the green plastic. Then he practiced swinging the hammer the way we had all seen in more than one crime show. He paced. Watching the drainage hole entrance, he took out his phone a few times. He texted manically, the glow of his phone showing his handsome, contorted features in blue-white light. She was glad she had left her phone behind. She prayed silently that he would give up and go away. She wasn't sure what she would do if he turned his flashlight her way, at least until he finally did.

"Then the mother deer came in with her babies," she breathed. Tears slid down her cheeks and Quanah and I exchanged a look. "Antlers or not, you don't mess with a mama like that."

Lisa wouldn't say anything else.

Quanah ordered her another Dr Pepper. We sat in silence.

"You have his phone?" Quanah said quietly.

Lisa nodded and pulled it out of her backpack. It was smashed. It no longer turned on.

I ate the last of the cheese curds; after all, fried food makes the worst leftovers. We put the car windows up, air-conditioning on high. We began to talk about what to do. "Nobody's going to believe your Deer Woman story," I said.

Neither Quanah nor I mentioned our other doubts. "I think he wanted you to keep everything secret so you could disappear." Quanah was starting to get emotional. "Like my cousin . . ." she paused. Then took a deep breath before speaking again. "Maybe his plot will keep you in the clear as long as you don't tell on yourself." We were both watching Lisa through the rear view mirror.

"If you tell anyone, ever, it's going to be bad for us too. You understand? You need to decide now if you can do this. If you can't, then say so now, Lisa," I said.

Lisa nodded immediately.

"Is that a yes?" Quanah asked.

"Yes," Lisa responded.

I reached over and turned on the stereo. We had a playlist we had all made together. I heard the strains of "Truth Hurts." Lizzo had the right questions and answers. I turned the stereo up and Quanah and I sang along.

I had an uncle with a small farm near Skiatook. Outside of Tulsa County it was still legal to burn trash. Lighting the burn barrel on Saturday night was par for the course. Once that was decided, I pulled Lisa's phone out of the glove compartment. "Lisa, call your mom and tell her we're spending the night at my house to work on the art project."

Lisa did as she was told. "No, Mama, I'm fine. Just tired." A pause. "I don't know why the school called. I was there," she lied smoothly. Then another pause. "We stayed up too late last night, but I'll go to bed early tonight." Another pause. "I promise, Mama. I love you, too." When she got off the phone she stared at it vacantly. When I looked back at her she was turned away, looking out the window.

I called my mom to let her know Quanah and Lisa were coming over. I used Quanah's phone and texted her mom the same.

"Tomorrow we go to school like normal," I said.

Quanah and I looked at each other. Now that the adrenaline had worn off, I felt shaky. Quanah looked tired. It was not an ideal way to start the evening. We stopped at a Family Dollar and bought some clothes for Lisa to wear. The sun was setting as we drove to my uncle's place. We buried the clothes deep in the burn barrel. We put the phone in the Sonic bags and smashed it between some concrete blocks until it broke into pieces. We carefully wedged it into the barrel, as well. Then we drove back to my house.

My parents were both awake and watching television in the front room. When we walked in Edoda handed the box with what was left of a pizza to Quanah. Funny, how my parents only ate fast food when I was out. Other nights it was dinner at the dining table with more vegetables than I, generally, cared for.

"Did you hear about that boy?" my mom said, as we turned to go down the hall. I stopped, but Quanah and Lisa kept going and disappeared into my room. I looked at my mom. My face all innocent confusion.

"The one who killed the girl," she said.

My ears began pounding with my heart.

"What girl, Mom?"

"At the high school in Owasso? That's why we had a lock-down drill today." I remembered Ms. M showing Quanah her phone during the drill. I remembered the note under the table.

"Oh," I said. "No, I didn't know. We were just hanging out and listening to music. Haven't been on my phone much."

"The parent group is buying doughnuts for the entire school tomorrow. I need you girls to help me deliver them to the class-rooms. We'll have to get there early."

"Yeah, sure, Mom. Let's get there really early."

I went to my room where Quanah and Lisa were waiting for me and told them my plan. In the morning I'd use my mom's master key to take doughnuts to leave on Ms. M's desk in the art room. I'd also do a little cleaning of the tables as long as I was there.

I thought of Ms. M. crying during yet another lockdown, over a girl being killed in another high school, over a world where learning in safety was neither a right nor a possibility. Ms. M was afraid for all the lives she thought hadn't really yet begun, as well as her own. It wasn't enough that she teach, she also had to protect the students in her care from a world that didn't make the safety of children a priority. Being a teacher nowadays is hard.

Almost as hard as being a teenage girl.

# I Come from the Water

*y*

Walela King Preston
Anvhyi 3, 2029
03/03/2029

Walela

The night before Edoda had his car wreck, I woke when I heard the cry of the Koga. To me the name echoes their sound. Most Cherokees don't care to hear an owl at night, but the cry of Koga in the dark is a bad omen, too. It took me a long time to fall asleep after that. It was doubly strange because agasga. It was coming down in sheets, lightning filled the skies. That I heard the crows in the tree in our yard kept me from falling asleep for what seemed like forever.

Sakonige, the Alien from the Ocean

We were sleeping. With a crack our craft boomeranged back into the planet's atmosphere, then silence. Something had gone wrong. Back home, in the deep of Oceania, they would receive a transmission, error messages would explain what happened, why the ship exploded over the earth before crashing into a prairie on the edge of a city. They would know why the rescue pod deployed, rolling far from the wreckage. They would know why we fell from the sky full of lightning and rain before we did.

The elder awoke to deal with it. I know this because I am still alive. I reviewed the echoes. If they hadn't awakened and pulled the right emergency switches the ship would have blown apart high above your houses and radio towers. They saved me and they died badly, as did the other refugees. I was left behind to hide the escape pod, immolate their bodies, and kill the feral dogs and coyotes that came for the dying.

## Koga

We were sleeping, most of us, when the storm came, and lightning flashed. A fiery craft fell out of the sky. It hit the ground. There was stillness for a moment, then out rolled a small shiny ball. This glassy sphere rolled far from the burning metal craft. Once clear, the ship seemed to breathe. Then it exploded into millions of pieces of shrapnel. We were far enough away in the cedar to be protected from the nearly dustlike shards. In a lesser storm the prairie's buffalo grass would have burned. The smaller silvery sphere had rolled into the space beneath a fallen oak, frightening a family of rabbits from their hiding place. It was still storming when the wet creature crawled up out of the tunnel. A few of us flew down to investigate. Their body smelled of ocean. In the dark they glimmered with wet. We watched. A few of us followed them, but we were quiet. As the rain began to lighten, the coyotes came. They dogged their path, then, emboldened, they surrounded them. We waited, not knowing whose side to take in the conflict.

Finally, one attacked them. It parried forward. They wrapped around the coyote. It yelped. Then it froze, as if paralyzed. It began to shrink from the inside out. It was like watching weeks of decay happen in minutes. The planet barely moved in the time it took them to leave behind an empty skin and gaping eyes. Still the coyotes circled them. They leaned toward another one. Foolishly, it tried to attack them, too. There was no contest. The rest of the pack slunk away, leaving behind the bodies. Some of us made short work of the eyes. A few others followed them.

Walela

We were at home sleeping when the fatal accident happened to my edoda. He's not Indian, but Etsi, Anna, and I are. The night before, it had stormed, and in the morning all the digital clocks were flashing to let us know at some point in the night we had lost power.

Before dawn, the doorbell app chimed loudly on the phone of Etsi. She checked the security camera feed. There was a policeman standing at the door.

I didn't know that part. When I rolled over in bed and listened there was quiet talk, muffled, low. Too much like silence. Then I heard my mom rushing around the house, opening and closing things: a dryer, the cabinet where she kept her keys, her feet rushing up the stairs to the bedrooms.

"Sissy, get up," she said, as she opened my door. "We have to go."

My name is Walela King Preston. King is my mom's maiden name, which she never changed. Only Edoda calls me Walela. Everyone else calls me Sissy.

My dad called me Walela, I mean.

I stood up and stumbled around wondering what was going on. I went to my drawer and pulled on some shorts. Etsi was back at my door carrying my sister, Anna. Anna was six and always in her puppy pj's.

"Let's go," Mom said softly. "Grab a jacket. Hospitals are always cold." Then she turned and headed back downstairs.

Sakonige

Sometimes you have to kill several predators before they will leave you alone.

251

When they attacked, I pierced their skin and filled their bodies with acid. It melts the inside bones and bits so you can drink them whole. The dogs are slow learners, so I had to do it a second time. Eventually, the rest of the pack was frightened off. They watched me from the scrub. They waited to trail me as I staggered to the next hiding place. Perhaps they dragged the empty skins of their brethren off and fought over them after I crawled away.

I was searching for salt water on the dry plains, a sea in the land of grass and cedar.

## Koga

The creature travelled purposely, toward something, following a scent, perhaps? We flew down near them. They paid us no mind. They smelled of salt and seaweed. They were far from home.

They stopped. Tiny pits opened along their skin as if they detected a whiff of water and salt, real water, not the lingering grit of an ocean that covered this prairie eons ago. The human pool they detected was higher up the hill, the home of the father who feeds us. They stopped again and smeared themself with oil, a fishy scent that made us hungry. We have seen what they can do to a threat, though. And we are not foolish, hungry coyotes. In the dark they seemed to see the worst of the jagged rocks. They crawled snakelike, avoiding the pricklies and brambles. They crawled toward the back gate of the house, slithered over dangerous barbed wire. They blobbed in through a metal gate and over a sandstone walkway. Just as the father's car pulled out of the driveway of the home, the creature dropped into the saltwater pool. We homed into our tree overhead.

Seven of us roosted just over the circle of water. A blue jay had started following the creature as they made their way up the hill, but with our arrival he fled. They swam in circles and learned the edges of the pool, where the walls ended in sandstone rock. It was like watching a fish play. They swam faster and faster, circles within circles, building up speed as if they meant to fly out of the pool on velocity alone. We watched and we waited and then, when they seemed to be going impossibly fast, they suddenly disappeared.

## Sakonige

In spite of the rain the night before, the land was harsh. Beneath the drying dirt is the thinly disguised profile of an ancient ocean floor. Tiny, thinwalled snail shells are scattered about, water creatures unaccountably living on the land. There are green plants shaped like coral, jutting up from the sandy dirt and covered in thin spikes like needles. In places the earth is cushioned by dry brown leaves that have sharp edges, curved crisply up at the ends. Round rocks are scattered about, worn smooth once by old waves. Shale and flint and sticks make the way jagged and treacherous for my skin. The oils I have covered my skin in for protection from the sun and the elements wear off quickly where I must touch the earth to walk.

There is the smell of salt on the air a mere fifteen hundred meters from where the pod landed. If only we had been closer to the ocean. Even a human-made pond would have been better. I dip into a stream littered with plastic. There are deep places, green with algae and foaming with froth, the runoff from grass covered in chemicals. The wet is nice, but the concentrated poison starts to burn before long, the acid irritating my skin.

In the deep, in our ocean, the ratio of pollution to water can be mitigated where we live, the microplastics filtered by our living biosphere, a bubble unseen by humans. But the men threaten this space, too, now. This is why we had to leave. We had to find another ocean far from the pipes running through our home. We didn't know if it would be permanent or temporary, but we couldn't be there while the submarines and machines were constructing stands and pods for human workers.

I crawl up the hill slanting up the other side of the creek. There is an old metal fence, two strands of rusty wire interspliced with jagged crosspieces, but I can slide under the barrier in places. I crawl slowly until I reach the top of the hill. There is another sturdier obstruction. I hope there aren't more coyotes as I jiggle the lock on the gate and wait. There is only a screeching blue bird following, warning anyone who will listen that I am coming.

I slip between a piece of square stone and a metal portal. On the other side, the pool is blue and still. Moving quickly, I slip into the water. The bottom of the pool is lightly dusted with sandy rock bits that have broken off the edges. I am grateful for the salt-water. I swim and cry. I cry and swim. All alone, I don't want to die here. I want to swim forever. I don't want to cry. I can't stop crying. I keep swimming in circles. I turn and swim the other direction. On one side I swim curving left, the other curving right. The two circles cross in the middle of the pool. I swim and cry until too tired to swim and cry anymore. Then I fall asleep and wait.

## Walela

I grabbed a jacket and the book I had been reading before running downstairs.

She drove fast. She was telling me quietly that there had been an accident. Her eyes glanced back at my sister sleeping in the back seat. When Etsi said that my dad was in surgery, her shaking voice terrified me. I looked out the window. My eyes welled with tears. Edoda left the house early that Saturday morning. He was going to go fishing with a friend from his work. Sometimes my unwell grandmother would call in the middle of the night and scream drunkenly at whoever answered the phone, so both my parents kept their ringers off at night. The phone of Etsi never rang.

Last night Edoda had wanted me to watch a movie with him and Etsi and Anna. I only wanted to read my book. I told them I was too tired after swimming that evening. I went upstairs to hide in my room with Carmen Maria Machado's *Her Body and Other Parties*. It occurred to me that it was the birthday of Chloe, the BFF who dumped me last year. Stupidly, I had told her I kind of had a crush on her. So much for "forever." Freshman year had been hard.

At a stoplight, Etsi asked me to get her phone from her purse. There were a lot of missed calls, including two voicemails from Edoda. I played the second one over the phone's speaker.

His voice was groggy. "Dani, there's been an accident. I'm definitely going to the hospital." There was a long chaotic pause. "I love you. Tell the girls I love them." Another groggy pause. "I'm sorry," he finished. The speakers filled the car with chaotic noise. We sat through the green light and listened to the noise on the open line. It was interrupted by the voice of someone talking to my dad, yelling to someone that my dad was unconscious. And then the call ended.

"Etsi?" Anna questioned from the back seat.

When a car behind us honked we all startled. Etsi made the left turn carefully. She drove quickly to the hospital. As fast as she drove it would never be fast enough. The only way she could drive fast enough was if she could drive backward in time, back to 4:00 a.m. when my dad left the house. If she could drive fast enough, we could circle back in time, and it would be last night, and I would stay on the couch in between my parents and just be with them. If she could drive fast enough Anna and I will still have Edoda and Mom will still have a best friend.

## Koga

The man doesn't come into the yard to leave us peanuts anymore. Now a creature lives in the pool and a young girl comes out and throws food onto the compost pile near the dying backyard garden. Then she goes back into the house. There is more food than there used to be. So, we keep visiting the yard even though there are no peanuts.

Occasionally, the water beastie crawls out of the pool and hunts small creatures and puts their emptied carcasses behind the gate. We carry most of them away and fight over the eyes. In this way, we are making friends with the creature. Being that creature's friend seems better than being their enemy.

The day after the crash, two humans in a black truck, black clothes, and black glasses search the park. They have found the crater where the ship struck. But not the beastie. They are looking, though.

## Sakonige

Occasionally, I have to leave the water. The emergency pod is biological. It can repair itself given the right stimuli. Some of that information and material I can provide. Other information must come from our scientists in Oceania. In the park behind the pool there is a road. It is gravel and rock and dirt. It's blocked off at one end with chains and locks, not meant for traffic. The day after the crash I went back to check that the distress signal was working. On the road behind the house, I saw a vehicle had broached the barriers. One adult human was walking the road, carrying a small machine. I dropped into the deeper part of the poisoned stream. A second human was kicking the dark vehicle's round feet and muttering.

"So much for turnaround, don't drown."

The other human glanced up. "We didn't drown. You just got stuck."

In response the human shoved a piece of wood under the vehicle's feet. He got back into the machine. It roared.

"You better scoot back," he hollered over the machine's roar at the human walking along the creek. I darted into the shadows.

The black feet of the vehicle spun and caught, lifting the machine out of the hole it had dug for itself.

"Let's go," the pilot shouted.

The other human frowned and turned and looked in the direction of my hidden pod.

"Supposed to keep raining," he said.

"Let's come back when it stops," the pilot hollered.

The other human walked back to the car.

I stayed in the water until they were gone, until they relocked the road's barrier.

Today it was dry. I wondered if they had come back. I would know if they had found the pod. If the pod was discovered there would be more than one dark vehicle. Being caught was not an option. Being caught would be the end for us. Human curiosity and greed had swiftly wiped out species with much larger populations than ours. In the last four hundred years animals and tribes of people have been destroyed by human hunting and pollution and diseases.

I cannot be found.

For me the only two options are death or the deep.

## Walela

When we drove to the hospital two weeks earlier, it was with hope. We hadn't known that my father was dying because a Good Samaritan had dragged him out of a vehicle that wasn't on fire, further damaging his broken spine in the process. The weight of bearing this on my own, with no best friend, was a lot. I had half hoped Chloe and her family would show up to support us. They sent flowers. I guess they figured a gay kid didn't deserve their in-person support.

Emily Dickinson said, "Hope is the thing with feathers." More like hope is the thing with stones. Life is a lottery. Not the kind you want to win.

"Sissy!"

I was stretched out on the couch watching a favorite Steven Universe episode of Edoda's. From upstairs my mother's voice called me, as if it was for the umpteenth time. Too late, I realized my little sister had intruded on her sanctum. Once more my six-year-old sister, Anna, had broken her promise to me to let our mother sleep this time so I could watch a show and eat ice cream. Because Edoda died and Etsi was having a breakdown, I didn't get to be a normal kid anymore. Maybe it's normal in an animated movie. Well, I guess in those movies it's the mom who dies. I can tell you now those movies are unrealistic garbage. Having a parent die is nothing like a kid's film. Nothing gets you ready for this. Except maybe *Dumbo*. I know, the mom doesn't die in that one. But it's complicated.

"Yeah, Mom!" I turned off the television. Upstairs, I stopped outside her room and waited for the next sound that might clue me in on what to do next. Finally, I knocked on the door. Anna opened it. Then she went back in and crawled back in bed with our very depressed mother.

"Sissy?" Mom spoke as if she was half asleep.

"Yeah, Mom?"

"Honey, have you emptied the pool's skimmers today?"

I paused before speaking. No, I hadn't emptied the skimmers. I had seen my father clean the skimmers, but it had never occurred to me that this was one more job I would get to take over. None of us had actually used the pool since my dad died. I think it made me and Etsi too sad. Anna wasn't allowed to use it without one of us, since she couldn't swim.

Since my dad's death, I noticed Mom's code switching in a new way. She had been a high school biology teacher before she stopped doing most everything. There was definitely a difference between her teacher voice and her mom voice.

Now, when she used a term of endearment like *honey* or *sweetheart*, she inevitably asked me to do jobs she previously would have expected my father to do. So, of course when she asked me if the skimmers had been cleaned, she knew they hadn't been cleaned.

Dad's last night home he had done maintenance on the pool while he tried to teach Anna how to swim. Our pool was no deeper than five feet, but you know what they say, kids can drown in less than two inches of water. The world is a dangerous place.

"You want me to do the pool first or make dinner?" I said flatly. My mother was immune to hints of irritation in my voice.

Her voice lifted, a false happy note: "I got a lasagna at Braum's and some pool salt at Lowe's this morning. And a frozen creamed spinach and stuff to make sundaes . . ." Her voice drifted off as if speaking exhausted her. I wondered if she was taking too many of the pills her doctor had given for her crying jags.

Finally, I prompted, "Yeah, Mom?" a little too loudly.

"Can you stick the lasagna and the veggies in the oven and dump the salt in the pool and clean the skimmers?"

Lasagna. Lasagna in the oven took over eighty minutes. Anna was supposed to be asleep in eighty minutes. Nope, chunks of that lasagna were going in the microwave. When you delegate, sometimes you can't be all micromanagey.

"C'mon, Anna," I held my hand out to my six-year-old sister.

"No!" Mom suddenly seemed awake.

"We're going to watch *Scooby*!" Anna exclaimed as she jumped out of bed to grab my father's tablet where it sat charging on his nightstand. It was propped amid his wallet, watch, and wedding ring, as if he were merely in the bathroom getting ready for bed.

At least *Scooby* was a safe show for them to watch together. It fed Anna's current dog obsession and there were no dead parents like so many of the kid movies Anna had always loved. I saved my sighing for the hallway.

Who were sighs for anyway? Most exclamations were for communicating with others, but a sigh? Though even dogs sighed and you knew exactly what they meant. I did it again, louder and deeper. It felt good.

Before my dad died, it had taken two years to get Anna to stay in her own bed. His death had relocated her to our parents' room more strongly than before. It seemed like a terrible idea to me, but what did I know? I sometimes heard my mother crying when she was in her room alone, and when Anna was in the room with her, she didn't weep. At least not too loudly. Occasionally, the aloneness in the dark was a bit much for me, too. But when I was awake, I stayed busy. My mother's mourning saw to that. Or didn't see. Maybe that's a good definition of depression.

I had never wished for another responsible adult to have an interest in me and Anna so hard in all my life. My parents had always been enough. When I saw cousins back in the Cherokee Nation posting on Facebook about gatherings and funerals and getting together, I only envied them a little before. Mom talked about taking us to powwows or Wild Onion dinners, but things never seemed to work out. My parents were always busy with work. Suddenly, without my dad, our family no longer worked. At least it wasn't working for me. I thought about my etlogi, Aunt Ama, my mom's relative who was an over-the-road truck driver. She was this tiny woman who drove these big rigs all over North America. Her size belied her powerful presence. I figured she had no idea what was going on. Doubted my mom had called and told her. Mom hadn't even called the woman who ran the American Indian program she worked for, though we spent two solid weeks together every summer. The funeral had, mostly, consisted of Dad's coworkers. Private and self-sufficient doesn't even begin to describe it. My mom didn't know how to ask for help, although she always tried to help other people when she saw they needed it. "When it comes down to it," she would say, when someone else had let her down, "you can't depend on anyone but yourself."

I was beginning to understand how she felt.

Sakonige

The park is a big dark. There are large swaths of grasses where the sky isn't blocked by the trees and there are no lights for meters, and you can see the stars like islands and streams of water that pour into the sky. Our stories say we came from the sky, left a drying planet, for a blue oasis in space. Are there others like us in the deep ocean we were fleeing to? Do we have relatives out there on another star or planet? In Oceania we stopped building things we didn't need in order not to call attention to ourselves. We had water, food, and shelter. Our lives were good and full of story and family and loved ones. Our elders maintained a fleet of evacuation crafts complete with biological escape pods. The knowledge to access them and maintain them and pilot them had been passed down.

I use starlight to guide me back to the pod in the dark. I pay special attention to Venus. Our messages will bounce off the planets in space and back into the oceans. My people won't forget about us. I just have to help them find us. I just have to sing to them. They will be listening for our song.

## Walela

I went downstairs and started the lasagna. Before I went out to the pool, I soaked my skin in mosquito repellent.

It was the first day in two weeks that it hadn't rained. It started the night before Edoda died. There had been a raging storm, too, full of lightning and thunder. At one point there was been a huge explosion in the park behind our house. It shook the walls and was bright enough for a moment to seem like daylight.

Last night, just south of Fort Worth, there had been what the weather people called a five-hundred-year flood. It was the second five-hundred-year flood in three years in that part of Texas.

A layer of leaves covered the pool's bottom.

I flipped the switch that controlled the pool's pump and, normally, the bottom-sweeping robot. However, today the robot and its long hose sat neatly at the bottom of the pool, detached from the wall, sweeping nothing. It was strange that it was detached. I realized Edoda had unplugged it, maybe, while he was teaching Anna to swim. Anna was terrified the robot would sweep her. She swore, very dramatically, that it chased her as she bobbed along in her life vest, splashing madly away.

I pulled the robot's hose to me with a long pole and then reattached it to its port in the wall. I emptied the robot's leaf bag and then dropped it back in at the deep end.

I removed the lids that covered the skimmer baskets and debated whether or not to retrieve a fishnet from the house in order to clean out the debris. I poked through the stuff in the very full skimmer with a stick and didn't see anything moving of its own volition, so I began to scoop it out by hand. The first scoop was rotting leaves, exposing the next level of swollen cater-pillar bodies, centipedes, and a drowned rat. Its body was swollen and it looked like a wet fur stole, its pink wormlike tail curled under the leaves, its eyes squinted shut like it was sleeping.

I retched for a moment, thinking of my fingers scraping along the ragged corpse.

Disgusted, I went back into the house to check on the lasa-gna and get some long dishwashing gloves from beneath the sink. I pulled them on dramatically, like a surgeon, then stomped back outside.

The robot's hose was once more at the bottom of the pool and the robot sat still. "That's weird," I said aloud.

I finished cleaning out the first skimmer and tossed the dead creatures over the fence into the lower backyard that backed up to the prairie. The prairie was 160 acres. A local group was try-ing to rehabilitate the park back into grassland, but a lot of it was dense brush and invasive cedar and mesquite trees. Tall oaks towered and leaned toward the fence, always threatening to fall over and die from the heat and regular droughts.

The second skimmer was just as full. I emptied it. Then I reattached the robot's hose to the wall before turning the pump on again.

I went back in the kitchen to plate Anna's dinner. I covered the spinach in butter, salt, and cheese. If it was unspinachy enough, Anna might at least take a bite of it. I stuck it in the microwave before going back outside.

Once more the hose floated free of the wall.

"I must not be doing that right," I muttered.

It seemed odd that I suddenly didn't know how to do some-thing I had watched my father do for years. I wondered if some-thing had broken on the hose or the port. I didn't want to get into the rain-cooled pool, so I grabbed the long pole with the leaf net and began to push it along the bottom of the pool. I started scooping up the gunk in the shallow end with the net, removing it from the pool. Then I used the edge to push the smaller debris toward the drain on just the other side of the pool's middle. It would be sucked into the drain and then filtered out. When that side was cleanish, I moved to the deep end. Almost immediately it felt like the pole bumped into something solid, solid enough that it shocked me not to see anything where the pole had come to a sudden stop. I pressed the leaf net forward, hard, and it bounced back into my chest with just as much force. My arm registered a slight electrical shock.

"Stop." The word seemed to come from inside my own head.

I dropped the leaf skimmer and it floated to the bottom of the pool. Auditory hallucinations, I thought. This was new.

"Stop, please," the voice repeated.

Wow, I thought, my auditory hallucinations have manners. My heart was thudding. I felt it in my ears. I began to feel light-headed. I bent over at my waist and breathed deep. The dimming sunlight had me figuring it was almost eight. I hadn't eaten lunch that day, as usual. I thought to myself, You're just hungry. I walked quickly back into the house, making sure to lock the door behind me. I was afraid to look back through the glass into the backyard.

## Sakonige

I've grown stronger, recovered from the wreck. The clean salt water strengthens. There are a lot of trees over the pool. So much shade the water doesn't get too hot during the day. The humans have stayed out. That's been a big bit of luck.

I wonder if today is when the luck ends. A girl came. She hit me with a metal pole.

Do I stay and dare to speak to her again? I feel her thoughts, anger, sadness, loneliness. If I could make her understand I feel those same things, might she help? I don't want to die here, far from home, far from kith and kin. I don't want to die at all.

## Walela

I set out the lasagna and spinach and called Anna down to eat. Several minutes later Anna came downstairs carrying our mother's car keys.

"Mom said the salt's still in the trunk of her car."

"Crap," I said.

Anna gave me a look, a look that said, "a month ago I would have ratted on you for swearing in front of me, but now what's the point?" With one parent gone and the other using Anna as a security blanket, there was no longer any competition between us. Anna got the affection and bleary-eyed attention. I kept the infrastructure going, a poor substitute parent.

We sat down to eat. We talked about pasta and creamed spinach and getting another dog and whether or not Anna had done her reading and of course she hadn't, but I signed her reading log anyway. I made Anna write down the title of *The Giving Tree* because it was the darkest children's title I could think of. I wondered how anyone really expected a first grader whose father had died weeks ago to keep a reading log. I rather doubted it. I also knew the person I was doing this for was not Anna's teacher, but Anna's etsi.

After dinner, I walked Anna back upstairs, supervised tooth brushing, then hugged her good night. She disappeared into our mother's room.

"Good night, honey," Mom called, as Anna shut the bedroom door.

"Good night," I shouted back. Then added, "I love you." It seemed to bounce back at me from the closed bedroom door.

I went downstairs and turned all the lights on in the back of the house. Then I turned on the back deck light and the single light in the pool. I wished we had a security camera in the backyard. After I unlocked the car, I started hauling the six fifty-pound bags of salt to the pool. It isn't as easy as you'd think.

I sat down in a chair and rested a few minutes. The rain had left the world humid. I focused on listening. The crows were chatty.

"Koga!" I hollered back. I guess that was kind of like hollering "cow" when you saw one as you were driving in the country. I wished I was fluent in crow. For that matter, I wished I was fluent in Cherokee.

I shoved the first bag of salt to the edge of the pool. I tore it open. Salt crystals poured into the deep end. I opened the next bag, all the while watching the salt fall straight to the bottom. Suddenly, it wasn't falling straight to the bottom of the pool. It was falling on either side of a large, ovoid emptiness. I stared. Then I stopped dumping the salt into the water. I went to turn off the pump, wondering if the water being sucked toward the skimmers or the drain was creating the strange shape.

When the water became still, I slit open another bag. The salt poured in. The large white crystals still fell on either side of a large oval. It reminded me of the shape of my mother sleeping the many times I had found her beneath a thin sheet on her bed or the couch. I dropped the bag. I begin to back away. When the salt stopped falling, the soft, warm voice in my head spoke again.

"More," they whispered.

I was struck by the voice, in tone, so much like my mother's. A moment later I heard it in my head again,

"More."

I cut open the last three bags of salt. I dumped them into the pool. When I finished the last bag, all was silent. I turned the pool light off. I turned the pump back on. I didn't bother with the robot.

Before I left, I called out, "Who are you?" I glanced toward the house to make sure my family didn't hear me.

"Sakonige," I heard from someplace in my brain. I doubted that was right. That couldn't be right. This was definitely me losing it. I knew the word sakonige.

"Weird," I said, aloud. "Sakonige means 'blue' in Cherokee."

There was no response and finally, I went back into the house, making sure to lock the back door and set the alarm.

Sakonige

Digitsi is my best friend. Her name translates to "fast swimmer." Digitsi had left in an earlier evacuation. Before we left, I got messages from her describing the new waters. The mother of Digitsi would often ask me what I had heard. Families were sent separately. There was a fear entire clans would be wiped out if everyone from one family evacuated in the same pod.

Not unrealistic, apparently.

Walela

Sleep escaped me for hours. In my phone I tapped random search words into Google like *invisible + sea + creatures*. The only thing that came up was a crustacean called a Sea Sapphire. I got up out of bed and crossed the hallway to listen at my mom's door. From inside I heard her using my father's phone. From the sounds I could tell she was rewatching videos with his voice in the background, looking at our family through his eyes, going through his pictures and selfies. As much as I didn't want to be alone, I didn't want to intrude on my mother in her sadness either.

Warily, I went back downstairs to the kitchen and stared into the backyard, toward the pool. The moonlight's reflection rippled, but I didn't think it rippled any more than normal. When I checked the clock it was midnight, so I made lunches for the three of us. Then I crawled into bed and cried myself to sleep.

The pool was the first thing I thought of in the morning. I was awake an hour earlier than usual. I went downstairs and set up the coffeepot for my mother. I stood at the back door and felt progressively braver as the sky started to lighten. Dressed in my pajamas I went outside and sat next to the deep end of the pool.

The pump was on, but the robot still lay useless at the bottom of the pool where I had left it. However, the debris, sand, and small bits of leaves were not strewn about randomly. Instead, the pool was lined with concentric figure eights, circles within circles, an infinity symbol within an infinity symbol.

I checked the skimmers. For the most part, the normal abundance of green leaves and crêpe myrtle blossoms was absent. The surface of the pool was clean. So, I thought, You're a vegetarian?

"Sometimes," a voice inside my head cooed.

I froze. I heard the blue jays in the trees behind the yard. Then I heard the call of the crows. Finally, I stepped closer to the pool's edge. "Hello?"

No voice answered this time. The lights upstairs came on, reflected in the pool's water. I returned to the house, spooked again.

Sometimes? I thought. What does that mean?

September in Texas is unpredictable. You never knew once school started if you would be able to swim again. Truthfully, the pool had been our father's thing. He dove in each morning before work. He often swam when everyone else in the family glanced at the clouds or the thermometer and shook their heads.

Now that there seemed to be a thing in the pool, I couldn't

imagine swimming. I wished I had someone to talk to. Since being outed as a lesbian at my school, I didn't really have any friends. Teachers who had only known me as the loner now knew me as the girl with the recently deceased father whose mother— who she wasn't out to—no longer came to work.

I felt their eyes avoid me in class, as if I were bad luck, as if an unintentionally long look might invite a problematic conversation, something they would have to write up and speak to a counselor about. Perhaps even follow up on. As if they had the time. For the most part, I did us all a favor and avoided them as well.

## Sakonige

The girl does her best to keep the water clean, but I can't live here much longer. Thinking is slow. I wake up sad. Perhaps I'll wander out to the dogs.

When I start thinking like this, I tell myself stories. Tales new and old. We are a narrative people, made of stars and stories. In Oceania, there are sea stars everywhere. It is the most perfect shape, the most beautiful. This is why we think people are, also, made of stars. They are four limbs and a head. Telling myself this, I believe we could be relations. I believe the girl might save me.

Then I start to make lists of ways to get the pod to the ocean, though I'm too tired to visit it every night. The heat barely relents. The water is too warm.

There is comfort in the knowledge that my friend's pod made it. In death, I will once more be with my beloveds who have gone before.

Until escape or death, I am alone.

## Walela

I found myself staring at the aquarium after class in science that day, not moving from my seat. My teacher stared at his computer.

It was obvious he was checking the time, on the wall clock, his phone, his watch. I knew I was cutting into his forty-minute duty-free lunch period. Finally, he jingled his keys in his pocket.

Instead of looking at him, I said, "Do you think there are invisible sea creatures?"

Dr. Oludipe seemed very confused. "There may be creatures we haven't seen in the deepest parts of the ocean. Do you mean clear like jellyfish? Hard to see?"

I thought of the shock I had received when the leaf net had bumped the creature's body. Jelly, a telepathic jellyfish in a pool in Fort Worth? I wanted to laugh, but I was sure that this was the type of inappropriate response that would get me another free counseling session.

So, instead I said, "That's right, the mysteries of the ocean deep."

Dr. Oludipe changed the topic of conversation. "Your mother is the sea-life expert in the department." He paused. "Do you think she's coming back to work soon?" Dr. Oludipe was the department chair of science at our school. I was pretty sure she had not been returning his phone calls. I understood that my mom was questioning her life choices in the midst of her mourning. Did I think she wanted to go back to teach fourteen-year-olds biology? To return to professional observations and state testing? Did I think she wanted to keep trying to get students (who only wanted to pass) to love the earth and its creatures the way she did, while they made hand puppets out of the poor abandoned cats the biological supply company sold for dissection? No, I'm pretty sure my mother was no longer seeing the point of getting out of bed for the professional beatings anymore, honestly, I wanted to say. Of course, I had learned the hard way that honesty was rarely the best possible policy.

"Yeah sure. I mean she loves teaching. She's just really sad right now." I had been half honest. It was the best I could manage anymore.

## Sakonige

Why are things sometimes all bad, but rarely all good? The escape pod is mostly repaired. There turned out to be a backlog of messages from Oceania and New Oceania. Though they had not been audible to me, the repair instructions have been directing the healing of the pod. Everything that is alive, all living things have spirit. To be able to communicate across species is a wonderful thing.

Unfortunately, the humans in black were back, as well. They are camped out at the crater. There are cameras and traps set up throughout the park. Just when it looked like the pod would be ready, I fear it is too late.

## Walela

The temperature was a low of 101 that day. I made a salad and chopped up a rotisserie chicken for dinner in order not to overheat the kitchen. The air-conditioning seemed to be struggling. Afterward, I fell asleep in the front room watching *Tiny House Builders* on HGTV. I wished I could jump in the pool, but the creature at the bottom made that impossible. I went outside and stared at the bottom of the pool, the infinity symbols of sand crafting a path underwater. It made me think of the paths in meditation gardens that fancy churches and schools installed.

The pool had never looked better. I dumped more salt into the shallow end of the pool. Something swam through the salt, tossing it in all directions.

"More?" I said out loud.

"More," I heard in my head. I poured in more and then I waited. There was only silence and the sound of the pump.

As I started to walk away, instead of "More," I heard, "Hungry." It gave me chills. I waited. A few minutes later, I heard "hungry" once more.

"What do you mean?" I said.

"So hungry."

"I don't know what to do," I replied.

The voice mumbled once more, "So hungry." Then the voice disappeared. I felt uneasy. The silence seemed ominous. Humans can do terrible things when they are hungry. What would a sea monster do?

I looked around the yard. It was mid-September in Texas. If I were a sometimes vegetarian sea monster, what would I eat?

I wandered upstairs to brainstorm with my mother. Etsi and Anna had brought a fan into the bedroom. I told Etsi I was making up a large sea creature for a class project.

"Krill," she said, not taking her eyes off the tablet Anna held. "Absolutely." In the past my mother would've been thrilled if I had shown any interest in marine biology. "Whales eat krill. Dolphins eat fish, though."

I thought of my sister's five goldfish downstairs, but quickly dismissed the idea. The death of a pet was supposed to be practice for the death of a human being, a family member. My sister didn't need practice.

It occurred to me that several grocery stores nearby sold live tilapia. I would just have to get to the grocery store. Maybe that would satisfy the pool being. In the meantime, I wandered back downstairs and pulled out all the frozen fish from the freezer. There were two large boxes of fish sticks, six fillets, two packages of salmon, two small trout, and one large whole bass. Etsi must have gotten them on sale and never had a chance to cook them before Edoda died. I wondered if I should defrost them. I put everything back but the trout and the bass, which I set in running warm water. I hoped my mother wouldn't wander downstairs.

When the fish was mostly thawed, I walked outside to the pool. I went to the deep end and set one of the trout into the water. It began to sink, but then it suddenly stopped and floated a foot or two above the pool's bottom. The fish seemed to be shrinking, its sides being sucked in, its dead eyes melting, staring at me. Empty it floated to the bottom of the pool. I grabbed the net on the long handle and fished the trout husk out of the water. I shook the net. It was a mere skin, boneless, no longer carrying any serious weight. I took it and dumped it over the back fence. Even before I walked back to the pool, the voice in my head whispered, "More."

I dropped the second trout into the pool. The same thing happened. I waited for the request for "more" before setting the bass in the water. It was heavier and I accidentally let my hand sink lower into the water than I meant to. Suddenly, I felt a warmth spread up through my fingers, past my wrist and across my chest. It was a perfect warmth, as if I had been cold and not known I needed heat. The feeling spread throughout my entire body. I hardly noticed the disappearance of the bass from my hand. It feels cheesy to say, but I felt a peace unlike anything I remembered feeling before. Is this what it feels like to not be sad, to feel unwanting? I walked back into the house on air.

For the first time in a long time, I fell into a peaceful sleep without a worry. When the air conditioner went out that night I simply went downstairs to sleep on the couch, stopping by my mother's room to get Anna. The upstairs would be well over ninety degrees before morning. My mother was awake. She assured me she was fine in her own bed, wrapped in a sweat-soaked sheet. Anna didn't argue, however, when I carried her to the much-cooler front-room couch.

Sakonige

The live pod is sending me messages, relaying those of Oceania and New Oceania. Warning me that the humans are circling closer to our hiding place. The task of getting the pod out and to the gulf that is a gateway to New Oceania is daunting. All I can do is focus on the feeling of being loved and missed and valued. In the embrace of my kith and kin, this can be borne a little longer . . .

Walela

As Mom dropped me off at school the next morning, she assured me she would call someone to look at the air-conditioning when she returned to the house. I suddenly remembered the fish emptied of their insides and before she drove off, I said, "Don't let Anna swim this evening, even if the house is hot. The pool chemistry's off, she'll get an ear infection."

My mother sighed before driving away.

The temperature hit one hundred and five by three o'clock. It was a record for that day in September.

For the first time since Edoda passed, I stayed at school for orchestra practice. A friendly girl named Hope dropped me off. The house was still miserably hot when I walked in. For the first time since Edoda died, NPR radiated through the radio's speakers in the kitchen. Beneath it a voice in my head spoke urgently, "Come!"

"Mom!" I hollered. "Anna?" I made my way to the back door.

As I stepped off the back porch, I saw Anna's head and shoulders bobbing awkwardly in the pool, her arms flailing, her life preserver nowhere in sight.

"Come!" Now the voice in my brain was shrieking.

I ran to the pool and jumped in, wrapping my arms around my sister and screaming, "Mom!" Anna struggled, nearly dragging me underwater, while the creature supported her legs.

My mother stumbled out of the house in her swimsuit muttering only, "Oh my God. Oh my God," over and over.

I stumbled up the pool steps, Anna clinging to me.

"How did this happen?" I yelled, not at Anna, but at my mother. My mother reached out for Anna, but she clung tight to me.

"I thought I could swim without my lifesaver," Anna cried.

My mother stammered. "The house was so hot. She wanted to go swimming. I told her to wait for me." She was blubbering now.

"What is wrong with you?" I hissed. "She could have died! You are her mother! You don't get to sleepwalk through your life because you're in pain. You don't get to ruin our lives because you're sad!"

My mother wasn't saying anything I could understand other than "I fell asleep after I put on my suit." She started crying. "Oh my God, I am so so sorry."

I was struggling to hold Anna who refused to be set down or taken by my mother. Her long skinny legs wrapped tight around my torso. I turned to go into the house and Mom rushed ahead of me to open the door, squeezing through right behind me to tell Anna she was sorry. I decided it was time for me to call Etlogi Ama. We definitely needed more help than I could manage. I gave her a call and explained to her what had been going on.

That night Ama called my mom. I heard Etsi go into her bedroom and shut the door. I listened through the door, but her side of the call was just a series of long silences, finishing with "Donadagohvi."

Suddenly, the bedroom door opened.

"Ama wants to talk to you," Etsi said, handing me her phone.

"Oh."

Etsi disappeared into Anna's room to help her get ready for bed.

"Ama?"

"It's a good thing you got in touch with me, Walela. You should have done it sooner."

"I guess so," I said.

"Your mom loves you. She just forgot." Ama waited for me to respond.

"That she loves me?" I finally said. There was a catch in my voice.

"She just forgot that when we pass we go where we want for nothing. Your father will be there when it's her time. She forgot how to mourn. This isn't the way. She needs to let him go. She needs to be where others can be there for her."

I didn't know what to say.

"I'll be there tomorrow. It's time your mom moved home. I'll see what I can do. You shouldn't be the only Cherokee people you know."

Etsi stayed in Anna's room talking to her and reading to her until she fell asleep. Eventually, I heard her go downstairs and out the back door. I was exhausted and trying to decide whether to follow her or go brush my teeth. Instead, I dozed off in my own bed. I jerked awake when I heard my mom open my bedroom door. She was wet. She dripped all over the beige carpet.

"Sissy, how long have they been in the bottom of our pool?" my mom asked.

I hesitated. She didn't sound accusatory. Finally, I just said, "Excuse me?"

Mom breathed in slow and deep. "Anna told me there was an alien at the bottom of our pool who saved her. She said they're dying."

I didn't say anything.

"Anna told me when she started sinking, they hugged her and took her to the air so she could breathe. She said while they held her, she could see their memories. She said a spaceship crashed into the prairie while they were on their way to another ocean."

I stared at Mom wide-eyed. "Wow," I said. "Just wow."

"Walela, I went down and checked. I didn't trust, but I did verify."

"Oh," I said. "Well, then . . ." I waited a moment. "Well, I just call them Sakonige."

My mother closed her eyes and tilted her head back, deep in thought.

"Sakonige saved her life, Walela. Anna was in the pool at least fifteen minutes." Tears were running from my mother's eyes now. "Anna could have died and it's my fault."

She was crying quietly now. I hated how guilty I suddenly felt. It didn't seem fair. Mom was the adult, not me. I was only fifteen and, yes, I had the benefit of mostly present parents that had allowed me to grow up semi-self-sufficient, but Anna was only six and still needed her etsi.

"Please don't call the police," I finally said.

It was my mother's turn to look incredulous. "Do you think I want to see Child Protective Services here? Get carted off?" A moment later she continued, "No one else would believe or understand. It doesn't sound wild to you because you've known for—how long?"

"A while," I finally admitted. "But I didn't know they were an alien."

We stared at each other.

As she walked into my room, she closed the door behind her and said, "Anna says they'll die if we don't get them to the ocean."

"What?"

"They're dying. They can't live in captivity. We have to get them to the ocean."

I took this in. I had no idea. "You know how to do that,

though, right? From when you worked at Sea World. I remember. You helped move dolphins."

My mother guffawed. "What you don't know is how hard and expensive it is. Sometimes they die anyway."

"Oh," was all I could say.

Suddenly Anna burst into my room. "We can't let them die." She put her arms around her mother. "They saved me when they didn't have to. Even though it was dangerous."

"Yeah, Mom," I agreed.

Mom leaned down and picked up my sister who was too big to be carried around.

"You're right," she said, hugging Anna. "Well, your Etlogi Ama will be here around dinnertime. Maybe we can all figure something out."

Realization dawned on me. "Ama drives a truck."

My mom nodded. Anna hugged her tight.

I walked out to the pool and thought hard to Sakonige. "You're going home," I said. "We're going to try to help you get home."

Home, I heard in my head. Home is where they love us. Home is where they are always waiting.

Home was what I lost when I lost my father. My mother and I have been homesick ever since.

Ama was there just as it started to get dark. The windows of the cab of her semi are tinted, so you can't see who is driving when you try to have a look. She is about five foot five and wears Ray-Bans all the time, her dark hair that frames her face making it hard to see her features. She looks rather like my mom's younger sister than her Aunt or second Aunt or whatever. Ama parked the truck near one of the unofficial roads into the park. It was a place other neighbors parked semis and campers they weren't allowed to park along the street. Etsi had already explained the situation to her. Etsi said she took it in stride. We drove her back to our house, then all of us went out to the pool.

Ama dove into the water. She swam several figure eights in the pool beneath the water. I was amazed at her ability to stay underwater so long.

Finally, she stepped out of the pool.

"'There are more things in heaven and earth, Horatio, than are dreamt of in your philosophy,'" she said.

"Well?" Etsi said.

"Looks like we're driving to Galveston."


Sakonige

I told them about the escape pod, hidden in the earth. I explained that the pod was alive, could shudder forward, roll toward us. The woman, Ama, is different from the others. Like me she sees in the dark. Together, we were able to guide the pod around the humans guarding the area. She walked out into the woods. She let me know how to avoid them. The mother and daughter waited at the wheel of the large truck, the back open, the truck's ramp down. As fast as Ama was, the pod was faster. Guided by Ama it avoided the humans and the surveillance equipment. Even the birds were quiet that night, though they warily watched the clear sphere speeding on its circuitous route across the prairie. Zipping out of a valley, it sped up a hill, flying into the air, targeting the back of the big truck where they waited. In the dark I made my way in too. Walela slammed the door shut.

Anna trusts me completely, but she hasn't watched me feed,

yet. Walela and her mother have a healthy amount of respect and fear. The feeling is mutual. Ama and me, we understand each other.

Their mother understands water and pH and sea creatures. Between us we are ready for a trip to the gulf.

Of course, knowing what these creatures are capable of, I'm wary. Some of them burrow into the deep, poisoning my family along with other creatures they have never seen in order to fuel their world. Harming the world that is their home, too. For now, we are refugees, but we are refugees who can fight when there is no longer anyplace to go.

## Koga

The people in black are confused. They stare at their devices and look where they can see nothing. They chase dots on a screen, but see nothing. They radio one another, asking what they see, but they see nothing. Signs are for people who know what they are looking for. You can't see what you don't understand.

## Walela

Last June before my father died, I made some rainbow bracelets with pony beads at Indian Summer Camp. Mom was teaching, too, but she spent most of that day outside helping students run water tests and teaching about things like turbidity and life in the water, the microscopic creatures that thrive or die depending on the quality of the Trinity River. There are places where the rights of rivers and creatures have been recognized, accepted as part of living with the planet. Not here, though—yet.

Indian Summer Camp is fun and I get to hang out with other urban Indian kids who aren't growing up on their homeland, for the most part. For a week I had friends, instead of being the queer kid who everyone talked about and not to. None of them raised their eyebrows or gave me a hard time about my choice of beading colors. A couple of them asked if I would make them one, too.

Ms. Arin wouldn't have put up with us being mean to each other. She would have noticed any low-key bullying. Some of the other kids had two moms or dads, so they just helped me find the beads I needed to repeat the rainbow around my wrist. I put the bracelet in my backpack and took it home. I never wore it, though. I just couldn't imagine talking to my etsi or edoda about something that personal.

When Etsi had tried to have the talk about periods I thought I would die of embarrassment, I said, "I have the internet, Mom. This is so unnecessary. And awkward."

Mom had pursed her lips and taken a deep breath. Then, as she turned and walked away, she said, "Well, as you already know, the supplies are in the bathroom." She sounded hurt, but I just couldn't talk to her about it.

As we got ready for our trip to the ocean, I pulled the bracelet out of my desk and put it on. I wasn't going to hide this part of me anymore.

### Sakonige

I'm going home. To our new home. My kin and kith are there waiting. My best friend and my teachers and the elders and my siblings. It's a new home, but it's where my family is. That is what makes it a home.

### Walela

Anna rode with my Aunt Ama in the truck cab. Mom and I followed closely behind in her car. She drove. I watched out for black vehicles following too closely. Mom was letting me control the music, her mind elsewhere while she navigated the dark road. Finally, I turned off the stereo.

"So, Etsi, do you support gay rights?"

My mom turned and looked at me, questioningly, but quickly returned her focus to the road. "Of course, I do. Have I ever given you any reason to believe otherwise?" Her face looked troubled.

I had to think about that for a minute. Had she? I'd never seen her laugh at or make fun of gay people. In a world that taught you homosexuality was wrong or abnormal through headlines and television broadcasts, you could never assume anyone was an ally. My experience in high school had certainly confirmed that some people who hadn't previously brought up the subject, sure had an opinion on it.

I ignored her question.

"I've been doing a lot of research on the internet."

"Research?" My mom was starting to get her alarmed tone.

"Yeah, I've taken some quizzes and I'm pretty sure I'm gay."

My mom's face froze.

I waited.

She took a deep breath. "So, you found out you're gay through an internet quiz?"

"Well, that, and I had a crush on Chloe."

"Oh."

Sometimes you can see your parents thinking. Teachers, too. Because you share a past, you can see them scanning their memory banks and processing things in real time. I saw her hastily brush a tear away before it could roll down her cheek. This was a terrible reaction. I realized I should not have started this conversation.

I pushed back anyway. "Are you crying because I'm a lesbian?"

Mom shook her head. She was watching the road. "I have to pull over," she said. "Text your etlogi."

I did. felt like there was a huge weight pressing into me and I felt like crying. What was she going to do? Mom pulled into the parking lot of a Braum's. When she turned off the car, she turned toward me.

"I was crying because I remember what it's like to lose a friend you have a crush on. And I hate that my daughter had to go through that."

I spoke without thinking, "Yeah, but was your friend a girl in your class who was supposed to be your BFF? Who rejected you and then told everyone else?"

Mom was really crying now. Then she nodded.

This wasn't how I thought this was going to go.

"So, are you telling me you're not straight, either?" I asked.

Mom shrugged and nodded, kind of at the same time. "I guess. I mean, I didn't have any role models for any kind of healthy relationships when I was your age. Not in my world or even in books, really. I just kind of stuffed all that down so my life would be easier. So nobody would talk about me or beat me up because of who I loved. That happened to the kids who were out a lot when I was in high school."

I nodded, "It still happens."

She nodded again. "I'm not as brave as you."

We were both quiet for several minutes. When she seemed to be done crying, I handed her a napkin from the glove compartment. Something was nagging me. I wanted to ask her while we were both already uncomfortable. Otherwise, I figured I never would.

"Well, what about Dad?" I said quietly.

Mom laughed, "Well, I always seemed to fall in love with my best friends. Your dad was the last best friend I ever had." Tears were pouring down her cheeks now.

I reached over and hugged her. My right shoulder was quickly soaked with her crying. I let go of her and fished another napkin from the glove box.

"Thanks," she sniffed. Then she said, "You still have to be careful, you know?" She raised her eyebrows, so it was clear I knew she was talking about sex. I cringed.

"God, Mom. See this is why I can't talk to you."

"I'm sorry," she wiped her arm across her weepy face.

"It's okay," I shrugged.

"I want some chocolate-raspberry ice cream," she said, gesturing toward the store. "Do you want something?"

"Yeah. We need some protein for Sakonige, too." I looked at her. "You're a mess. Let me go in and get it."

Mom handed me some cash and I went in. I got some fish for Sakonige and ordered french fries and gravy, because that's my mom's favorite comfort food. I got her that raspberry-chocolate cone and myself a rainbow sundae, just because. When I showed it to her, we laughed. We ate and we laughed.

And that was how I found out my mom was queer.

## Sakonige

Ama parked her truck on a deserted road that ran along the coast and opened the back doors. She reached out and touched the sphere and said, "You be careful out there. And if you see Uktena, tell him to stay put."

The pod was almost invisible as it rolled onto the beach in the moonlight. The rest of the family stood on the beach.

In my heart, I could feel my family waiting for me, singing songs that would help me find my way. Anna was already running along the edges of the waves, her bare feet dancing across the sand. Walela and Dani seemed lighter than before. A sadness had lifted.

Among my kind we don't speak farewells or love or thank

you. There is no need to say the things that are obvious in the way you treat each other. You feel it the same way you feel electricity, the wind, water, the sun. It is both wonderful and difficult to never be misunderstood.

Anna, Walela, Dani, and Ama could feel my relief, my gratitude. Words would have been poor substitutes. As my sphere rolled toward the water, the mother sat down on the beach. She watched as my escape pod rolled out, seemingly just adrift on the waves.

"Welcome home," I heard my people call.

"Home is where they love you," I responded.

Before taking the escape pod below the waves, I looked back once more at the people who had saved me. If there were more people who cared, who believed in the rights of all living things, maybe the planet could be saved. The mother welcomed her two daughters to sit beside her. Ama stood behind them, a gentle hand on the mother's shoulder. They were still waving and holding each other when I took my pod deep into the ocean.

# The Zombies Attack the Drive-In!

*q*

Charlotte Henry
Kyyegwona 4, 2039
07/04/2039

"Your parents will always disappoint you, Charlotte," Etsi said as she set down the yellowed Easter card she had found. She glanced over at my sister who was sleeping after a bout of asthmatic wheezing, before she added, "And loving your kids will break your heart."

Etsi was sitting at the dining table, the one with the yellow Formica top and chrome legs, reading letters and cards she had never seen before from a father who was merely a name on a birth certificate. When her mother died in California, someone had sent back boxes of her things, and inside this box was a variety of mail. Postmarks with dates spanning twelve years of absence and addresses from both coasts were arranged across the table. All were addressed to my mother and had been, previously, unopened. Etsi was careful to keep each card with its envelope as she tried to piece together the life of a father she didn't know. We had taken refuge in her childhood home a couple years ago. Her Aunt Audrey had helped raise her here along with her Grandma and Grandpa Spears. She had married our father, taking the name Dawson, but once our world started over, we began using Mom's maiden name.

"I think my mother kept all the money my dad sent me," Etsi remarked.

A sudden bang at the front door made us both jump. Twilight had snuck up on us and now our front doorknob shook. Etsi looked through the peephole.

"It's Old Bob," she said. She reached for the compound bow we kept by the door.

My sister stirred on the couch. Etsi used her lips to point toward her as she grabbed one of the masks hanging next to the front door. It was time to use the defense plan we had practiced regularly for a year after fleeing my father. If it had been my father, Ruth and I would have hidden in the pantry, locked it from the dark inside.

Before I went to my sister, I peered out the peephole. Old Bob had shuffled across a long field and crossed the road that separated our properties. He had that fresh-dead look. His milky blue eyes rolled in his skull, searching for movement. Old Bob was the first zombie to wander up to our door since the power grid went down.

I knelt next to the couch beside my sister. Beneath Ruth's lids her eyeballs flickered. I patted her sweaty arm. Old Bob sniffed loudly along the door frame.

I was going to count to seven loudly, so Mom had time sneak out the back door. My sister startled awake. I put my hand on her to calm her.

"Sagwu, tali, tsoi, nvgi, hisgi, sudali, gahlgwogi." Then I hollered loudly, "Who is it?"

Old Bob slammed his body violently against the door. It shuddered in its frame. The knob began to yank back and forth. Fright erupted in my body, though I tried to stay calm when I heard Mom yell and a low moan escaped Old Bob. Arrows are silent and deadly. I held my breath until Mom finally called my name. I leaned down and kissed my little sister's cheek before I grabbed the ax, leather gloves, and another mask from the pantry. By the time I unbolted the door, Mom was already dragging Bob's body to the ditch across the road. A smear of red gore left a path worthy of a post-apocalyptic Hansel and Gretel.

Etsi fished Bob's truck keys out of his pocket before taking the ax and making a messy job of chopping off his head.

"We'll move him a few miles away later," she said. "Let's go get the truck." Our own car was out of gas and hadn't been reliable even before the plague.

In the house, Ruth already had her shoes and mask on when I went to fetch her.

We scavenged what we could from outside of Old Bob's house. Even with masks and gloves, we wouldn't risk entering the house until the weather turned cold. This wasn't our first plague. Without contact with the world outside we still didn't know how long the virus lived, how likely it was that we'd catch it. We quickly filled the bed of the blue Ford with tools, a roll of barbed wire, another ax, and some new plywood. Then we drove back to our place.

Looking up at the sky, Mom muttered, "Dammit."

Already vultures soared above Bob's body. They wouldn't land, smelling disease, but they might attract unwanted and dangerous attention.

Etsi told Ruth to stay inside the truck while she and I dealt with moving Bob's body. His eyes crawled with flies and they kept landing on the homemade bandage stained brown and yellow between his left wrist and elbow. He hadn't believed the Zombie Flu would touch us out here and railed against an as-yet-unavailable vaccine.

"You watch," he said, before the world fell apart. "Somebody is going to report you if you cough and the CDC will show up at your door and haul you away." When he spoke like this, it was with such vitriol you could see the spit shooting from his mouth. The tribe had sent masks and sanitizer and commodities before the power grid went down. We made sure to make use of it all when Bob came to our door.

We had seen zombies in the streets of cities before the television went out a few weeks earlier. Seeing a neighbor dead because of the sickness was different.

Etsi noticed my fear. She made sure her plastic gloves were intact and then stepped up next to Bob and pulled the bandage away with care. A bloody crescent bite mark was in the center of a forearm—swollen and red—and yellowed skin and dried blood accompanied the fading bruises.

"He was bitten," she reassured me. "But leave your mask on and wash up when we get home." We were lucky we had a spring house in the backyard.

Etsi stretched out the tarp. She put one edge over Old Bob, then she rolled him up like an unwanted carpet. I helped her lift him into the back of the truck. Then I helped her left him out at the end of a deserted gravel road. Etsi said a prayer to Unelanvhi as we laid the tarp in the field.

Ruth started singing the first two lines of *Amazing Grace,* "Unelanvhi uwetsi-igaguyvhei-" Mom and I joined her. For the most part, the Zombie Flu had made funerals obsolete. But hymns and prayers were still important.

Back home, I picked up the Easter card. The cartoon bunny smelled of cigarette smoke and dust. A fluffy cotton tail and googly eyes were slightly smashed. Inside, a handwritten message said:

"The Easter bunny asked me to send five dollars so you can get some eggs."

Etsi took the card from me and dropped it back in the box. "It looks like my father thought my mother was taking care of me. He was sending her money electronically. She never even told him she dumped me on Grandma and Grandpa Spears and Aunt Sissy."

Two years earlier, my father had broken my mother's arm and threatened to kill me and Ruth. I thought of what she had said about being let down by your parents. "You haven't disappointed me," I said.

My mother shrugged and took the box back to her grandmother's closet.

The post-domestic-violence-pre-apocalyptic period of our life had lasted almost two years. We lived in survival mode in my grandparents' house in the woods of Cherokee County. We never went back to our home in Tulsa. We kept an ax by the door and a handgun above the sill. We had a rifle, but it was for right-handed shooters, so I struggled using it. Etsi bought an antique portable DVD player and started collecting cheap classic movies and musicals at thrift stores and pawnshops.

For nearly a year, she was afraid to send us to school, so instead we watched movies and educational television broadcasts from Arkansas. I learned about sex from *Grease*, irritating my mother by humming "There Are Worse Things I Could Do" while I did the dishes. We borrowed a left-handed rifle from Old Bob and she taught me how to use it. When we heard that Dad had filed for divorce because he met someone else, Etsi and Aunt Sissy decided it was safe for us to return to school. A lawyer handled the paperwork so we never had to see him. We ordered new birth certificates and got a second round of vaccinations because Dad had destroyed everything we left behind. I tried not to think about what might have happened to our pet rabbit. Forgetting is an art. It can be practiced and perfected.

Etsi picked me up a journal in a thrift store, not realizing it was lightly written in. I read the stories of a girl named Joy and her irritation with her brother, Dylan, and her love for her Grandma Stone, a talented beader. After those entries, I made lists of the things we lost when we ran.

1. Our pet rabbit, Harvey.

2. Letters and postcards from my Aunt Ama who lived in Europe.

3. Old family photos that Mom never scanned.

There were plenty of more recent photos on my mom's phone. Certainly, no shortage of my father. My father had a charming smile and twinkly blue eyes that made him seem kinder than he was. He was left-handed, too. In every photograph, he wore the leather motorcycle jacket with AIM patches all over it that my mother had found at Goodwill. My father had never been a member of the American Indian Movement. He had issues about not looking Cherokee enough, though, so maybe that's why he wore it all the time.

Those were the kinds of things that mattered before the Zombie Flu.

Fear of zombie attack wasn't that much different than the way we had feared our father for a year. Except now we didn't have to pay the electric bill and could no longer watch old movies, and we added face masks to the hooks beside the door. Old Bob gave us the compound bow when the power grid went down.

"Noise draws them," he said, standing on our porch without a mask. "Heard it on my radio."

After the pandemic began, Mom, Ruth, and I stayed together almost all the time, once again. Being together felt safe, but I was fifteen and the togetherness quickly got on my nerves. We went outside to gather supplies, hunt with the compound bow, and garden or harvest plants. We missed the too-brief months when we had had a Cherokee community.

During that time, we had met Etlogi King and our cousins. At school we had started to make friends. With Etlogi Sissy we attended the Cherokee Methodist Church where the choir sang hymns in Cherokee. When Aunt Sissy took sick, all the older women in the church brought food to the house. My mom's dear friend, who we called Edutsi Dagsi, brought his granddaughter Elissa and cooked the meal for Etlogi Sissy's funeral. We went to beginner Cherokee language classes at our schools. We went to stomp dances and Hog Fries and Wild Onion dinners.

At Christmas, Edutsi Turtle invited Etsi to help him cook for the Christmas powwow in Park Hill. Etsi turned the golden bread in the hot oil for hours until there was enough to feed over two hundred people. They served fried pork, fried chicken, frybread, fried potatoes, and a variety of cakes. Ruth and I sat in some chairs on a Pendleton. We watched the dancing. Uncle Turtle had brought his daughter's shawls for us to borrow. His granddaughter Elissa, who was Cherokee and Seminole, showed us how to line up to dance during the intertribals. Later in the evening, the powwow committee invited Edutsi Turtle and Etsi out to be honored with a cook's song. They laid a blanket on the floor in front of Edutsi Turtle and Etsi and the Park Hill Thunder Drum group played and sang, while the community danced to honor them. At the end the blanket was covered in dollar bills, and Edutsi Turtle gave it to my etsi to count. Then he told her to keep half to get Christmas for Ruth and me. Etsi was stunned and grateful. Being in a tribal community wasn't always perfect. Like anyplace else, there was jealousy, infighting, politics. But that Christmas powwow was perfect. We have the photos on our phone to prove it. We used to have the social media posts. I don't know if it's good or bad that scrapbooks moved online. So much to remember, so much to forget.

At night, we covered the windows with plywood and burned candles or oil lamps while we ate and talked. Sometimes my mother would have us pick out a classic DVD and we'd take turns telling each other what happened in it. When Ruth and Mom retold the stories, they never went the way I remembered them.

Etsi tried to take over teaching us Cherokee from some books Elisi Agayvli Mary Spears had bought her, even though neither one of them had grown up speaking our language.

"ah. ay. ee. oh. oo. uhn," she would say, pointing at the first line of the syllabary. Ruth and I knew it from school, but we complied.

"ah ay ee oh oo uhn," we would repeat.

Etsi tried to give our days structure. She had saved an article by Will Chavez about the thirteen Cherokee Lunar Months. They had cool names like Bone Moon or Green Corn, names that referred to natural time, a time structured around the earth and the seasons. In the spring we gathered the wild onions that grew along the creeks. We cooked them into eggs, served them over frybread with a bowl of beans. Sweetened it all with honey that tasted like clover fields. It was the best meal we ever ate. We ignored holidays celebrating violence. Certain holidays had always been bittersweet to Etsi anyway, knowing history. She loved a big winter meal. She loved fireworks, but said she felt funny celebrating the birth of a country that, even in 1776, was well on its way to trying to eradicate or assimilate the Indigenous population.

We had to admit, though, we had once been grateful for a day off for any national holiday. Previously, we usually spent the Fourth in a cool movie theater. We ate popcorn and chocolate almonds for dinner and kept refilling the Slurpee we shared. We hung out in the cinema until just before the fireworks shows started.

My sister was once a rambunctious kid. She wore skirts with

shorts under them so she could hang upside down on the monkey bars or climb trees without showing her panties. The stress of the Zombie Flu wore on her, though, and her asthma had gotten worse. At night, Ruth began to sleep right next to my mother. I tried not to feel left out as they squished together on the couch. To show I didn't care, I made a pallet on the floor on the other side of the room. Sometimes, though, I woke up and crawled over to put my hand on my sister's small body, waiting for the rise and fall of breath so I could be sure she was still breathing when everything was too quiet.

We were lucky that most of the land surrounding the house had been cleared for fields. No one could sneak up on us if we were vigilant. They had to cross dead field after dead field. I wanted a gitli, but Etsi said the barking might be dangerous. I didn't know how hard it would be to find a barkless dog in the end times.

There was a large sedi tree next to the house which we made sure to keep watered. Once we broke them open, the meat from the walnuts was so good. And the shells could be boiled to make a natural dye. I found a rope and hung a tire from it. I climbed in and swung myself as hard as I could. I pushed with both legs when I got close to the ground. The weight of the tire answered my jump. I leaned back and closed my eyes, trying to remember not to squeal, though my stomach had other ideas. When I tired of pushing myself I just let the rope spin, watching as the world seemed to rotate around me.

Then I went in to get Ruth. I made her promise not to make a lot of noise. You never knew what might be drawn to a scream. Etsi came out and sat watching from the back stoop. I pushed and pushed, throwing my whole body into it. Eventually, the rope stretched so much even Ruth's feet were dragging the ground. Etsi asked if we could modify the design. I said sure. It was too low and I would have to adjust it anyway. Etsi went back in the house to get some tools. She came out with a box cutter and an old-fashioned hand drill.

We took the tire off the rope. We set an old outdoor table under the tire just below where the rope dropped. Etsi and I drilled three holes equidistant apart. Then she tied two pieces of extra rope to the main rope and I helped her get the whole thing re-hung level. When we were done, all three of us were able to swing together. Some nights we went out and watched the stars. On cloudless nights they were brilliant. You could see the constellations, could see why people believed the stars were shiny bright beings, or some Cherokee boys who only wanted to play, and escaped their families and the cornfield by going to live in the sky and becoming what others call the Pleiades. Or how the Milky Way looked like corn spilled across the sky by a hungry gitli. The dog story always led to Ruth asking Etsi about the Doberman her grandma once had, that would grab the rope of a tire swing and pull the kids around the base of another tree.

Occasionally, after Ruth fell asleep, my mom would try to talk to me. Her voice was edged with a loneliness that frightened me, a longing for a friend. I recognized that hunger in myself and it bothered me. I was afraid that if I started talking, I would tell her too much, admit things I would later feel embarrassed to have said out loud, especially to my mother. Sometimes it's better not to know someone too well, I thought. I didn't want to know how afraid she was. I wanted her to tell me everything was going to be okay, that no matter what happened she could fix it. Sometimes I would pretend I was asleep. She would whisper my name a few times and then sigh. I think she knew I was awake. I wonder sometimes if I will ever forgive myself for refusing to be my mother's friend.

Ruth had been having more trouble at night, wheezing and needing her inhaler more frequently. One night, I awoke and noticed
her labored breathing.

"Mom," I said, standing over them both. I was already holding Ruth's inhaler.

Etsi woke, unconfused about why I was waking her. This was
happening often enough that she probably dreamed about it.

Ruth was groggy. I held a flashlight to her hand and saw her
fingernails had a dark tint.

"My chest hurts," Ruth stammered. She had already taken
two puffs, but they didn't seem to be working. Scavenging inhalers had been one of the first things Etsi did. The last time she had
gone out alone to scavenge and look for people, though, she
had come back shook, and covered in blood and bruises. Since
then she had stayed close to home, said leaving wasn't worth it
just yet. We thought we had what we needed.

I guess the expiration dates on medicine are there for a
reason.

I felt myself start to cry. I didn't want Ruth to see how scared
I was. Etsi sent me to the pantry for the other inhalers we had
stored there.

It made no difference. Ruth died there on the couch in our
arms.

Etsi carried Ruth to Grandmother's bedroom. She shut the
door, but I could hear her wails. I curled up on the couch and
cried. It was too unfair. We should never have been hiding from
my father in a house far from medicine and doctors. What if we
had been closer to other people, people who cared about protect-
ing our community, instead of forty-five minutes from town, the
nearest neighbors on their own 160 acres? We didn't even know
what was going on outside in the world. We were ignorant and
imprisoned and it was my father's fault. And I knew wherever he

was, my father was alive, that was the kind of man he was. Not a survivor in a noble way, but the kind of man who would sacrifice everyone around him to save his worthless self.

Suddenly, I heard Mom's crying stop.

I got up and went to the bedroom door and found it locked. "Mom?"

"Don't come in!" Etsi screamed.

"Mom, what's happening? Please open the door," I cried.

"Don't come in!" Etsi yelled. "I'm sorry. I didn't know. I love you, Charlie."

I heard growls, a throaty, ferocious sound, and then my mother screamed in pain.

"Don't come in, Charlie! Don't ever come in." There was a scuffling sound and something heavy struck the other side of the door.

"Charlie, I'm going to block the door. But you should go, baby—" The voice of my etsi cut off. The violent noises increased. The door shook with the weight of bodies pressing into it.

"Mom!" I screamed.

"Run, baby—" I heard the sound of heavy furniture sliding across the wood floors and thudding.

"Etsi!" I sobbed. I was so loud I was oblivious to anything else. I finally stopped to take a breath, but the sounds I could then hear were too horrible. I ran and got the ax and ran toward the back door, the emergency exit, the escape path. I locked the door behind me and pushed it shut. My mother wasn't crying anymore. In the dark, I stumbled toward Old Bob's Ford. Not knowing what else to do, I climbed in and locked the doors. I thought of my mom returning from the outside world covered in bruises and blood. I sat on the floorboards of the passenger seat and wept most of the night.

When I stopped crying, I foolishly wondered if my mother

had allowed herself to be killed in order to escape. Made a Sophie's Choice, left me behind, less loved, more alone than I had ever imagined. Etsi used to say, "When you're a parent, you really only have one job. To keep your kids alive." Now with Etsi gone, who was going to make sure I didn't die?

In the morning I took the truck keys and an empty water bottle from the truck's floorboards and filled it at the spring house. Then I got back into the truck and locked myself in. We had a good garden and a few times I carefully got out of the truck, ever aware of the house. I grabbed some tomatoes or a melon and got back in the Ford. I turned on the truck's electrical long enough to put the windows down a little, but it was hot anyway. I thought hard about what to do, but did nothing except what I had to that whole day. I would put the windows most of the way up, grateful the truck was in shade, and fall asleep for short spans of time. I was terrified I would wake to the face of my little sister, trying to reach in and grab me, and I startled from bad dreams more than I slept.

I've learned a lot about zombies since then. Zombies prefer darkness. They lumber around from just before twilight to dawn, but they're loud and don't hear well. They stir out of the woods as it gets dark. They're slow, but plenty dangerous. They follow their noses. If you bump into a zombie in the dark, you're dead. A zombie is all olfactory and teeth and hunger. If you want to hunt zombies, you go after them in the dark with a bright flashlight and a compound bow. The problem is the people who aren't zombies, but aren't good, either. They wander around day and night.

On the second day, I saw the figure on the horse coming down the road at twilight. I held on to the ax and wished I had a more long-distance weapon. Why hadn't I grabbed the compound bow? Oh, yeah, because I was afraid my family was wandering around inside the house that was no longer a home.

A dog ran alongside the horse and rider, sometimes running ahead, but not barking, then turning back toward the rider. I was afraid to move, make a noise, roll up the windows. As they got closer, I saw the dog run toward the truck. I ducked lower.

"Go away, you stupid gitli," I prayed silently.

The dog never barked. I smelled the horse as it came alongside the truck. From my spot in the floorboard, I was looking into the face of my mother astride the horse. For a moment I was relieved.

"Auntie?" I whispered.

Ama climbed down off the horse. I reached up and unlocked the truck door.

"Charlie?" She reached in and helped me up from the floor of the truck. My legs were stiff and I was clumsy. She took the ax from my hands and laid it across the bench seat. I stood shakily with my arms at my sides, not quite knowing what to do. I was grateful when she reached out and pulled me to her. I began to cry hard. When I gasped for air, I breathed in the scent of horse and the strangely clean smell of Ama. She let me cry until I was spent, holding me tight, running her hand down the back of my head to my back occasionally, comforting me the way I had comforted Ruth so many times.

It seemed impossible that Etlogi Ama was standing in our yard. She held me tight. "I'm sorry," she whispered into my black hair.

"I know," I said, through sniffles.

Finally, she whispered, "Tell me what happened." And I did. I started with my father breaking my mother's arm when she refused to listen to one more excuse, and ended with Mom's dying in the house in the arms of my undead little sister.

Anger burned in my aunt's eyes. "Do you know where your father is?"

I shook my head. I hated him. If he wasn't dead, I wanted him dead. I never wanted to see him again.

Ama looked toward the house.

"Get back in the truck and lock the doors," she said. "Go ahead and put the windows down. Amegwoi will let you know if there are any others around." She indicated the horse with her lips. "Don't worry. I may be a bit." Ama reached into the truck and picked up the ax. I got back in the truck to wait. She tied the horse's reins to the truck mirror. "C'mon, Gitli," she said to the dog.

Overhead the moon was full and a cloud floated over it. The world was light enough to see Ama and the dog disappear into the dark house. I nodded off for a while. I woke when Ama came back, her face and hair wet with spring water.

"Let's go in," she said, meaning all of us. I looked at her quizzically. "It's okay," she reassured me. "Just don't go down the hall. Ocean is a very clean horse, but she'll stay in the kitchen."

Once in the house, Ama made me something to eat. We were lucky the propane tank had been filled before the world broke down. I didn't much want the spaghetti squash she boiled, but I picked at it.

"I am going to work tonight and sleep tomorrow. It'll be up to you to watch over us, then," she said, as I lay down on my pallet. She had found the good shovel in the pantry and disappeared with it out the back door.

I was grateful that she let me sleep while she prepared the bodies. She also dug the single grave. At dawn the birds began to sing to each other, announcing they had made it through one more night. Ama and I went outside to the old family cemetery.

We prayed over Etsi and Ruth. There was no dirt hitting the top of a coffin, only the soft fall of soil onto the quilt my Elisi Agayvli Spears had made. I remembered the before times of open coffins in funeral homes and large community dinners afterwards. I missed that, but I didn't think it would have been much comfort in my dazed state. It would have just been something to get through, the food tasteless. I didn't need to see them in a coffin to know they were gone. Maybe we all are, I thought, numbly.

When we finished Ama said, "Tonight, we'll go to town. We'll take the truck."

At dusk, Ama had me lead Amegwoi into the kitchen, where she would be safe and the linoleum easiest to clean. Before I did, Ama warned me, "You know, people and animals aren't supposed to share a house. That's how diseases start. So, be real careful, wash up when you're done seeing to her."

On the bench seat of the truck between us sat Gitli, the compound bow, a rifle, and the pistol. On the way to Tahlequah we drove by Old Bob's, and Ama went in and retrieved Bob's other compound bow. She filled up a can of gas from Bob's reserve in the shed and refilled the truck's tanks.

The streets of the capital of the Cherokee Nation were empty. Ama drove straight to the pharmacy. Etsi had practiced the syllabary with us each morning and I could read the street signs lit up by the moon. They were in English and Cherokee. I wouldn't have known what most of them said, but I knew how to say the words.

"You know," Ama said, "this building has always been a pharmacy."

I looked around to see where she had read that, then remembered she grew up in the area. She probably knew lots of stuff about the town I didn't. She handed me a flashlight and told me to keep it pointed down at the ground. I wondered why she didn't need one. We got out and walked into the brick building to see what was left. Before we opened the door, I adjusted my mask and face shield.

The door was unlocked. I followed Ama inside. It had been ransacked, the shelves left mostly empty. I wondered if this was where Mom had come the last time and the hairs on the back of my neck tingled. Ama held the compound bow at the ready and went to check the back. She returned quickly.

"Let's go," she said, quietly. But before she opened the door, she stopped. On the front door was a movie poster, a piece of red, black, and white artwork.

Ama pulled it off and read it, before handing it to me. The silk-screened print advertised a limited run of *The Shining* at a place called the Lost City Drive-In. When I was twelve, my mom had begged me to watch that movie with her. I fled from the room when it was over, telling her I never wanted to see it again, never wanted to see Jack Nicholson again.

"That guy's a monster," I cried. Too close to home, I guess.

*Showing every Friday in August in perfect 35 mm*, the poster screamed. *Price of admission: Cherokee Language mate-rials, DVDs, ammo, canned food, celluloid, medicine. People needed: Cherokee speakers and culture experts, medical, solar, and hydro technicians, electrical engineers, horticulturists, projectionists. A free can of soda with every DVD from the Crite-rion Collection. Soda + popcorn for every Wes Studi film.* On a separate sheet of paper was the schedule for Saturday night, a family film early, followed by something for the older crowd. Was it sweet, the attempt for normalcy? Or a ploy to lure suckers into the Drive-In?

In spite of myself, for the first time in a year, hope spread like fever in my body. It was the kind of hope that will kill you (or somebody) if it's thwarted. My mother's classic DVD collection had seemed worthless once the power went off. Now it was a highly desired property.

I handed the poster back, though I kind of wanted to keep it. Ama returned it to the door. On the way back to the truck I tried to walk quietly, to not make the kind of stupid mistakes people in horror movies make while the audience screams, "Don't go in there!" What we had to offer was my mother's legacy to me. From *Whatever Happened to Baby Jane?* to Lon Chaney's *Wolf Man*, the films had promised a better time, a shared culture like the stories we still tell that are old and timeless. I wondered what actors and directors and writers had survived, seen the great flood that washed the scum off the earth.

"We'll go tomorrow night," Ama said. "When we get back, pack up some things. I need to get a horse trailer, do some other stuff. We'll sleep tomorrow and go in the dark."

"Please stay, Ama, or let me go with you." I was begging. I know I was. "It's dangerous out there." She had been so close when Ruth died. If she had been there, things might have been different, I thought. What if she didn't come back?

"They don't bother me," she said, as she shook her head. "I'll be close by. Stay in the house until I come back."

Tears burned the corners of my eyes, but I agreed.

When we got back, she made sure I had a flashlight. She checked the pantry door to make sure it was secure, in case I had to hide in there while she was gone. She gave me several weapons, including a bayonet she said was from World War I. Then she had me lock the door from the inside one last time. In the dead quiet, I heard Ama checking the house. I almost cried when I heard her start up the truck. Once more she didn't turn on the headlights, but I heard her drive away. I didn't think I could drive in the dark like Ama.

I packed bags and boxes with useful things. DVDs, Cherokee

language books, canned food, sleeping bags, all the guns and bows and fishing and frog gigs. I moved everything to the back door, stopping occasionally to pet Amegwoi. She was a gentle giant. Ocean is an interesting name for a horse. When Ama returned close to dawn, I saw blood on her white T-shirt. I felt my chest clench.

"Ama? Were you bitten?"

Ama gave me an odd look and I pointed with my chin toward the blood splatter on her shirt.

"No," she said. "I told you, those things don't bother me."

We made pallets in the pantry, but I had trouble falling asleep. I found myself telling Ama, again, about the last time I had seen my father. It was outside of Claremore Indian Hospital, where my mother had just had her arm set, and was supposed to stay a few hours for observation for a head injury. He was shaking me and screaming, "Don't you ever hang up on me!" before he ended up in the back of a police car. He glared at my mother, his face close to the window, warning her that if she left, he would find her and kill us all. He spent a night in jail while we packed what few things we could in a cousin's car.

I tried not to envy Ruth and Mom leaving this broken world, and I wished they were still here. My ancestors had been forced from Georgia onto this plot of land. It had passed down to Etsi and Ama. When we fled my father it was our fortress. I imagined there had always been a rifle next to the door. How different were zombies from the soldiers and settlers who wanted our land? The spiral that was history was exhausting when you could recognize it.

Ama drove us toward the Lost City Drive-In. Two miles away, she pulled off along a dirt road. Gitli hopped out of the back of the truck. Ama unloaded Amegwoi from the trailer, then helped me up onto the horse's back and climbed up behind me. We each carried a compound bow. Around my neck hung a pair of binoculars. We could hear the drive-in before we could see it. "Immigrant Song" was playing through many speakers. We headed in its direction using the road until we got close. Then we crossed a field and climbed an obsolete cell tower. I heard the weird echoey ricochet of a single rifle shot firing away from our direction. In the cell tower's nest, I trained my binoculars on the people on a wall of scaffolding and wire and boards surrounding an area much larger than the drive-in grounds. They were armed with rifles, and, occasionally, swept their scopes to the edges of the woods and grasses growing around the drive-in.

We could see and hear the film from our vantage point. When the first film began, I began to cry. Ama pulled me to lean against her as I wept through the story of an old guy who realizes people matter more than stuff, after he and his cartoon wife work hard all their lives, never go anywhere, and can't have a baby. At intermission, through swollen eyes, I scanned the crowd through the binoculars. I wondered if there would be people down there, good people, people that would have made Etsi happy.

"They're watching us," Ama said.

A watcher on the wall had been looking at me through a pair of binoculars. As soon as he saw that I was looking at him, he smiled and waved. His long hair was tied back in a braid.

I sat down in the tower's nest again and breathed heavily.

"What should we do?" I asked Ama.

Intermission was over.

"I guess we should check it out."

"Will you stay?"

Ama didn't answer. She took the binoculars and scanned the drive-in. "I miss movies," she said.

"The popcorn smells really good," I prodded.

"Does it?"

There were people over there. People who made art, and loved movies, and wanted to speak Cherokee, and they had popcorn with movie butter flavoring. We climbed back down and rode Ocean to the packed truck.

"We don't have to go," Ama said. "I can stay with you at the house. We'll be fine."

"I'm tired of hiding," I sniffled. I thought of Mom and how much she loved *The Shining*. Suddenly, I wanted to get to the drive-in before Shelley Duvall completely lost her mind.

The Lost City Drive-In turned out to be a community of college students, artists, Cherokees and other Indians, and the staff of Hastings Indian Hospital. The college students had been trying to figure out a way to reopen the drive-in before the Zombie Flu hit.

"When Creator closes a door, he opens a window," one of the artists told me, laughing. Small homes and tents dotted the edges of the grounds. Children ran around hollering at each other in Cherokee. No one was in charge. People did what they were good at. Some people didn't like it and left. Some people didn't fit and were asked to leave. Some people talked about sovereignty and threw around words like *post-colonial* and *post-tribal*. Clearing rivers was a priority and there was talk of sending ambassadors to other tribes. Ama said the Navajo Nation had organized, too, and the Blackfoot Confederacy had spread back out across the land that was once a man-made border between Canada and the United States. According to her, First Nation reserves were more worried about white invaders than zombies. In our community, there was talk of electing a chief, but enough people said we needed seven like in the old days, so a vote hasn't yet been organized. Others maintained that instead of recreating the old world, we should be cautious, not accidentally recreate the same problematic one that had destroyed itself. Be intentional, we told ourselves, recognize the rights of the land and the water. In the remaking of the world was a life my mother, my etsi, would have loved, a place she would have liked to have raised us within. Instead of being sad she never got to see it, I tried to live the way she wanted me to, to live like she was in the room with me. My life became an honor song for Etsi and my sister.

Ama didn't exactly make friends. People gave her a wide berth. The people who worked in the language department sometimes showed up toward evening to talk to her about words they couldn't recall. A lot of times she'd shake her head, say she just couldn't remember herself, hadn't used it in so long. Then later she might be talking about something and suddenly she would remember. She'd write it down. I'd run it to the Cherokee schoolteachers the next morning.

I took work hunting and gathering and went on sentry with Ama the nights she worked the wall. I wanted to be able to defend my new family the way I hadn't been able to when we lived in fear from my dad. I didn't want to be afraid anymore. There were tribal policemen called the Lighthorse, but Ama didn't join them, though she took night work. The Lighthorse had existed since the 1800s. They patrolled the area, cleared nearby zombies, and looked for survivors. If people had to be run off or needed an ear cropping, the Lighthorse did that. In Cherokee traditional law, it had once been up to your family to avenge a murder or a rape, but now the Lighthorse had taken that over as well. Some families were extended. Most were like mine, small. Decimated.

On the fourth of Kuyegwona, I volunteered Ama and I to be on the wall. It's not really a wall. It's the scaffolding the students used to repaint the lower half of the drive-in's damaged screen, then expanded. It puts you higher than the twelve-foot wooden fence, higher than the sixteen-foot barbed wire and chain link that surrounds the drive-in. Each night, as the sunlight faded, the noise of the films and movie soundtracks lured the undead from the woods.

At sunset, they began playing "Ride of the Valkyries." This was like petitioning the universe for a celluloid version of *Apocalypse Now*. It was an audio prayer wheel, mourning the perfect things of the imperfect world that had destroyed itself.

Until it got dark enough for the screen, they played the soundtrack from the first film of the night. While the music from *Grease* pulsed, I scanned the perimeter for the zombies that wander out of the darker woods when our stereos kick on. I noticed crows moving around the wood's edges, calling to one another in warning. I saw Ama was watching closely, too. Something big was moving around.

A zombie lurched out of the pecan grove into the field of grass. His senses were keyed in to the smell of popcorn and Olivia Newton-John and John Travolta singing, "You're the One That I Want."

"I got chills, they're multiplying," I sang. Ama let me take aim at the zombie. I targeted his nose in my sight. Sweat rolled into my left eye, blinding me briefly. I blinked several times. Up this high, there was a slight breeze. I felt it when I shifted my shoulders, my perspiration-damp hoodie touching the back of my recently shaved neck. I had my finger on the trigger when I saw the zombie's head explode and heard a shot. The zombie took three more steps, then went down. I looked toward the woods.

A man stepped slowly from between the trees, his rifle still perched on his left shoulder. He lowered his gun and a woman walked up next to him. She was carrying a small child. She handed him the baby and took a machete from his belt. She could have been a younger version of my mother. She even had one black eye. She walked toward the zombie to finish the job. The man turned and looked back into the woods. He was still wearing the motorcycle jacket my mother had given him, the AIM patch on the shoulder. The toddler girl he carried resembled the baby pictures of the little sister I had watched die a year earlier.

The woman put the machete in her belt and took the baby. It occurred to me that the girl might also be my sister. My father reshouldered the rifle. I watched him scan the perimeter before finding me and Ama. Ama, who looks like my mother. I pulled my hoodie away from my face and I wondered if he recognized me. Somehow it didn't surprise me that he had a gun pointed at my head. I think I always worried this is how it could end for me. People who knew my mother said I looked like her. We have the same black hair, the same single dimple in our right cheek. I lowered my rifle for a moment, so he could see my face clearly.

He sighted in and then quickly lowered his weapon.

He took his finger away from the rifle's trigger, as if he were trying to show that he wasn't a threat, the big liar. His face brightened up, that charming smile, with a few more lines around his blue eyes than I remembered. He raised his hand up to wave. I raised the sight back up to my eye.

Stockard Channing started to sing, and I joined in, softly. "There are worse things, I could do." I breathed slowly out and then back in, the way my mother had taught. I thought of my father grabbing me and shaking me, screaming at me to never, ever, ever hang up on him again, while my mother screamed at him to stop, unable to protect me because of her broken arm. I thought of our house with the rifle ever beside the door. I held my breath while I aimed directly into his beautiful smile.

Ama's arm swung up and under my gun, knocking the rifle into the air. My finger squeezed the trigger. The shot spooked my father and the woman with him, the pretty girl with a black eye. They both ducked, then turned and ran back toward the woods.

I turned and stared at Ama. She grabbed me by the side of my head and pulled my face close to hers. Long, sharp teeth gleamed in the moonlight. "Never give up everything you love for a man," she snarled. "If you kill him, you will have to leave your people."

She shoved me away. I fell onto the wood slats. She handed me her rifle. Her face was a warning. Then she stood up and stepped off the wall.

I jumped up to see if she had fallen the many feet to the ground. Instead, she had cleared the wire surrounding the fence and was already running. She ran past the woman and the child, a dark flying shadow. She overtook my father and turned, standing in front of him, speaking. He stopped and she stepped toward him, her arms open as if to embrace him. Once more, with shaking arms, I lifted up my rifle. I felt ill and confused as she took him in her arms. His hands slid up into her hair, as if pulling her to him for a kiss. My finger itched on the trigger again. Suddenly, Ama's mouth was at his neck, and my father's arms were flailing. He struggled to pull back from her, to get away. He fell backward as they tumbled in the long grass, all but her black-dressed form hidden. The woman with the child stared, slowly backing away. After a few moments Ama sat up and said something to the woman. The woman turned and ran toward our gate. The little girl in her arms was crying. The gate swung open.

Aunt Ama stood up and began to walk toward the woods without looking back. The sun was going down and she started to disappear into darkness. I picked up the night-vision goggles and switched them on.

"Ama!" I screamed.

Ama kept walking.

"Auntie!"

Ama stopped.

Once more I screamed, "Etlogi!"

Ama turned quickly. She looked up to where I was standing. She drew her left arm across her face to wipe the blood from her lips. Then, she lifted her hand to her lips and blew me a kiss across the darkness. I lifted my arms up in the air, not to wave, but to catch her, leaning over the wall's edge to pull her back into my world. Ama shook her head slowly. Then, she turned and began to run toward the woods.

"Ama!" I screamed. My despair was incongruent with the soundtrack that was so much louder than my cry. John Travolta and Olivia Newton-John's voices bounced back at me from the dark.

I dropped down on my knees and stared at nothing. As long as I thought my father was alive, I would have been afraid. I would have been angry. How many times had he promised to change, suckered my mom back in using her love and pity as the cruelest weapon? I would have never not been bitter and afraid. He was the kind of man who really only loved himself, a monster that destroyed the lives of those around him, the lives of those who loved him. My Aunt Ama had ended things the only way she could—to save me, to bring balance to our world, to make up for him killing Etsi and my sister.

Like so many of my ancestors before me, my parents and grandparents could only guide me from within now. But I had a community. I was learning our language, our history, the things that had been schooled out of many of my ancestors. It was a journey my mother had begun, had enjoyed for a short time, had deeply craved.

There were people who understood being Cherokee together was more than being Cherokee apart. Before me would be a lifetime of choices that would bring me into balance with the world, or make me a threat to the balance of our community. My mother was no longer here to tell me what to do, how to be, assign me lessons in our language.

The rest of my life is on me.

## THE END

# Glossary

I am a learner of Cherokee. In creating this glossary I used https://cherokeedictionary.net/about (thanks Tim Nuttle, et al.) Most often, I defer to the entries from the work of Cherokee linguist and speaker, Dr. Durbin Feeling (Cherokee English Dictionary 1975); the resources provided online by the Cherokee Nation Language program; and *Beginning Cherokee* by Ruth Bradley Holmes and Betty Sharp Smith; as well as my Instructor Andy (Lawrence) Panther; Ed Fields, Meli Ray, and Eva Garroute; and my friend, Keetoowah Knight.

A brief guide to Cherokee phonetics:
a=ah e=ay i=ee o=oh u=oo v=uhn

## MONTHS

| | | |
|---|---|---|
| Unolvtana | January | OⁿZ-ꭺꮃꮎ |
| Kagali | February | ꭷꮝꭾ |
| Anvhyi | March | Dꮳ~ꮒ |
| Kawohni | April | ꮳꭺꮠ |
| Ansgvti | May | Dꭽꮋꭼꭻ |
| Dehaluyi | June | Sꮝꮇꮙꮒ |
| Kuyegwona | July | ꭻꮠꮕꭼꮎ |
| Galohni | August | ꮝꮆꭾ |
| Dulisdi | September | ꮝꭺꮿꮦ |
| Duninhdi | October | ꮝꭾꮒ |
| Nvdadegwa | November | Oꮝꮷꭲ |
| Vsgihyi | December | iꮣꭹ~ꮒ |

## (DIRECT ADDRESS) RELATIONS

| | | |
|---|---|---|
| Achuja | Boy (often shortened to "Chooch" as a nickname) | DꮰꮐG |
| Ageyutsa | Girl | DꮀꭶꮐG |
| Edoda | Dad | RꮴꮆU |

| Edudu | Grandpa | RSS |
| Edutsi | Uncle | RSᏲ |
| Elisi | Grandma | RᏢᏏ |
| Elisi Agayvli | Great Grandma | RᏢᏏ ᎠᏍᏴᏢ |
| Etlogi | Aunt | RᎤᎩ |
| Etsi | Mom, Momma | RᏲ |

## WORDS AND PHRASES

| adalonige | orange (color) | ᎠᏓᏟᏂᏆ |
| Agasga. | It's raining. | ᎠᏍᎦᏍᎦ |
| Aliheliga. | I am grateful. | ᎠᏟᎮᏟᎦ |
| ama | water, salt | ᎠᎹ |
| amegwoi | ocean | ᎠᎺᏌᎾᎢ |
| anitsgili | ghosts (skilly or skillies) | ᎠᏂᏲᎩᏟ |
| dagsi | turtle | ᏓᏍᏊ |
| digitsi | tadpole, pollywog | ᏗᎩᏲ |
| Dododagohvi. | Let's you and I see each other again. (Plural) | ᏴᏴᏓᎪᎠᏉᏔ. |
| Donadagohvi. | Let's you and I see each other again. (Singular) | ᏴᎾᏓᎪᎠᏉᏔ. |
| dosvdali | ant | ᏴᏣᏛᏟ |
| gigage | red | ᎩᏍᏲ |
| gogi | summer | ᎠᎩ |
| Gutiha. | It's snowing. | ᏌᏗᎲᏙ |
| Gvgeyui. | I love you. (Literally, I'm stingy with you.) | ᎬᏲᎬᏔ. |
| Hadita | Drink! | ᏱᏤᏔᏔ |
| Hawa. | Alright, okay. | ᏱᏤᏓ. |
| Hlesdi! | Quit it! | ᏞᏍᏗ |
| jisdu | rabbit | ᏠᏎᎠᏚ |
| nigadv | everyone | ᏂᎦᏛ |
| oginalii | friend | ᎣᎩᎾᏟᏘ |
| osda | good | ᎣᏍᏓ |
| osiyo/siyo | hello/hi | ᎣᏏᏲ/ᏏᏲ |
| Otsitsalagi. | We are Cherokee. (Two) | ᎣᏥᏣᎳᎩ. |
| sakonige | blue (color) | ᎤᏆᏂᏆ |
| sedi | walnut | ᏁᏗ |

| Tsalagi | Cherokee (language, people) | ᏣᎳᎩ |
| Tsitsalagi. | I am Cherokee | ᏥᏣᎳᎩ. |
| tsunalii | friends | ᏧᎾᎵᎢ |
| ujetsdi | possum | ᎤᏤᏥᏍᏗ |
| Uktena | Water monster | ᎤᎦᏔᎾ |
| Unelanvhi | Creator (One who made everything). | ᎤᏁᎳᏅᎯ |
| Uyvdla. | It's cold. | ᎤᏴᏓᎳ |
| Wado. | Thank you. | ᎠᏙ |
| walela | hummingbird | ᏩᎴᎳ |
| yona | bear | ᏲᎾ |
| | | |
| sagwu | 1 | ᏌᏊ |
| tali | 2 | ᏔᎵ |
| tsoi | 3 | ᏦᎢ |
| nvgi | 4 | ᏅᎩ |
| hisgi | 5 | ᎯᏍᎩ |
| sudali | 6 | ᏑᏓᎵ |
| gahlgwogi | 7 | ᎦᎵᏉᎩ |
| chanela | 8 | ᏣᏁᎳ |
| sonela | 9 | ᏐᏁᎳ |
| sgohi | 10 | ᏍᎪᎯ |

# ᏇᏉ. ᎠᏈᏈᏈᏍ.

ᏇᏉ, ᎣᏄᏓᎣᏩᎠ. Wado, Unelanvhi.

ᏇᏉ, ᏂᏍᏆ. ᎠᏈᏈᏈᏍ. Wado, nigadv. Aliheliga. I am grateful. Without readers, writers have no one to talk to. I appreciate you spending time with this family and the stories I made up and always have with me.

I was born at Claremore Indian Hospital, just like my father. But I grew up in Tulsa. "Maria, Most Likely" was the first story written in this collection while I was still living there in 2001. When we moved to Dallas, Maria entered and won a contest hosted by the Dallas Public Library. Since then, I am grateful for the places where versions of some of these stories have appeared. Wado, *Transmotion*, for publishing "Me & My Monster" in 2018; *Kweli Journal*, for publishing my love letter to Mary Shelley, "Man-Made Monsters", in 2018; *The Massachusetts Review* for publishing "Lens" in 2020; "Homecoming" in *River Styx* in 2020; "Ghost Cat" in *Waxwing Literary Journal* in 2020; "Manifesting Joy" in *Santa Fe Literary Review* in 2019; and "American Predators" in *Yellow Medicine Review* in 2019. An illustrated version of "Hell Hound in No Man's Land" appears in *A Howl*, edited by Elizabeth LaPensée from Native Realities Press and Lee Francis IV.

When I moved to Texas, I knew next to nothing about the history of Texas and the Indians who called that land home. The character of Ama Wilson was born when I read Gary Clayton

Anderson's *Conquest of Texas, Ethnic Cleansing in the Promised Land, 1820–1875*.

How do you thank all the people who made you who you are, inspired your stories, loved you?

I miss you, Dad. Cynthia Bechold Hawkins, you were right. There should be more time. I don't know how I manage to do much without the two of you.

If it weren't for my daughters, Elena, Ana, and Angie, I wouldn't be who I am. I'm lucky you chose me. I am grateful for the young women I taught at the all-girls public school in Fort Worth. The kids are better than alright. My mother (Grammie) and my sister, Angela, are two of the most generous and hard-working women I know. I'm glad we're family. My little brother, Jesse, was the first kid I loved like he was my own. I'm grateful for him and his wife Jennifer's, kindness. Heath Henry continues to be a loyal friend, partner, and good father to our girls. I appreciate him. Millie Kingbird, thanks for listening.

Wado to artist Jeff Edwards. You are a Rockstar. If people like this book, your work is a huge part of that. Thanks to Arthur Levine and his wonderful publishing house at LQ. You have given so many authors, including myself, a loving and supportive home. Thank you, Nick Thomas, for believing in this manuscript and sending all those e-mails. Thank you, Jonathan Yamakami, for the beautiful design work. Thank you, Irene Vázquez. Thank you to my agent, Emily Sylvan Kim of Prospect Agency, along with Ellen Brescia. Thank you, Christine Platt, for the introduction, friendship, and *Awiti*. Thank you, Laura Pegram and *Kweli*. Thank you, Melanie, for being my friend and telling me to check my junk e-mail.

Thank you, Tommy Orange, for being my mentor. You were the first person to read the manuscript. I was terrified. It was worth it. Thank you for questioning everything. Thank you for editing out the second space after those periods. Thank you, Cynthia Leitich Smith, for your keen eye and support; your work makes the book world exponentially better. Thank you, Stephen Graham Jones for doing what you do.

I've only met Louise Erdrich and Eden Robinson once, but I doubt I would be doing this if it weren't for them. Thank you, Mona Susan Power, for your work. Thank you, Terese Mailhot, for naming the things that needed naming.

I am grateful for the resources provided by the Cherokee Nation. Wado, Roy Boney and the Cherokee Language Department. Ed Fields, thank you for your expertise and teaching Cherokee during isolation. Lawrence Panther, wado, for being the first teacher of Cherokee language at the University of Arkansas. Wado, my Cherokee brother Keetoowah Knight for answering language questions. Your dad was right, without our language, what makes us Cherokee? Eva Garroute and Meli (ᎣᎯᎵ), thanks for parsing the tough stuff with me. Aliheliga for Durbin Feeling and his legacy to the Tsalagi language. I am a learner of the language, so all mistakes are my own. If it's correct, I owe that to everyone I mentioned. Wado, Matthew Anderson and Spider Art Gallery. Without you, my walls would be naked. Thank you, Traci Sorell, for writing the books we needed when we were kids. Thank you, Kelli Jo Ford and Brandon Hobson, for your work and support. Dododagohvi. ᏩᏝᎪᏋᏒᎢ.

Wado to the Low Rez Program at IAIA. Thank you, Byron Aspaas. Toni Jensen for always listening. Thank you, everyone who supports the Institute of American Indian Arts in Santa Fe. Without that Lannan Foundation partial scholarship, this manuscript may have taken a few more years. Glad we met, Luann Chalifoux.

Thank you, Nicka Sewell-Smith, Bryan Hurt, and Mackenzie

Kiera, for putting eyes on some work. Thank you, Vasantha and Lily, for letting me read to you. Thank you, David Cornsilk, for suggesting readers. Thank you, Eric Rasmussen, for the comedy, tragedy, and letters of recommendation, Dr. Roberts for taking the supernatural and popular culture seriously. Dr. Yandell, for teaching about Indigenous women. Thank you, Julia Nall, Dr. Joshua Byron Smith, Dr. Teuton, Dr. Jensen, Dr. Linda Carol Jones, Summer Wilkie, Dr. Colleen Thurston, Marty Matlock, and everyone else who helped to get Cherokee taught at UARK. Thank you, Robert Hall, for your replies to my language questions.

Twila Barnes, thanks for looking at my made-up family trees. Thank you, my teacher friends: Dorice Warren, Dr. Mia Hall, Jones, Gaynell Bellizan, Chapa, Amber Bailey, Doc Martinez, Tyler Harris, Sean Florence, Coach Bruce, Flores, Colby Allen, Dehn, Schmid, Clark, Nurse Miles, Skipper, Strange, and Montoya. Wado, Melanie Archuleta, Jessamine Lewis, Shalini Rana, and Aakash Tripathi, for your friendship. Venus Monroe, I wish Irene Owens and Jewell were still around so we could talk about Goat Man. Thanks, especially, to the *NATVs Write* critique group. Ruby Hansen Murray, I appreciate all the last-minute reads of stuff I want to get right. Marcie Rendon, when you told me you wanted to know more, that was what I needed to hear. Kim Rogers, you are so kind while reading deeply. I wish we had met at that Def Leppard concert. Stacy Wells, thanks for being ready to hit the road when I had a plan. Blue Tarpalechee, Mvto for all the conversations and feedback. It always matters. Darcie Little Badger, I will always be grateful for your work. Brian Young and Dawn Quigley, you rock!

Please know, I appreciate all of you. If you have stories you want to tell, go write them. We are made of stars and stories.

ᏩᏛᎠᏎᏔ. Dododagohvi.

ᎠᏆᏇᏋ.

Andrea L. Rogers

A big thank you to Andrea L, Rogers for having faith in me and giving me the opportunity to illustrate *Man Made Monsters*. I will never forget the day she came by my office. She introduced herself, told me what she did, and after some chit chat she asked me if I would be interested in illustrating crazy things that go bump in the night? I was out of my comfort zone because I had never done anything like this, so to say I was unsure of myself would be an understatement. But she continued to encourage me and sent me a rough draft of the book and asked that I read a few stories and then make my decision. So, I started reading, and at the end of the story, just like with all of my artwork, I had formed a mental image of what I would create. I continued reading and with each chapter the mental image was made. I reached the end of the book and all of the images were there and stuck in my head, so I had to let them out. I told her I was on board, started creating, and never looked back.

To Nick Thomas of Levine Querido, thank you for giving me complete and total control of the artwork. I read the story, created the artwork, turned it in, and moved on to the next piece. The Cherokee Syllabary is very important to me in both my personal life as well as in my art career, so being able to display it through artwork for all to see without resistance is truly a blessing.

To Roy Boney Jr: Thank you for your patience and countless hours of training. I owe my art career to you my friend. You have given me a very particular set of skills, skills that I have honed over a ten-year art career, skills that, when needed, make me an artistic force to be reckoned with.

A Simple Call Out:
Dear United States Dawes Commission,

Being Cherokee is not achieved from guessing one's blood quantum by visually inspecting how dark/the color of one's skin and assigning them a fraction. A fraction is simply a small or tiny part, amount, or proportion of something. It is not a whole.

Being Cherokee is knowing and practicing your culture, traditions, and language and contributing to the Cherokee Community, as a whole, every day, for your whole life. So, I regret to inform you that I am not a fraction, your Lordships, I am a Cherokee.

Sincerely,

Jeff Edwards

Cherokee Graphic Artist

## About the Author

**Andrea L. Rogers** is a citizen of the Cherokee Nation. She grew up in Tulsa, Oklahoma and graduated with an MFA from the Institute of American Indian Arts in Santa Fe. Her stories have appeared in several literary journals. In 2020, Capstone published *Mary and the Trail of Tears*. Her work has also appeared in *You Too? 25 Voices Share Their #METoo stories* from Inkyard Press; *Ancestor Approved: Intertribal Stories for Kids* from Heartdrum; and the anthology *Allies* by DK. Her picture book called *When We Gather* is forthcoming from Heartdrum.

## About the Illustrator

**Jeff Edwards**, of Vian, OK, is an award-winning Cherokee graphic artist who has worked for the Cherokee Nation for over 20 years. He is a language activist and has worked on numerous projects that have projected the Cherokee language into the global spotlight. He attended Haskell Indian Nations University in Lawrence, KS and received his Associates Degree in Liberal Arts, and completed his Bachelor of Arts in Graphic Design at Northeastern State University in Tahlequah. His artwork is almost exclusively Cherokee themed and he prefers using the Cherokee Syllabary as opposed to English, to promote the Cherokee language. He likes using old cultural concepts but expressing them with modern electronic tools.

## SOME NOTES ON THIS BOOK'S PRODUCTION

The jacket, case, and interiors feature artwork and designs by Jeff Edwards, who used Adobe Illustrator. The text was set by Westchester Publishing Services, in Danbury, CT, in two typefaces: Miller Text, a transitional serif created by British designer Matthew Carter and released through Font Bureau in 1997, and Noto Sans Cherokee, a typeface designed by Google for the Cherokee syllabary originally created by Sequoyah. The display was set in Eksell Display, a 1962 type from legendary Swedish designer Olle Eksell. Each part opener also includes a Cherokee numeral originally created by Sequoyah and hand-drawn by Jeff Edwards. The book was printed on 98 gsm Yunshidai Ivory uncoated woodfree FSC™-certified paper and bound in China.

Production supervised by Freesia Blizard
Book design by Jonathan Yamakami
Editor: Nick Thomas
Editorial Assistant: Irene Vázquez

LEVINE QUERIDO